DEVIANTS

c j skuse

ONE PLACE. MANY STORIES

C.J. Skuse is the author of the YA novels PRETTY BAD THINGS, ROCKOHOLIC and DEAD ROMANTIC. She was born in 1980 in Weston-super-Mare, England. She has First Class degrees in Creative Writing and Writing for Children and, aside from writing novels, lectures in Writing for Children at Bath Spa University where she is planning to do her PhD. THE DEVIANTS is her fifth novel.

HQ
An imprint of HarperCollinsPublishers
1 London Bridge Street
London SE1 9GF

1
First published in Great Britain by
HQ, an imprint of HarperCollinsPublishers Ltd. 2016

A catalogue record for this book is
available from the British Library

ISBN: 978-1-84845-526-9

Printed and bound in Great Britain
by CPI Group (UK) Ltd, Croydon, CR0 4YY

For my Auntie Margaret and Uncle Roy Snead,
Thank you for the days, those sacred days you gave me.

1

A Day at the Beach

I'm sitting beside the café window when I see the man running up the beach and I instantly know it's washed ashore. The sand flicks up behind him as he sprints. And he's screaming.

His face is alive with fear. He's running so hard to get away from it, what he's found. In those brief moments, I am the only person in the café to see him. But, within seconds, the quiet crumbles into chaos.

'Somebody! Help!'

'What's he saying?'

'Did he say a body?'

Someone calls my name, but I don't turn around. I keep walking, out of the café, into the morning air, along the Esplanade, down the steps and onto the wet sand, like the sea is a magnet and I am metal.

People overtake me. Someone shouts, 'Call the police.' Thudding footsteps, snatches of breath. The sand's covered in a billion worm hills and tiny white shells. A group of crows squawks nearby. They're all clustered around an object, pecking at it.

'Let the police handle it.'

'Don't look. Don't look.'

I keep walking towards the mound, until I can see for myself what the man was running from. Until I can see for myself what I have done.

'Tell me everything. Start with what was happening between you and Max.'

2

Moonlight Adventure
Saturday, 1 August

It's like those really old paintings you see in art galleries – if you look at them from a distance, they're beautiful. A quick glance, it's a masterpiece. But as you get closer, you start to see all the cracks. We were a masterpiece, me and Max. We'd known each other for ever. We had the same taste in music. We finished each other's sentences. We ate Carte d'Or watching *Botched Up Bodies* and he'd pretend not to wince. We watched romantic comedies and he'd pretend not to cry. And he had these marvellous arms and always wore sleeveless hoodies in summer.

But close up, there were problems. And these problems were becoming harder to ignore. I was snipping at him more and he took nothing seriously.

He could still impress me though. This one night, he arranged a big surprise for me at the garden centre. I had no idea what the occasion was.

'You don't remember, do you?'

There had to be a good reason why he'd gone to so much trouble. Not only had he stolen Neil's keys and broken us in after hours, he'd set up a table in the café, with lit candles, buttered teacakes and two glasses of milkshake. It looked like something from a honeymoon brochure, with all the fairy lights strung up in the palm trees and the white cloth on the table. Essentially, though, we were still *in a garden centre*. I'd worn an actual dress and shaved my actual legs to be taken to a place that sold worm poo and weed killer.

'Of course I remember,' I lied. 'This is nice. Thanks.'

He folded his arms. 'I could get quite offended, you know.'

'What?'

'You don't have a Scooby, do you?'

'Ummmm, well… I'm pretty sure it's not my birthday. And you've just had *your* birthday, so that must mean that it's…' I scanned my brain for something, anything. What did 1 August mean? But I had nothing. Max looked so disappointed it was almost painful.

And then I got it. It was the synthetic strawberry smell of the shakes that did it.

Our first proper date, five years ago, when I was twelve and he was nearly thirteen and we realised we liked each other more than as the best friends we'd been since primary school. It had been here, in the café, supervised by our mums on another table. We'd had teacakes and strawberry milkshakes, and Max paid for it with his own money from his Pokemon wallet, even though his dad owned the store. Then we had our first proper kiss, inside one of the sheds, while the mums went to look at geraniums. On the way out, Max had held my hand.

My whole body flashed over with goosebumps. 'Oh God. I'm so sorry!'

'It's all right.' He shrugged. 'I wanted to do something without my parents or your dad being around. Something for us.' He pulled out a chair for me and sat down opposite.

'So I thought we could come here when no one else was around, hang out and have teacakes and milkshakes, just like then. Well, *I* could, anyway.'

'What do you mean?'

Like a sadistic magician, Max whipped away my buttery teacake and creamy shake, replacing them with a bowl of freshly chopped fruit and an ice-cold bottle of Evian.

'I figured you'd be on low cal till breakfast. There's no orange or lemon, don't worry.'

I smiled, but my heart sank. My summer training plan meant I was on a strict low-carb low-fat diet. 'Oh, goodie.' It was sweet that he'd remembered to leave out the citrus, though. Only Max would know to do that.

'Happy anniversary, Ella Bella Boodles,' he said, leaning across to kiss me.

'Happy anniversary, Max,' I said.

We tucked in by the light of a salted caramel Yankee Candle. The fruit was freezing, and burst against my sensitive teeth like I was crushing gemstones. It was weird, being there when no one else was around. Normally when me and Max met for lunch there'd be loads of shuffling grannies with walking sticks, or kids on the next table having food fights or pasting stickers all over the undersides of their chairs. Tonight, but for the trickle of a water feature somewhere, the place was silent.

Outside, the night had coloured everything dangerous. Through the large glass windows, the looming mass of Brynstan Hill was just visible. They called our town Volcano Town. Apparently, in Old English, Brynstan meant 'brimstone' – that biblical 'hell hath no fury' stuff. That was the only exciting thing about this little place – the fact that the huge green hill we lived around could spew out molten lava any old time, and blow all the sheep and Iron

Age remains to bits. At Easter they put three crosses on it. In November, they held a huge bonfire on the top with fireworks – from afar, it looked like an eruption. I liked the night. It was the only time of day I didn't have to stare at the bloody thing.

'Did I tell you Dad's bought a new car?' said Max, around a gobful of teacake.

I winced as I bit down on a freezing chunk of melon. 'Another one?'

'Limited edition Porsche 911 Turbo S. Over a hundred and forty grand. Grey leather seats.'

'Grim.'

'No, it's sweet. The ride on it is unbelievable. Top speed's, like, two hundred miles an hour. Nought to sixty in three seconds. It's, like, one of the fastest cars in the world.'

'*Like* one of the fastest or *actually* one of the fastest?'

'One of the fastest,' he said, his face alive with joy.

I chomped down on an apple chunk. 'Don't say "like" then. If it's one of the fastest, *say* it's one of the fastest.'

'All right, all right, easy, Tiger.'

'What's the point of a car that fast anyway? Can't drive it anywhere at that speed. It's ridic.'

'Why are you so snippy?'

'I'm not snippy. It winds me up, that's all. Your dad spends money like it's going out of fashion, and my dad reuses tin foil.'

I hadn't realised how much my anger levels had risen in the last five minutes. Max was always the one who pointed out my potential bitchplosions; like a scientist keeping an eye on the heat levels inside the crater. But Neil – his dad – always had that effect on me. Everywhere he went in the town he was treated like royalty, all blinding smiles and two-handed handshakes, but to me he was a show-off who stank of aftershave and wore too much gold.

'Dad's earned it, Ells. You can't say he hasn't.'

'How many new cars is that this year?'

'Only three,' he said. 'It's being delivered from Germany in a couple of weeks. Oh yeah, Mum asked me to ask you to come over for lunch tomorrow.'

'Bit late notice, isn't it?'

'You haven't got anything on, have you?'

'Yes, I have. Training.'

'You don't train at weekends.'

'Summer regime.'

'What about next Sunday then?'

'I can't, Max. I can't mess Pete about.'

He closed up. I could tell he was pissed.

'Maybe the weekend after next?' I suggested, more to cheer him up than anything.

'Yeah, yeah. I won't hold my breath. It's not haunted, you know. I know you said it freaks you out, but Jess isn't there, I promise.'

'I know. I'm sorry.' I felt bad about lying to him about that.

'I wish she *did* haunt it,' he said, a pink line of milkshake framing his top lip.

'Funny thing to wish,' I said, still feeling awful. I reached out to thumb away the mark from his mouth.

'I know. Sometimes you just need someone to talk to who's not your parents, don't you? Like a big sister.'

I reached out to him and pulled his hand towards me. I held it between both mine. 'You can always talk to me.'

'Yeah, I know,' he said, with a smile. 'So, you'll come for lunch next Sunday then?'

I sank back in my chair. 'Your mum always cooks everything in tons of lard.'

'You can just have the veg, can't you?'

'Oh, cheers. I'd rather just be with you anyway, not all your family.'

'It's not all my family. It's just my aunts and uncles. And we don't have to stay with the olds all afternoon, do we? We can go into town, or across to the island, or something?'

That gave me actual chills, despite the warmth of the restaurant. 'No, not the island.'

'We could hire a boat like we used to.'

'I don't *want* to hire a boat like we used to.'

'All right, all right.' He threw down his half-eaten teacake and sat back.

'There's just no point, is there? There's nothing to see. Just trees and a few old rocks.'

'It doesn't matter, does it? We can just go there for some alone time. We used to spend whole days there when we were kids.'

'Yeah, well. We're not kids any more, are we?' Max's face was still doing that scrunched-up thing. 'I'll come over for lunch soon, I promise.'

'How about when the new car's there? That weekend, yeah? Please? I'll tell Mum to do your potatoes in Fry Light. She won't mind.'

'OK. I'll change my training schedule that weekend.'

His face lightened at once, but I could feel my forearms heating up – my rash was coming on. It was always worse in summer. He reached across the table for my hand and just held on to it for the longest time. As my stress levels dropped, my body cooled, with a comforting sweep of goosebumps.

'Anyway,' he said, fiddling with something under the

table and pulling out a small turquoise box and a large white envelope. 'This is for you. Just to say I love you to Pluto and back.' He handed them to me.

I couldn't hold back my smile. 'Not the Moon?'

'Pluto's further away, innit?' He stuffed the second half of his teacake in his mouth and grinned crumbily at me.

I set down the envelope and opened the box. Inside, on a crushed velvet bed, was a silver chain with a solid silver teddy pendant in the middle. 'Oh, it's gorgeous.'

'Cos I gave you a teddy bear on our first date.' He took the necklace from the box, coming round to my side of the table. The original bear was still on the shelf above my bed – a little koala he'd brought back from Australia after one of his many holidays.

I felt the cold chain graze my neck, and the even colder metal of the teddy bear slide and come to rest at the base of my throat. Max did up the clasp. I looked down to see it and moved the teddy's little arms and legs. The box said 'Tiffany'.

'This looks expensive, Max.'

'It's fine.'

'Your dad gave you a loan, didn't he?' I said, unable to mask my disappointment.

'Well, yeah – but when I start here next month, I can pay him back. It's cool.'

Max was such a sponger where Neil was concerned. He never had to work for anything. He'd coasted through his GCSEs because Neil said he could just work for him at the garden centre. He was only doing A levels because I nagged him to. My dad said he could be so much more if he 'applied himself'. The thing was, even when Max *didn't* apply himself he got grades most kids would kill for. It was so annoying.

'So it's not actually from you, it's from your dad, isn't it?' I said. 'Same as your driving lessons, your car, our Glastonbury tickets…'

'Do you like it?' he said.

'Yes,' I said, touching the teddy bear – a mistake, as he spotted my scabby knuckles.

'Christ, what happened to your hands?'

I toyed with telling him the truth, but then thought better of it. 'I fell over on the track a few days ago.'

'How did you manage to fall on the *backs* of your hands?' He lifted up my other one and looked at it, gently tracing his fingertips over the scabs. 'This one's even worse.'

'I tripped. I think my new spikes are too big.' I flexed my fingers – the deep ache was still there, but if I didn't concentrate on it too much, it didn't matter. Quickly, I diverted his attention back to the necklace. 'This is beautiful. Thank you.'

I opened the envelope. Inside was an oversized card, covered in pictures of us. He must have spent ages sticking them down, shaking on glitter. There were pictures of us on swings. Our school Nativity, with me as Mary, with a cushion up my dress and Max as the innkeeper, with a scribbly black beard. Selfies in Starbucks. Selfies outside the arena in Cardiff waiting to see The Regulators. Selfies on bonfire night in woolly hats and scarves. Snuggly Duddlies in our Christmas onesies. There was one photo he hadn't cropped – it was a day we'd spent on the island with some other kids we used to hang around with – Zane, Corey and Fallon. We all had wet hair and chocolate or jam around our mouths, and we were all laughing.

'God, look at us,' I said. My throat grew sore.

'Yeah. I didn't want to cut that one up,' said Max. 'I love that picture.'

'Me too,' I said, clearing my throat. I never saw them any more. Even though we'd all gone to the same school, walked the same streets, breathed the same salty air, we were virtual strangers now. Zane had turned out to be the world's biggest bully, we hadn't seen hide nor hair of Fallon since the funeral, and though Corey still lived just down the road from me, we rarely spoke any more. Weird, wasn't it? One day spending every second of the holidays together, the next barely acknowledging each other's existence.

I opened the card. The message inside read: *To my Ella Bella Boodles, who owns my heart and every beat in it. Love you always and 4 ever Maxxxxxxxxxxxxxxxxxxxxxxxxxxxx*.

I looked at the front again. At the picture of us all as kids. Me, Max, Zane, Fallon and Corey. 'Do you remember going to the town carnival? Us all sitting in Zane's mum's hairdresser's window, eating tomato soup?'

'Yeah, I do.'

'And watching the fireworks on the hill on Bonfire Night. And that time we went to the island and Corey got stuck up the tree and Zane had to talk him down. God, we'd spend whole days out there in the summer, wouldn't we? Do you remember camping out?'

'Ella…'

I'd have given anything for just five minutes back inside that photograph. Before the island had become this evil cancerous lump sticking out of the sea that I could barely look at. It used to be called Grebe Island. Supposedly formed thousands of years ago from a huge blast of debris the volcano spewed out. Another local legend says there's precious stones buried there. When the council put it up for auction, Max told Neil about the stones and the next thing I knew, he'd bought it and renamed it Ella's Island.

The council and a few birdwatchers were up in arms about that. I hadn't been back there for years.

Max was looking at me, all glassy-eyed and cheesy smiley.

'What?' I said, a mouthful of freezing-cold fruit.

'I really love you, Estella Grace Newhall.'

I looked up at him. 'I love you too, Maximus Decimus Meridius.'

'Oi,' he said, with a bat of eyelids. 'I'm trying to be meaningful here.'

'I love you too, Max Alexander Rittman.' I couldn't say anything else. Why did looking at that photograph make me pine so much? Me and Max weren't even going out then, just friends; friends who knew there *was* buried treasure on that island, and spent years looking for it. Friends who gurned for photos, who ate chips not caring about what we weighed, not caring whether our tans were even. That's why I loved Max, I guessed. Because of what he represented. I'd hung around with various Beckys or Laurens at school and I knew girls at the track who did the same distances, but none of them were Max. He was my constant.

'Estella, to the last hour of my life, you cannot choose but to remain part of my character, part of the good in me, part of the evil...'

I couldn't help it – I laughed. I was glad for the break in the tension in my throat. 'You did *not* just come up with that.'

'No, it's from *Great Expectations*. I memorised it.'

'My dad named me after her from that book.'

'Seriously?'

'Yeah. We're all named after Dickens characters. David, Oliver, then me. Apparently Estella's a right bitch in the book too.' I laughed an ugly laugh and I hated myself for it.

'You're always so hard on yourself.'

'It's the athlete in me. Nothing's ever good enough. Everything can be improved.'

'How come I didn't know that about your name?'

I swallowed as tears stung my eyes. Luckily, he didn't seem to notice. 'There's lots of things you don't know about me.'

Stroking my hand, he stared at me. There was meaning in that stare. I tensed up, flaring with realisation; tonight wasn't just about 'marking the occasion'. This was a prelude – he wanted us to try sex again. Here. *Tonight*. I pulled away.

'What's wrong?'

'Nothing.' I scratched my arm. 'My hives are up. I had a satsuma earlier, it's probably that. I need to cool down. Do you fancy a dip in the pool?'

'Sure.' He blew out the Yankee Candle and we both scraped back our chairs on the hardwood floor and walked out of the café, through the sliding doors and into the night.

Hidden between all the rose beds and ferns, bronze statues, ceramic ladybirds and smirking Buddhas, lay the large rectangular pool with the statue in the middle; a laughing pearl fisherman, spouting water from his ears. It all looked so beautiful, lit by outdoor nightlights, making the water look as appealing as an icy blue cocktail on a hot beach. People had thrown coins in, and the bottom was green with algae in patches, but otherwise it was quite clear. A string of lights that looked like blue ice cubes hung around the edge of the pool.

Max had known me when I swam – in the days when my dad used to call me 'Little Fish' because I could hold my breath underwater for a whole minute. Now, I was 'Volcano Girl' – the Commonwealth Games hopeful with a county record for the 400 metres. In the days before dieting and

6 a.m. jogs got their claws into me, I'd loved to swim. But I didn't even own a costume any more. And Dad hadn't called me Little Fish for years.

'Good idea, this,' said Max, kicking off his trainers and ruffling his socks down over his feet. 'I didn't shower after football.' He pulled his T-shirt up over his back. I took off my top and skirt, until I had on only my black sports bra and Snoopy knickers. It never used to bother me that my underwear didn't match.

I got in as Max lowered himself beneath the surface. I watched his body shimmer through the blue water until he bobbed up in front of me with a smile, a dolphin expecting chum. He put his hands on the ledge, either side of me.

'Hello,' he said, droplets of water peppering his skin all over.

'It's colder than I thought.' I shivered. His hair looked darker when it was wet.

'Your rash any better?'

I looked down at my elbow creases. 'Yeah.'

I hugged him towards me and we stayed like that until he pulled back and kissed me in a desperate smash of lips and tongues and teeth. I wanted to lie down with him and just kiss, stroking his bare back like I sometimes did. I liked the feel of his body against me, and I felt safe, holding him. That was all I wanted to do. But he wanted more. He was so ready. I'd thought that if I kissed him long enough I would be ready too—that I'd get the feeling. The hunger. The throb between my legs. But it wasn't there. There was something in the way.

'Come on,' I said, and started moving away from him, climbing out of the pool.

'Where are we going now?' he said.

'Where do you think?' I said, reaching over for his hand.

He scrunched his face up. 'I better stay here. Got a kind of – situation going on.'

'It's *because* of that. Come on.

We padded through to Garden Furnishings to grab some picnic blankets, and then back out between the foliage towards the sheds, like Adam and Eve in the Garden of Eden. We chose a two-storey Wendy house with window boxes then we spread out the blankets on the floor and lay down. Our breaths were hot. Our skin was wet. He moved on top of me and kissed me all over my face, gentle as a moth bumping a light bulb.

'You're shaking like a jelly,' he chuckled.

'I'm fine. I'm just cold.'

Maybe it would be all right this time. It was no big deal. Everyone did it. I stroked across the span of his back, his skin as soft as catmint.

Before my brain could catch up with my body, I moved him away and reached down to peel off my wet Snoopy pants. I flung them outside the shed and they landed with a splat on the path. It *would* be all right.

'Are you sure you want to?' Smiling like Christmas had just arrived, he started wriggling out of his boxers.

'Come on, quickly. Before I change my mind.'

I couldn't have felt less in the mood than if he was measuring me up for my coffin.

'Why do we have to be quick? We've got all night.'

'Before I lose my nerve then,' I laughed, and shuffled back underneath him. I didn't want to think too much about it this time. I just wanted it done.

'Ella, if you don't want to . . .'

'No I do, I *do* want to. Please. Come on.'

'I haven't got any condoms.'

'I don't care this time. Come on, please – quickly. Kiss me again.'

As we kissed, Max's hands were in my hair, then at my neck, my side, around my hips and my bottom before one of them sneaked around the front. He was going 'there'.

'Kiss me again.'

I kept my eyes open. I wasn't worried. This was Max and he loved me. I was safe in his arms. We both wanted this.

'You smell so good.'

'You do too,' I said in breaths, even though the only thing I could smell was the intense spicy smell of the wooden shed. 'Tell me you love me.'

His fingers were going deeper. 'I love you so much, Ella. God, I want you.' He un-clicked my sports bra and pulled it off. 'I want you so badly.'

I held his head against my neck as my tears rolled down my cheeks into my ears. The necklace had slid down – the bear was resting on my sweaty shoulder, looking at me.

His tongue flicked inside my mouth. 'I want you so much.'

I slid my hand into his hair and grabbed a tuft. Any second now, I'd want this too.

'You're gorgeous,' he said. Silently, a dragon roared in my belly. Max wriggled about, positioning himself so every inch of his naked body was against some naked part of mine. 'Kinda need you to open your legs a bit though, Ells,' he laughed.

I was lying like a corpse. 'Oh sorry.'

Oh God, this was it. We were actually going to do it. I wasn't going to be scared. I grabbed on to his back. I looked up through the roof of the Wendy house, and through a crack in the wood I saw starlight. I drew up my knees. He was going to put it inside me. Any second now. The starlight grew blurry in my eyes.

I closed my eyes and found a memory. Fallon and me, dancing on rocks, laughing so hard about something. Max and Zane were pulling at branches in the woods – making a den. Corey was sitting on a pebble beach, trying to catch a fish with a stick and some string. We were best friends who danced, built dens, fished, had picnics and swam whole summers away. And we had the best big sister to look after us and tell us stories.

'*Who wants to hear my new story? I just finished it.*'

'*Me! Me! Me! I do! I do!*'

'*Right, get over here, then.*'

There weren't always five of us. Sometimes, it had been six.

Then I realised where we were. We were on the island – the sea had swallowed the land. I looked around. I was alone. They'd all gone. I was stuck there, forever screaming.

'Ella?'

With a jolt of panic, I was wrenched back to now, back to the hard shed floor, Max's heavy body on top of me, waiting for the pain I knew was coming.

'Ella?'

I was panting. 'Just do it, Max. Do it, please. I'm ready. I'm ready. I'm ready.'

But I wasn't ready. I was crying. The only thing I was ready to do at that moment was vomit. And just as he pulled away from me, a thick surge raced up my throat.

'Oh God,' I managed to squeak, lunging for the open shed door as everything I'd eaten that day erupted from my mouth before I'd reached the nearest bush.

How to Kill a Moment, by Estella Grace Newhall.

For the next minute, the only sound was me yacking into

a yucca. When I was done, I looked behind me. Max was sitting on an upturned flowerpot. Naked and embarrassed, just like Adam. And there was I. Naked and embarrassed, just like Eve. 'I'm sorry.'

'I'll get our clothes.' He stood up, snatched up his sodden boxers from the path and walked back towards the pool.

I followed him. 'I feel better now.'

He turned around, his eyes as sad as I'd ever seen them, and grabbed his trousers from a bronze giraffe's ear, scrabbling them on. A plastic sachet fell out of his back pocket. I picked it up, but before I could look at it, he snatched it away.

'What was that?'

He stashed the packet back in his jeans. 'Condoms.'

'I thought you said you didn't have any?'

He didn't answer.

'I hate that I keep doing this to you.'

'All you had to say was no!' he yelled. 'Have I *ever* pressured you? Why do you even lead me down the road if you can't go there?'

'I thought it would be OK this time.'

'You thought that *last* time. And the time before that. And every time, we end up like this – having a massive barney.' He trailed off and scratched his head on both sides, like he was trying to scratch his brain out. 'I'm sorry, I'm sorry.'

He was so angry. He'd never been this angry before. I saw what I was doing to him, his strange fury, and I hated myself even more. I started gathering up my clothes. It wasn't until I'd laced my trainers and he was sitting on the edge of the pool with a roll-up that he spoke again.

'I Googled it,' he said, reaching for my hand. 'Genophobia. It's a proper thing.'

I sat down next to him on the edge of the pool. 'Is there a cure?'

He rubbed his mouth and reached for my hand. 'Don't think so.'

'We'll be OK though, won't we?'

He surrounded me in a hug. 'Yeah. 'Course we will.'

'Did you talk to anyone about it?'

3

Thumping Good Fun

I didn't want to talk about it, but I was finding it more difficult to keep it to myself. The relationship was becoming so one-sided. He started sexting me just before Christmas last year – this picture of him naked except for a bath towel, and a text saying *Wanna see beneath, my beautiful? Wink wink*.

I didn't know how to reply. I'd seen his you-know-what a few times before but it was never something I wanted to see, and certainly not in an excited state. So I kept sending back jokey answers, like *No you're all right, I've just eaten. Wink wink*.

Then he sent back *I'm in bed, just thinkin bout my baby.* ♥

So I sent back *I'm in bed trying to remember if I put the bins out.* 🐵

So he stopped, just like that. I liked the kissing and the hugging. I loved tiny, insignificant things we did like playing Round and Round the Garden on each other's palms. I loved us playing with each other's hair and I loved how he always sent me text kisses first thing in the morning and last thing at night – but it wasn't enough. I didn't want dicktures, I didn't want sex aids he said he'd order me off the internet or him nibbling my neck or pressing against me. For me that was love with a grenade attached – it said *I love you so much, I want to hurt you.*

If things had been different, maybe it would have turned me on. Maybe we'd have booty-called each other from our beds, like he said his mates did with random women on Snapchat and Skype. But things *weren't* different. Things were the way they were.

I had a bit of a meltdown about it at training the next morning.

'Come on, don't let me down, keep going, work through it, work through it…'

The sweltering sun attacked us like a baying crowd as we climbed the east-facing slope of Brynstan Hill. My body did as Pete was yelling at it to do, but my head was everywhere – on the white butterflies shimmering through the long grass, the sheep lying in the shade, the tractor ambling along in a faraway meadow. The distant cars. Hay bales wrapped in shiny black plastic, like large body bags.

'Come on. Push it, Ella, push it! All the way now, all the way…'

Sweat streamed down my face, and the taste of tiny flies and hot hay clogged my nose and my throat. Pete pushed me harder and harder up the hill, until all my willpower left me and I stopped and bent over to grab my ankles and catch my breath.

'What are you doing? We're nowhere near the top yet,' he panted.

'I've had enough,' I gasped, reaching behind me for the Evian in my rucksack.

'Come on, just a bit further. You've got to punch through it.'

I shook my head, chugging down the cool water like I'd crossed a desert. 'I don't want to do any more today.' I swigged again and bent over, every muscle torn up and my lungs aching when I breathed in or out. 'I hate this damn hill.'

'You have been keeping up with your diet, haven't you?'

I said nothing, wiping my face on my T-shirt hem.

'You're sluggish today. Perhaps we should look at reeling back on the carbs.'

'OK, I had a day off yesterday. My dad made me a bacon sandwich. It's not a crime.'

Pete Hamlin had been our school's Teacher You Most Want to Bang – they called him the Pied Piper, cos wherever he went there was always a line of girls following him. I wasn't interested in him that way, but I could see that he was good-looking. He was twenty-five, with a big, happy smile, and he spoke with a posh accent, like he'd done ten years' training with the Royal Shakespeare Company. We talked a lot. I knew he wanted to move back to London, that he liked going to see plays but hated the cinema, even that he still carried a picture of his ex-girlfriend in his wallet. We'd run up Brynstan Hill like coach and student, but we'd come back down as friends, chatting about music and books.

'Come on then. Back at it.'

I shook my head. 'This is as far as I want to go today.'

'That's not an athlete talking, Estella.'

I started undoing the Velcro on my running gloves but left them on. 'Yeah well, maybe I don't want to be an athlete today, *Peter*.'

'This isn't like you. Where's my Volcano Girl?'

'Extinct,' I said, and started walking back down the hill. The local paper had started the whole Volcano Girl thing, because of the way I 'erupted' out of the blocks on the track. I didn't mind it. It was pretty apt if you think about it.

'Ella, I'm being paid a lot of money to train you.'

'Then what do you care?' I stopped walking. 'Why can't we just *say* we ran, just for once? Why do we always have to bloody run everywhere?'

He laughed and started back down the hill to where I was standing. 'Uh, well, there's this little thing called the Commonwealth Games? And the fact that you're the best runner in the county, probably the best runner in the South-West when you set your mind to it? That enough for you to be going on with? Come on, I'll race you to the top.'

'No, I can't.'

'I'll give you a head start.'

That was when I blew. 'WHY DOESN'T ANYONE EVER LISTEN TO ME?'

I didn't look at him. I marched back down the hill like a belligerent Grand Old Duke of York; my one man staying exactly where he was. For a while. Until I heard his footsteps coming up behind me.

'Is it your dad? He's still in remission, isn't he?'

'Yeah, my dad's OK. Well, at the moment he is.'

'Has your mum called again? Your brothers? You're always fractious whenever they've been in touch.'

'No.' I sat down on the grass, narrowly avoiding a pat of dried sheep crap. I felt like crying so badly it was hurting my neck. I chugged back some more water to drown it.

He sat down next to me. 'Is it leaving school? I know it's a big step, sixth form, but you'll be all right. You should be excited about it. I think you'll do well.'

'It's not any of that.'

'Tell me,' he said, like he was settling in for a good movie. 'Come on, we need to clear out your brain, otherwise you're not going to get the most out of this. You may as well go home and eat twelve Krispy Kremes and a Nando's for all the good it's going to do.'

'You can't eat Nando's at home,' I said.

'You can,' he argued. 'They've got it in Waitrose. I've tried their pervy sauce. Believe me, it is *all* the noms.'

A smile tore at my lips. 'It's peri-peri sauce. And don't speak young. It sounds weird.'

He laughed. 'Come on then, what's the matter? Is it Max?'

Trying to form the sentence in my head was getting me nowhere. We sat in perfect silence, but for the buzzing in the grass around us. His eyes fixed on me.

'Yeah,' I said eventually. 'He's been my best friend since primary school. When we started going out together it was lovely, for a while. But he wants more now. And I don't.'

'Ah. I see.'

'It's so difficult cos he's my best friend. If I was going to kiss any boy, *be* with any boy, it would be him, no question. We make perfect sense. I miss him when he's not around. Sometimes I miss him when he goes to the toilet. I know, I know. It's so soppy.'

'No, it isn't. There's nothing soppy about it. You love him.'

I nodded. 'But I feel like I'm losing him.'

'If he loves you as much as you love him, then you won't lose him. He won't let it come between you.'

'It *is* coming between us. All his mates have these stunning girlfriends, and groupies who hang around the social club after his home games. Some are younger than me. Tight tops, all swigging cider. Any one of them would do it with him, I know they would. And then there's Shelby.'

'Who's Shelby?'

'His cousin, Shelby Gilmore. Well, step-cousin. His Auntie Manda's daughter. She's seventeen as well. They come over for Sunday lunch every single week. She's a walking, talking reason never to look in a mirror again.'

'So?' said Pete. 'That doesn't mean anything will happen with her, does it?'

'Maybe it already *has* happened, though. I don't know. They really get on. And she flirts with him all the time. Flicking her hair back. Smiling at him. Always talking to him about stuff they're both interested in but I'm not, like gaming and football. She's gorgeous. And she's so... experienced too. She's had more boyfriends than I've done time trials.'

'Have you tried getting to know her?' said Pete. 'You might have things in common.'

'I've hate-liked a few of her status updates on Facebook. But no, not really.'

I slowly peeled off my running gloves to show him the scabs on my knuckles. 'And then there's this.'

He cringed and gently lifted my left hand to look at it. He reached for the other one and studied it. 'How have you done this?'

'We've got a stone pillar in our lounge. When I'm home alone, sometimes I punch it. I gaffer tape a cushion to it so it doesn't hurt as much.'

Pete's face creased. 'How long have you been doing that?'

'Only just recently. It just gets too much sometimes. You know what I was like when we started training. Running helped me. But just lately it hasn't been enough.'

'Ella, this isn't right, what you're doing to yourself. You don't owe Max anything and you certainly shouldn't blame yourself for not being ready to sleep with him.'

'I *do* owe him though, don't I?' I said. 'I'm his girlfriend. It's what girlfriends do. He's waited ages.'

Pete's jaw dropped. 'Where is that written? Is this some law I don't know about?'

'It's just a fact.'

'It most certainly is not,' he said, getting to his feet. 'You don't owe him sex for any reason whatsoever. Sex isn't the prize you get for patience, Ella. The only reason to do it is because *you* want to. If he's the kind of person who will have sex with a girl who doesn't want to have sex with him, then ask yourself why would you want to be with a guy like that?'

'No, he's not, his… He's not pressuring me,' I said, scratching my shins. The fire was raging. Urticaria, our doctor called it – a completely random skin reaction to too much histamine in my blood. My training meant I couldn't take my antihistamines because they made me drowsy. The wild grass was making it worse. 'I just hate what we've turned into. And I don't feel like we can go back to how we were. Just friends. I hate myself.'

'How can you hate yourself? You're an incredible girl. I'm so proud of you, how you've come through it all – your mum leaving, and your dad's illness. You've stuck to your training plan, you're nailing your PBs on a regular basis. You're brilliant, Ella.'

'Don't give me compliments, Pete. You're just throwing stones into a bottomless pit.'

'You know, not talking about something that's hurting you always makes it worse. It starts feeding on you, like a parasite. Once you let it out, it's got nowhere else to go but away. Is there something else upsetting you? Other than the Max thing?'

The tractor in the far meadow had stopped baling. The

sheep under the tree were looking our way. The whole world seemed to be waiting for me to say it out loud.

I shook my head. 'No. I just need to work things out for myself, that's all.'

'By punching concrete?' I didn't answer that. 'Will you at least recognise that it's not good for you to keep doing this to yourself?' I shrugged. I couldn't promise. 'OK, well, if you're determined to punch for therapy, I can at least show you some proper technique.'

'Can you?'

'Yeah. I boxed a bit at university. It's a great stress reliever. I still do a bit now and then. It's great for stamina, too.'

'Where do you do it?'

'In my garage. Come on, let's go back and have a cuppa and I'll show you.'

We jogged back down the hill and walked across the churchyard into Church Lane, where Pete's cottage was. His garage wasn't like ours, with all Dad's dusty boxes of rusty tools, doorknobs, foreign editions of his *Jock of the Loch* romance novels and Christmas trimmings. Or Neil Rittman's immaculate garage, with the two luxury cars and giant speedboat. Pete's was smaller, like a boutique gymnasium with a wall TV, a fridge of isotonic drinks, weight machines, a treadmill, dumb-bells, a bench and, swinging from one of the low slung beams on a chain, a large black-and-red punchbag. He reached for something on top of the fridge and unravelled it.

'First we wrap your hands.' He set about coiling a length of red bandage right around both my hands, like I was being mummified, then tied it off on a Velcro strip. Then he reached for a pair of boxing gloves, tied to a nail on the wall next to the first aid box. He put them on me. It felt like some grand occasion, like I was putting on a crown. 'Right, relax your hand. Now make a fist. Keep your fingers all in there. Thumb on top but keep it in tight. OK, bounce on the balls of your feet. Keep everything relaxed but ready. Now, hit the bag.'

I did. Hard.

'OK, again. Breathe out on the punch.'

I did it again. Harder.

'Yep, good, exhale each time you let the punch fly. Don't hold it in. Make a noise if you have to. Both fists, elbows in tight, that's it, keep bouncing. Watch me. Don't fling it forward, *push* it. Good. Breathe out. OK, let's try some jabs. Keep breathing; let your breaths out, don't hold them back. Relax when you're bouncing, then let the punch fly and exhale. Good. Exhale. Good. Okay, cross. Upper cut.'

We stayed in his garage for the next hour – an hour when I should have been doing sprints and shuttle runs or burpees up on Brynstan Hill. Instead, I was Muhammad Ali. Strong and powerful and *so* angry. All bee – no butterfly.

'Let's try a few straight line punches. These'll wear you out quicker but they pack the most power. Keep those wrists loose, don't lock them. Keep those breaths coming out on each punch. Bounce. Jab jab jab. Quicker. Good. Now smash it! Lights out! You've picked it up quickly, Ella.'

My knuckles and wrists ached but there was no real pain, not like there was at home. By the end, the sweat was pouring from my face and arms. *Bang-bang-bang. Bang-bang-bang. Bang-bang-bang.* It was so fast. I was so ferocious. I loved it. I used my anger well in my running, Pete said, but I had too much of it, and had to burn some of it off.

'Like bleeding a radiator. We're just getting rid of your trapped wind, so you can function more efficiently.'

'You better not be calling me windy!' I carried on pummeling the bag.

He laughed. 'Believe me, I'm not going to mess with you while you're in this mood. That's great, keep going. Find the rhythm.'

It felt like each punch had meaning. Pete was right. What I'd been doing at home was just battering myself. This felt like it was working something out of me. Every time I punched, a tiny puff of poison flew away. I felt exhausted, but electric all over.

'OK, that's enough for today,' Pete laughed, holding the bag steady and starting to unlace my gloves. I was still bouncing on the balls of my feet, sweat sliding off me in rivers.

I folded up the hand wraps and put them back on the fridge. 'Can we do this again?'

He scratched his stubble. 'Neil Rittman's paying me a lot of money to train you in running the four hundred metres, Ella. It's not going to look great at Area Trials if you're first out the starting blocks with an upper cut and a straight right left, is it?'

'I know but just one more session doing this? Please? We don't have to tell anyone. We can run for half the session and box for the other half or something. Can we? Please?'

'Tell you what,' he said, fumbling in his pocket. He pulled out a small set of keys, unhooked one attached to a Brynstan Academy fob and gave it to me. 'How about we keep our training sessions to running, but any time you feel like punching the crap out of that pillar, you come here and use the bag and gloves. No more dry wall sessions on those fists.'

'OK,' I said, holding the key like it was a precious arte-fact. 'Thanks.'

'And you jog all the way here and all the way back, right?'

'Right.'

He looked at me for a long time, then rubbed the outside of my arm. 'And if you do want to talk, my door's always open.'

I held up the key and smiled. 'I won't. But thanks.'

'So, hang on, where does the missing cat come into it?'

4

The Mystery of the Disappearing Cat

Oh yeah, well it was the morning Max picked me up from training at Pete's house, which he never ever did. He was leaning on his Audi across the road from Pete's cottage when I emerged from the garage, fists shaking, sweat trickling down my forehead.

'What are you doing here?' I said, with an edge to my voice I hadn't meant.

'Oh that's nice,' he laughed. 'I thought I'd pick you up, save you the jog back.'

'I like the jog back.'

'All right, I'll go then, shall I?'

'No,' I said, wiping over my face again with my damp towel. 'Sorry. Thank you.' He was expecting a kiss, so I kissed him. Then I felt bad cos when he hugged me in to his chest, he rubbed my back like he did when we were kids and I was crying. I went round to open the passenger door.

Max got in too. 'Sweated up a storm today,' he commented. I didn't answer. He didn't switch the engine on either. He was just looking at me.

'What are you waiting for?'

'How was it?' he asked. He wasn't looking at my face,

though. He was looking at my hands, red-tinged and shaking.

'It's just adrenaline. I only did a quick warm down today.'

He was looking at me funny, the way he did sometimes when he didn't get something.

'Pied Piper on form today, was he?' He started up the engine.

'What do you mean?'

'You know. Did he push you all the way?'

The car started off down Church Lane. 'You don't like Pete, do you?'

'No,' he said.

'Why not?'

'Uh, cos I've met him? And cos he's a dick?' he said, stopping at the lights.

'He's not a dick.'

'He's posh.'

'So are you when you're not trying to sound like your dad.'

'I am not!'

'You so are, Max.'

'Am not.'

'So are.'

He stopped talking for at least a mile. Only when we came to the hospital roundabout just down the slope from my road did he open his mouth again.

'There's nothing wrong with my cock, is there?'

'Where did *that* come from?' I said, washed hot and cold with embarrassment.

'I was just thinking about last night at Greenland. You would tell me if that was the problem, wouldn't you? With us, I mean.'

I couldn't help laughing, and the ice between us broke and melted away. He'd obviously been stewing on this all night.

'The only thing wrong with you is you picked the wrong girlfriend.'

'Never.'

I clicked off my seat belt and leaned across to kiss him back. 'Thank you for picking me up. And for last night.' I kissed him again. 'And my card.' And again. 'And my necklace.'

He started doing Round and Round the Garden... on my neck with his fingertip and I cringed, remembering I wasn't wearing it. 'That tickles.'

'Where is it?' he said, looking at my neck where a pool of sweat had collected.

'Where's what?'

'Your teddy necklace?'

'Oh I can't wear it for training cos it keeps hitting me in the face,' I gabbled.' I couldn't actually remember taking it off.

'What are you doing later? Do you wanna go into town or something? Or we could, I don't know... Oh. You've got a visitor.'

I followed his eye line along the garden path towards our bungalow, where a figure sat crumpled in my doorway.

'It's Corey!' I yanked open the car door and slammed it behind me, running up the path. 'Corey? Are you OK?'

'Ella?' said Corey, un-crumpling. He was all bleary-eyed, and he had a noticeable scab on his eyebrow and a yellowing bruise on his chin. Old wounds.

'What are you doing here?'

'I was waiting for you.'

'Why? What's happened?'

Another car door slammed and Max ran up the steps, two at a time. 'What's up?'

'I'm still trying to find out,' I said. Corey was getting to his feet, adjusting his glasses with one hand and clutching his skateboard with the other. 'Why are you on my doorstep?'

'No one answered.'

'My dad's gone to Manchester to do a book signing and see my brother. He's just had a baby. What's happened? Is something wrong?'

'Ells,' said Max, folding his arms across his chest and nodding. I followed his eye line towards the bottom of the road. A figure stood beneath a lamp post opposite Corey's grandparents' house; a stocky figure with a shaved head, wearing a rugby top and jeans.

'Let's go inside,' I said, getting out my key and ushering both boys through the front door, keeping one eye on the distant stranger.

Me and Max had grown up with Corey Malinowski (his full name was Corneliusz, but we'd never called him that). We'd spent the summers together, us and him and Fallon and Zane. He'd gone to Brynstan Academy too, but he'd mostly been one of the school loners – he had a mild form of cerebral palsy, a hearing aid and two dead parents, so he was pretty much begging to be an outcast. But to us, he'd been vital. He was the reader of books, the architect of dens, darer of dares, encyclopedia of Harry Potter trivia (seriously, down to page numbers), and the only one who could get a fire going using just sticks. To the other kids, he was that skinny weirdo with the limp; to us, he was a genius.

He took off his tatty Converse by the pillar in our lounge and padded into the kitchen, standing in front of our French windows like they opened onto a long dark tunnel.

'He's gone,' he said, turning to me.

I knew his granddad had a bad heart. 'Oh, Corey, I'm sorry. Are you OK? How's your nan coping?'

'No, no,' he said, correcting me. 'Granddad and Nan are on their cruise to the Rhineland. For their anniversary.' His voice was shaky, and before each sentence, he would sort of rev up to get going. I'd forgotten he did that. 'No, it's Mort.'

His cat! Phew. 'What's happened to him?'

Corey sat down on one of the heavy pine chairs at the breakfast table. I got some Diet Cokes from the fridge. Max shook his head when I offered him one and leaned against the wall, taking a roll-up out of his tobacco pouch.

'Patio,' I said, ordering him towards the French windows. 'Go on, Corey.'

'I was outside on my skateboard yesterday, and Mort got in my way.'

'And you… ran him over?'

'No,' he said, his eyes creasing up. A single tear fell. 'I put him on my board. I was gonna Instagram it.'

I bit both my cheeks to stop the laugh. Corey was always doing things like this. His nan sometimes saw my dad – they both did the sugar-craft class at the community centre – and she told him how much Corey got on her nerves with his 'experiments'. Putting foil in the microwave, just to see. Trying to drive his granddad's car out the garage, just to see. Asking out a supply teacher, just to see. Nothing ever ended well.

Max poked his head through the gap in the French windows. 'Did I just hear right? You put your *cat* on your *skateboard*?'

I threw Max a death stare and turned back to Corey.

'OK, so you put him on your board. Then what?'

'The board went too fast. He got to the bottom of the

close where there's that hilly bit and then the kerb. And it flipped him up and he crashed into the wall.'

I felt bad for Corey, but not for Voldemort. I couldn't stand that cat. It was always wailing outside our French windows, waiting for my dad to make a fuss of it. He even bought tuna for it – from the Finest range. I didn't really like animals, anyway, and cats were the worst of all. And Mort was the worst of all cats. He hated me. His yellow eyes were full of it, like it was thinking, *I know your secret*.

'Right. Well, we better go and scrape him up then. I'll help you bury him.'

Corey pulled back, wiping his nose on his jumper sleeve. 'No, he's not dead,' he said. 'He got up straight away and ran off. I haven't seen him since. But he could be injured, Ella. Dying somewhere. We need to look for him.'

'Why didn't you start looking?' said Max, poking his head through again. 'Why wait for Ella?'

Corey didn't respond to that. 'Can you help me, Ella? Please? I don't know where to start. What if Zane's found him? He might do something to him.'

Then I knew for sure who the figure was, standing under the lamp post. It *had* been Zane. I'd seen him a few times in our road, or thought I'd seen him. He didn't live round here, though. He lived on the seafront.

'OK, Corey, let's get looking. We'll find Mort, I promise.'

Corey leaned in for a hug. 'I knew you'd help me,' he said.

'Max'll help too,' I said. 'Won't you, Max?'

Max rolled his eyes, but flicked his fag butt outside onto the flagstones. At once, I barged past him and went to stamp it out, just in case the world burned down.

'Why did you feel like you had to help?'

5

An Old Friend
One month earlier – 9 July

Corey'd had a crap life. Not only had he been born with a disability but his junkie dad died of an overdose when Corey was months old; his junkie mum killing herself a year later. He'd got lucky with his grandparents. They took him in, wrapped him in home knits, organised physio and speech therapists and treated him like a little prince. But at school, he was one of the loners; one of 'those' kids with an aura of stay-away about them. The last few years had leached something out of him. He looked like Kurt Cobain gone wrong, with his shaggy, dirty-blond hair, baggy jeans and cardigans. He had this low, almost apologetic voice. We'd barely spoken in months.

I still saw him around town, though; a headphone zombie skulking in doorways, sitting on walls eating pasties from a Greggs bag, or in the churchyard, reading comics and fantasy novels. He worked at the computer shop in town, had about six Twitter followers and idolized his cat, Mort. All his Instagram posts were pictures of Mort reaching up to paw at a toy mouse or wearing a little sombrero next to a stand-and-stuff taco.

Everyone knew what Zane was like with Corey. We'd seen the spit glistening in his hair, the bend in his glasses. I was afraid Zane *had* done something to Mort. And it would be my fault if he had. Our last day of school, I'd been in the girls' changing rooms when I heard noises outside:

'Please, please don't. I'm sorry. I didn't, I swear, I promise. No! Pleeeeease!'

'Go on, have it!'

Cough Cough. Nggghhhhhhhhh.

'Do it!' A burst of laughter.

Cough. Aaaarggghhh. Ngghhhh.

It was coming from outside, by the wheelie bins, so I stood up on the bench and peeked through the top-opening window. There were three of them around Corey, who was on the ground, curled up like one of those little cellophane fish you get in Christmas crackers. His cries echoed off the bins – muffled, because he had a banana skin in his mouth. Zane Walker kicked him in the stomach. Then the other two joined in, and I felt every kick like it was ricocheting back onto me. A fire started to glow in my belly.

'Streak of piss. You wet your pants yet? Let's have a look,' came Zane's unmistakable Essex twang. One of his mates yanked down Corey's trousers.

Without any more thinking, I grabbed a hockey stick from the pegs, ran to the fire exit and banged down on the bar, bursting through into the open air.

'Get off him!' I yelled, gripping the stick with both hands to stop them shaking.

Corey squirmed away to yank up his trousers as the other boys turned to me. Three pigs – Zane Walker, Danny Leech and Andrew Tanner. Danny Leech did rugby and was a good shot-putter. He was also a wuss. He ran off straightaway, sunshine bouncing off his highlights.

Andy Tanner's mum was a receptionist at our GP surgery. I also happened to know her pet name for him; I'd heard her call him once.

'Run along, *Piglet*. Unless you want me to call Mummy and rat you out?'

Tanner went violently puce in both cheeks, gobbing on Corey's hair as a parting shot. 'Hit me up when you're done, Walks. See you in town.' They fist-bumped and Piglet swaggered off, giving me a finger on each hand as he went.

And then there was Zane.

He was a big guy these days; all hench and shaven-headed with a scowl in his eyes that could shatter glass. But I knew all his weak points. Fear of horror stories, horror movies, bees. Fear of being fat. But he wasn't afraid of me. He'd taken me out in our judo bouts on Max's living room carpet a million times. And he was a superstar fly-half on the rugby team now. He looked me up, then down, and laughed. 'What do you care, *Estella*?'

The fury took over, and I ran forward, ramming my whole body into him until his back hit the wall. I was strong, but I couldn't hold him – he laughed, grabbing the stick and throwing it to the ground. Then he got right up in my face, so I could smell the Germolene on his zit scabs. Rage ran through my body like a bush fire. I got my stance, levelled my fists and swung my right arm back into a punch that I could hear sweeping the air. But I missed.

'Ha! Try again, babe. You got a good action there.'

To my horror, I found myself doing the exact same thing.

'You're lucky I'm in a good mood,' he said, killing himself laughing.

It was then that I saw the kitchen slop bucket by one of the bins.

'And you're lucky these are *today's* leftovers.' In one

movement, I lunged across for the bucket and launched the contents straight over his head. In seconds, Zane was covered in a chunky, vomity goo of custard, mince, mash, soggy bread, chips, rice pudding, pasta and peas. The raging fire inside me fizzled into joy like popping candy.

'Oh, you are DEAD,' the Abominable Lunch Man roared, lunging after me. By the grace of God – and the vomity goo – he slipped as he came, landing hard on his backside.

'Quick, come on!' I said, grabbing the hockey stick and practically dragging Corey back through the fire exit before Zane dived after us.

We headed for the girls' toilets, cuss words peppering the air behind us.

'You're dead! Both of you. *Deceased*!'

I locked the bathroom door behind us, barricading it with the hockey stick, then parked a shivering Corey on a toilet, his glasses hanging on his ear by one bent arm.

Within seconds, Zane was banging and kicking the door from the other side.

'Get out here, bitch!' *Bang bang bang.* 'I'm gonna kill you!'

The door pulsed and rattled but I tried to take no notice, although really I was petrified. 'He'll go away in a minute.'

I grabbed the roll of loo paper from the cistern behind Corey and wound it around and around my hand, then rinsed it under the cold tap.

Bang bang bang. 'I'll have you, bitch, I'll kill the pair of you! Get out here *now*!'

I crouched down beside Corey and inspected his face. Blood ran from his mouth.

'Don't worry, he won't get in,' I told him, dabbing with shaky hands. 'Do you remember when he wet his pants in the middle of our Nativity? And that picnic, when he got stung by the bee? And Jessica telling us horror stories on sleepovers – Zane was the *worst* wuss. They had to call his mum once!'

Bang bang BANG BANG BANG. Corey winced.

'Jessica told the best stories.' He bowed his head. 'The one about the Witch's Pool was my favourite. Remember when she told that on Halloween night? I go through the graveyard and sit beside her sometimes. Stupid.'

'It's not stupid, Corey. I've done that too,' I said. 'I always felt like she was my sister as well as Max's. I wished she was. Instead I've got two great big brothers who still think it's funny to fart on my head.'

Corey smiled.

'Oh, you think that's funny, do you? Olly once put blue food colouring on my toothbrush. I had blue teeth *all* day. My mum went mental.'

Corey laughed properly at that, the sound taking me way back. It was only then I realised the banging outside had stopped. There were appalled voices outside. Teachers. Zane wasn't about to admit a girl had thrown slops over him – he must have come up with an explanation for them. The voices died away into the distance.

'See? Told you he'd go away,' I said, holding the cold compress to Corey's eyebrow.

'I saw you at County Champs,' he said. 'You were amazing. Like Volcano Girl.'

'That's what they call me,' I said, recalling the recent headline in the local paper.

'No, the *real* Volcano Girl. She's a superhero in one of my comics. She's faster than Flash, and she's got lava coming out of her heels.'

'I'm not into comics.' I dropped the wad of bloody paper and bundled up another one, ready to wet it.

Corey sucked his bottom lip, split where Zane had punched it. 'I saw you erupt at your house, too. I was walking past and your lounge curtains were open. You were punching the pillar in your lounge.'

My cheeks burned. 'You might have a scar. It's going to look cool, though. Let's check your vision. OK, how many fingers am I holding up?'

'Three.'

'Er—'

'How many were you holding up?'

'Almost three.'

There was a depressed silence.

'I've never seen him go at anyone like he does with you,' I said, returning to the toilet cubicle with another batch of wet compresses. 'You used to be such good mates.'

'It's because I know his secret. He thinks I'll tell everyone. But I haven't. I wouldn't.'

'What secret?' My phone buzzed in my pocket. Without looking, I knew it was a text from Max.

Corey shrugged. 'I promised I wouldn't tell.'

Automatically, I pulled my phone out of my pocket and checked the message.

Are you done with education yet? Fancy coming over to mine? The olds are out. We've got all afternoon. Maxxx

I turned off my phone and looked back at Corey. 'School's over now. I don't have anywhere to be. So what's Zane's secret?'

'Did he tell you Zane's secret?'

6

An Adventure Beckons

No, he wouldn't tell me. He'd sworn to Zane that he would keep his secret, and he wasn't going to budge. That was the kind of boy Corey was. If not for his condition, he'd have been perfect for the SAS; no way was anything going to break him. He was a much better person than me.

Zane had gone by the time we trooped down the hill on our quest for Mort. Thank God. He'd always been a bit weird as a kid – he ate too much, swore too much, he insisted on always challenging us to duels or fights. He had this stupid habit of hiding our things and making us look for them and he was also the stopper of sneezes – surely the most evil of all vices. But at school, these things had been amplified. He swore at teachers, shagged around, picked fights with any 'poof' who dared to argue with him. Corey was exactly the kind of geek a brainless beefcake like Zane Walker grown up *would* bully, but I still didn't understand why you'd pick on someone who'd been one of your best friends.

We looked everywhere for Mort – all the Rittmans' businesses, the pubs, up and down the High Street, the bins in the alley at the back of the seafront hotels, Tesco car park, and finally the pier. Corey went inside the kiosk to ask the manager if he'd seen him – sometimes cats went there for fish scraps. It was starting to drizzle, and Max rubbed his hands up and down my arms. The breeze from the sea was a cold one, and my cheeks were getting sore with wind chill. Max must have been freezing too. He only had his Street Reaper sleeveless hoody on,

'He's a bloody nightmare, isn't he?' he said, teeth beginning to chatter.

'Dressed in a daydream,' I added, moving his hair from his eyes and cuddling him in close. He looked good today. He was wearing the basketball vest I'd bought him for his birthday, skinny jeans and his new Vans. 'You saw Zane hanging around, didn't you? Opposite Corey's house?'

'Yeah, I did.'

'I don't want to leave him on his own today, Max. Just in case.'

Just then, Corey came out of the shop with a massive bag of sweets, crisps and cans.

'For you guys,' he said. 'For helping me look for Mort.'

'Thanks,' I said. 'But we should get back. Maybe Mort's gone back to yours?'

Corey shook his head. 'He won't. He's too scared.' His face radiated terror. 'Oh my God – what if Rosie's got him?'

'Why would she have him? She lives in the back of beyond. It's a bit unlikely,' I said, trying to head him off.

'Ooh, I dunno,' said Max, suddenly enthusiastic. 'If a cat's gone missing in suspicious circumstances, Roadkill Rosie's got to be involved, hasn't she? Old Witchy Woo herself.'

The Brynstan-on-Sea grapevine had declared years ago that Rosie Hayes was a witch. Any animal that went missing, Rosie was the prime suspect. Sometimes we'd seen her as kids, hanging out at the farm with Fallon, but more often than not she'd be out in the tractor, or just going somewhere in the 'Torture Truck'. People said worse about them now: Fallon had been expelled for sleeping with a teaching assistant, and people said now she was some kind of prostitute. Rosie was a gypsy, possibly even a serial killer. They stole cattle, had bats in their cellar, fed their pigs on human remains. There was talk of skulls in the freezer, body parts left out for the bin men, even an amputated you-know-what in the kettle on her stove. You know how people talk – rumours appear like cracks in egg shells and before long giant eagles have taken to the air.

Neil had done a lot to help spread those rumours.

'I reckon Mort'll be in a pie by now,' said Max. 'Ooh, I've got a hell of a peck on for Mort 'n' chips. Remember Rosie's suspicious stews? You never saw the same cat twice round their house. And the stories Jess used to tell us about Witch's Pond?'

'Stop winding him up,' I said. 'All that stuff about the cannibalism and the Witch's Pool is crap. We know Rosie – at least, we used to.'

But Corey wasn't laughing. 'She might have picked him up, just by accident. She does that – we know she does. The farm was always crawling with stray cats when we used to go there. Could we go out and look? Just to see?'

'No way!' said Max, the smile wiped off his face. 'My dad would never forgive me.'

Corey looked confused so I filled him in. 'It was because of Rose that they recorded an open verdict at Jessica's inquest. Rose insisted she saw her walk in front of the bus. On purpose,' I added, quietly.

'Stupid cow,' Max grumbled. 'Mum'll go loopy if she knows we've even thought of going out there.'

'It's unlikely Rosie picked up Mort anyway,' I told Corey. 'I vote we go back to yours.'

'No! Please, we have to try. Missing animals *always* end up there.'

'Corey, come on, be logical. Rosie never comes into town any more.'

'But we've tried everywhere else. Please?' This time, he was brimming tears, his eyes all huge behind his glasses. Going to Whitehouse Farm meant nudging a hornets' nest, as I knew perfectly well, but I couldn't talk him out of it. He seemed desperate.

'Fine, we'll go out to Rosie's,' I sighed. Max made an outraged noise at once. 'We won't stay long. Your parents won't ever know we were there. You can drive us, can't you?'

'Uh, no,' he scoffed. 'My car's only two months old. Some of the roads out that way are just dirt tracks.'

'There's a bus to Cloud that stops twice a day at the bottom of our road,' Corey said. 'I've seen it on the timetable. There's one at lunch and one back at teatime. I'll pay.'

'Damn right you will,' said Max.

Just then, a car rolled along the seafront and came to a stop next to us. The driver's window rolled down. It was Neil, in his glimmering midnight-blue Jaguar.

'Alright, son?' He beamed, showing teeth whiter than the seagull slime on his windscreen. He always looked uglier, each time I saw him, despite the amount of surgery he'd had to fix his nose. Max beamed back at him, loping over to the car and leaning against the door frame.

'Alright, Dad? What time's the guy coming to pick it up?'

A Renault Clio beeped behind. Lazily, Neil threw a rude hand gesture as it overtook, gunning its engine.

'About six he said, give or take. Got a brand new Porsche

coming in a couple of weeks.' He was telling me, more than anyone else.

'What are you going to do till then?' I asked, though I already knew the answer. Max had told me.

'Garage is providing a hire car. Mercedes Sport. Just to tide me over. You coming round to see the Porsche when it arrives? Jo's going to do a lunch. Get all the family over.'

'Yeah,' I said, unenthusiastically. 'That'll be nice.'

'Good. What you up to now, then?'

Max spun Neil a yarn about how we were all going into town to look at some new phone as Corey hung back with me and we wandered over to the sea wall to watch the tide vomiting up clumps of seaweed and lager cans, leaving a trail of foamy spit on the steps.

'He hasn't changed then,' said Corey.

'Nope.' I smiled. 'Still a knob head.'

'Do they still live in that massive bungalow overlooking the bay? The one that backs onto the dunes with the big black gates...'

'... and panoramic views of Brynstan Bay and outdoor pool and three en suites and gold taps. JoNeille.'

Corey laughed. 'Jo and Neil. How corny? I always envied Max though, having a garden that backed onto the beach. Well, the dunes, anyway. Ours backs onto a dog toilet.'

'Don't be fooled, Corey. Something's rotten in the state of Denmark.'

'Huh?'

'Nothing. It's just this stupid quote Dad's got framed in his study.'

'Max'll inherit all that when they croak, won't he?'

'He's not interested in the money,' I said. 'Not really. Max would be happier working for a living, I know he would. He just hasn't got any incentive to at the moment. He's certainly not arsed about all the businesses, the arcades and the garden centre and that.'

'He owns the Pier now, doesn't he?'

A salty breeze stung my eyes. 'Yep. Yet another Rittman Inc property. It's like a cancer in this town.'

'Doesn't Greenland sponsor your running? He can't be that much of a knob head.'

'Oh he is, believe me. And it's only while I'm winning. He's still a twat.'

'Huge twat,' Corey added.

'Colossal.'

'Mammoth.'

'Gargantuan.'

'Humungulous!'

We were laughing by the time Neil sped off down the seafront and Max returned to us.

'What are you two giggling about?'

'Nothing,' I said. 'Come on, we've got a cat to find.'

'Yeah,' he said, flinging an arm around me. 'And a serial killer to ask about it.'

*

I don't know why I didn't try harder to talk Corey out of going to Whitehouse Farm. Maybe a part of me wanted to go back. A pretty sadistic part. Maybe I wanted to be reminded of a place I used to go as a child, before everything went wrong. I don't know, I really don't.

But anyway, we took the lunchtime bus to Cloud, the tiny village on the outskirts of Brynstan, where 'Roadkill Rosie' lived. It had been a while since any of us had been out there – Fallon had been the only reason. We'd befriended her in primary school, on the basis that she would do anything for a dare; 'Don't Dare Fallon' became one of our catchphrases. Take your knickers off and throw them at that windscreen. Jump off Devil's Rocks. Steal a Chocolate Orange. Flick a chip at that policeman. Go past the preaching Christians on the corner of the High Street singing that song about blow jobs. She'd do it all. She had no fear. She was also the kindest person I'd ever met.

The bus ride was endless, just like tomorrow seems like next year when you're a kid. I drifted into a daydream of the past. We were in the lounge at JoNeille – me, Max, Fallon, Corey and Zane – and we'd made a den out of the dining chairs, with some king size bed sheets draped over the top. All around the inside were sofa cushions, and in the middle we'd got ourselves a midnight feast of peanut butter and banana sandwiches, crisps, Haribos and cans of cherry Tango. Suddenly, a head parted the flimsy wall, giving a terrible cry.

'Wooooaoaaaaaaaaarrrrrgggggghhh!'

'Argh! Jessica, don't scare us like that!'

'Ha! What are you lot doing in here?'

'Dad said we could make a den and sleep in here tonight.'

'Have they gone out?'

'Yeah. Some dinner dance thing. Where have you been?'

'Just out, Beaky Boy.'

'Can you tell us a story, Jess?'

'Oh, not another story, Ella.'

'Yeah, please, Jess. Tell us a really scary one.'

'You can't handle a scary one, Zane. We had to call your mum when I read you some Silence of the Lambs, remember?'

'I won't cry this time, I promise. Please.'

'OK. Give me an idea, then, and I'll tell you a scary story about it.'

'Ummm...'

'Cats!'

'Cats? All right, then, Corey, cats it is. Hmm. Well, OK. There's this Edgar Allan Poe story called 'The Black Cat'. Have I told you that one before?'

'No. Tell us now!'

'OK, well, a long time ago, there once was this man who lived in this house with his wife and their cat—'

'What was the cat called?'

'I don't know. Maybe Claude or something. Yeah, Claude. Anyway, Claude was black, black as night, and the couple who owned him loved him very much. Then, as time went on, the man started to drink way more than he should—'

'Was he sad about something?'

'Yeah, he'd probably lost his job or something or he hated being married, something like that. Anyway, he started taking out all his problems on the cat. When he was drunk he got moody, and the cat was always around, rubbing against his legs and meowing for food. And one day, this cat got on the man's nerves so much that he took it out into his back garden...'

*

The bus dropped us off on the corner of Long Lane, and we walked the rest of the way until we came to the grubby sign for Whitehouse Farm, me with a gnawing throb of dread in my chest. Weirdly, it hadn't changed at all in the years since we'd last been there. The mud-spattered jeep was still parked in a garage next door; the field opposite was still barricaded with three rusty shopping trolleys, linked end to end with rope. The sweet smells of hay and dung still hung in the air, and, despite my fear, I felt strangely happy to be back.

'Go on then,' said Max, nudging Corey forward. 'Go and see if Mort's there. Then we can go.'

Corey took one look back at the everlasting lane we had just walked down from the bus. I saw him take a deep breath. Then he led us inside, one by one.

'Oh my GOD!'

FlapflapflapflapflutterflutterflutterScreeeeeech!

'Get it off! Get it off me!'

'AARGH!'

'What the HELL is THAT?'

'Jesus!'

Hell had been unleashed, and we were in the middle of it. Things squawked and screeched at me from branches, flapping about beneath the corrugated plastic roof. There were living things everywhere; creatures, birds, *things* crawling over my feet. Rabbits, ferrets, cats and an earless Jack Russell terrier brutally shagging a wig. Everywhere you looked were scruffy, eyeless or legless animals: a furry, flappy, feathery nightmare.

'Shut the door, quick!' a voice shouted, and Corey dived behind us to bang it shut.

All the way to Cloud, I'd held on to one hope – that Fallon Hayes might not be home. That we could just ask Rosie if she'd seen Mort, commiserate with Corey when she hadn't, then walk back to the pub on the main road and call a cab back into town. But the curt instruction had come from a girl – a long-legged, green-eyed girl with slightly buck teeth, a platinum blonde confusion of hair, and thick make-up. She had once been my best friend.

I took a deep breath. 'Hi, Fallon.'

'Was it strange, being back there again?'

7

Back at Whitehouse Farm

That's the weird thing. It was like the last four years hadn't happened.

'Oh, it's *you* guys!' she said, stroking a trembling white rabbit. 'Hi, Ella!'

'Yeah, hi.' I nudged away a teacup Chihuahua in a sailor suit that was trying to piss on my trainers. 'How are you, Fallon?'

She was smiling. A genuine smile, full of joy. She still had the same riot of freckles, like a leaf blower had blasted them to the four corners of her face. I hadn't expected her to be quite so happy to see us.

'I haven't seen you for ages!' The rabbit wriggled in her arms but she held it steady. 'Wow – you got cute, Max!' Max laughed and rubbed his mouth. 'And Corey! This is brilliant! Zane's not with you, is he?'

Max rose to the challenge of answering that one. 'No. We don't see him any more.'

'Oh,' she said. 'It's almost like the old times, isn't it?

'It was only four years ago,' said Corey.

The joy disappeared from her face as quickly as it had arrived. I knew she was thinking about the funeral – the last time she'd seen us. 'How are you, Max? How's your mum?'

'OK, thanks. Well, she has her days – you know. Dad's cool, though.'

'And, Corey, how's your nan and granddad? Have you still got all your Harry Potter stuff? How's baby Voldemort?'

I cut in at that point. 'Actually, Mort's the reason we're here. He's gone missing, and we were wondering if you'd seen him?'

I flapped away a rogue canary, nudging Corey. 'Has he got a collar on, Corey?'

'Yeah, a blue one. It's brand new,' he said, stepping behind me, cheeks so red I thought his head might explode. I'd forgotten he'd had a crush on Fallon four years ago. By the look of him, it had resurfaced.

'No, I would have recognised Voldy.'

'Mort,' Corey corrected.

'Actually, we haven't seen any gingers lately,' she pondered. 'We had one come in with one eye. That was ginger*ish*. You can have one of the tortoiseshells. Got loads of them.'

'No,' said Corey. 'His collar says "Malinowski" and it's got my number on it.'

'Can't you just take that one?' said Max, pointing to a scrawny black cat licking its backside on an upturned bucket.

'You can't have Esmerelda,' said Fallon. 'She's ours. Mum might have some more on the truck that she's picked up this morning, but she's not back yet. She shouldn't be too long though, if you want to wait?'

Max and Corey failed to answer – they were both in a trance, looking at her bottom as she bent over to put the rabbit down. She looked quite fat, under her frilly white vest, tiny denim shorts and mud-speckled moon boots. She started back up the steps to the farmhouse. 'You can wait for Mum inside, if you like. She should be back soon. We've got Sprite.'

Obediently, we all traipsed into the farmhouse behind Fallon, as if Sprite was the most golden carrot she could dangle. Cobwebs drooped in the corners of the kitchenette like forgotten Halloween decorations; the room opened up onto the same dingy lounge area, with the same tired leather three-piece and walls seemingly made from stacks of old newspapers. The shelving all around the top of the room was packed with ornaments, stuffed birds and woodland animals in small glass cases and clean white animal skulls acting as bookends and paperweights. The only light in the room came from two small windows and a box beside the fireplace with a nightlight inside, illuminating photos of Kate Middleton.

A little bird fluttered in from the lean-to and landed on a beam above our heads.

'Don't mind the mounts,' said Fallon, having seen Max staring up at the shelves of stuffed animals. 'They all died naturally.'

She retrieved three jam jars from a kitchen cupboard and put them on the breakfast bar. Not trendy jam jars like in some upmarket shabby chic restaurant either – actual old jam jars with the labels still glued on.

'Where's your mum gone?' I asked, moving aside a broken hamster cage to sit on a stool. Max stood beside me, hands still in his pockets.

'Gone to collect some pigs who died in the night. Sudden Pig Death Syndrome.'

'What does she do, exactly?' asked Max. 'I mean, I know she's a farmer or summing.'

Fallon turned to the fridge to get the Sprite and poured it

out into the empty jam jars, handing them to us. 'She *used* to be a farmer. She had to disintegrate, cos supermarkets are bastards with milk prices.'

Corey smiled. 'Do you mean diversify?'

'Yeah, that's it. We sold off most of our livestock; kept a couple back for milk and wool. Nowadays she's an ARS. Makes quite good money from that.'

'A what?'

'Animal Rescue Specialist. We look after sick animals, nurse them back to health. Kinda like vets, but a lot cheaper. We euthanise too, and cremate, all at cut-price. People report dead sheep or horses or large roadkill to Mum and she'll go out to them and pick them up. We've got a furnace out the back where we burn 'em, if they're no good for meat or black pudding.'

'Gross,' said Corey.

'No, it's not,' said Fallon. 'It's a good business. I help out when I can, but it's a bit difficult at the moment.' She looked at me and smiled again, so genuine it was kind of unnerving. A three-legged white cat, wearing a small plastic tiara, limped across the worktops, stopping by the stove to nuzzle the kettle; the kettle, potentially, with the you-know-what in it. A guinea pig ventured in and Fallon picked up a broken tennis racket and lightly tapped its tangly little arse back down the steps. While she was gone, Max moved over to the stove, prized off the lid of the kettle and peeked inside. Corey looked at him expectantly but he shook his head

After we'd gulped down the jam-jar Sprite and some stale smoky bacon Mini Cheddars, Rosie still wasn't back, so Fallon said she'd take us round the farm.

It was sad, really. The fantastic playground the farm used to be – giant tractors, rope swings, creeks, orchards, haunted corners and woods to ride our bikes through at breakneck speed – it was all still there, but we could see it now for what it was. Just a small, downtrodden smallholding in the middle of nowhere, housing dead or dumped animals, full of rust and mud. As kids, we saw the magic there. We saw magic in everything. Something about growing up kicks that out of you without you even realising it's happening.

'It's a shame Zane's not here,' said Fallon. 'Do you remember when those boys chased us at the swimming pool, Ella? We told them to get lost, but they kept on trying to kiss us.'

It was a memory I'd forgotten until Fallon unlocked it. 'God, yeah, I do.'

'Zane saw them off. He hated anything like that. His dad used to beat up his mum.'

'I never knew that,' said Max.

'Yeah,' said Fallon. 'They split up. Zane still lives in that ground floor flat on the seafront with her.'

'How do you know?' I asked her.

'I've seen him a few times since the – funeral,' she said, guiltily. 'I'm so sorry about what Mum said at Jessica's inquest, Max. She really didn't mean any harm, I promise you.'

There was a brief silence and awkward looks all round. Then:

'Where are we going, exactly?' asked Corey, bringing us back to the matter in hand.

'We could go down as far as the old railway line if you want,' said Fallon, as we crossed the road to the field gated by the three shopping trolleys. 'Nine times out of ten, if someone's lost a cat, that's where they'll be. Get loads of mice down there, cos loads of rubbish gets dumped. Mum's had to go down a few times cos of a fallen cow.'

So we headed across the lane to the fields and orchard, in the direction of the old railway line – a long road cut into the hillside, leading from Brynstan Bay through the interconnecting villages, and on towards Bristol. We used to race our bikes down there as kids. The big attraction was the Witch's Pool but you had to go miles down the track to get to it. There was an old railway tunnel halfway along the Cloud section of the line; we used to race through it at top speed, pretending a witch lived in the darkest part. If we went too slowly, there was a danger she'd reach out her bony fingers and grab us, dragging us screaming to our deaths. Zane was the most scared of all of us – I'd never seen anyone ride a bike as fast as him.

Past a chicken coop and a pen where four silky black goats were chomping on large heads of lettuce, we came to a rickety barn. Inside it, behind a mountain of hay bales, was a stash of small brown bottles. Each had a label on the front that read 'Acid Rain'.

'Mum's home brew,' said Fallon. 'We've got a ton of the stuff. Help yourselves.'

Max grabbed four bottles, and Corey put two in his bag of sweets from the Pier. I didn't take any, and Fallon said she preferred Capri-Suns. I couldn't work out if she was joking.

Fallon had grown up in a different way to us three. She hadn't grown up in the town like we had, so she was quite oblivious to a lot of the things we said, some of our slang. I almost envied her, a child wearing teenage skin that was never going to fit. I wanted to ask her if she had kept my secret, but I couldn't with the boys around. It was too much to hope she'd forgotten all about it.

Max pulled his phone out of his pocket to check the time. Along with it came a small see-through bag, with a clump of what looked like dried grass. I'd seen it before. He'd dropped it at the garden centre the other night. I was first to reach it this time.

'What's this?' I said, handing it back to him.

'Nothing. Just a bit of weed.'

'Weed? You mean, drugs?'

'Keep your voice down, or they'll want some.'

Still processing his answer, I followed Fallon through the orchard and across a field into the mottled darkness of the forest, making our way down a dirt track veined with tree roots. On either side of the track, the forest grew thinner and the pale yellow fields grew thicker. I scratched my now burning neck all over. I hadn't realised how annoyed I'd become.

'Can't you take a pill or summing?' said Max.

'Like you, you mean?' I snipped.

'What?'

'Nothing.'

'Oh, I get it. You're pissed I didn't tell you about the weed.'

'Yeah, all right, I am. I know everything about you, Max. I know that still sleep with the same Buddy Bear that your nan bought you when you were born.'

'Ssh,' he said, looking back for the others, but they were way behind us now.

'I know you love tomatoes but hate ketchup. I know where you got every single bracelet on your wrist, cos I was with you when you got them all. I know you still use the peach shampoo Jessica used to like. I even know why that little tuft of hair won't grow at the base of your neck. So why don't I know you do drugs?'

'It's not like it's heroin, Ells; just a bit of skunk. It's no big deal.'

'You said weed, now it's *skunk*? Isn't that the strongest one?'

'Nah, it's cool. It relaxes me. Seriously. Don't sweat it.'

'But people have gone mad on that, Max. Like, proper schiz. Are you high right now?'

'Stop making such a big deal out of it! It's nothing. I just didn't tell you cos I knew you'd get a hair up your ass about it.'

'How often?' I asked.

He was getting antsy. 'Just a few spliffs now and again.'

'What does that mean?'

'Oh for God's sake, just now and again, all right? A couple of spliffs in the morning. A shottie or summing before I go to bed. It helps me sleep.'

I couldn't believe what he was saying. I was waiting for him to smile and say he was joking. But he didn't.

'You should try it. Might loosen you up a bit.' He swigged from his Acid Rain bottle – the final straw.

'God, you are being the biggest arsehole today!'

'No, I just meant to relax you. I didn't mean…'

As I barged past him, he threw me a look like I'd taken his Buddy Bear and given him a bundle of barbed wire to cuddle.

The descent through the long grasses stopped at thick walls of leaves, and the long grey road of the Strawberry Line. The trains that used to run along there had taken strawberries and cheese to Bristol, and beyond. Now the tracks were gone and all the way along was an overgrown archway of trees and hedges, broken up in one direction by a huge black arc – the tunnel. A jogger huffed past and two cyclists were mere dots on the horizon. Apart from a dog walker with four elderly shih-tzus, we four were alone. We started walking, Fallon and Corey chattering away like old friends. Max was swigging Acid Rain, and I was ignoring him.

'Pete jogs down here,' I said. There was a definite eye roll from Max but I didn't draw attention to it. 'I've done some sprints along here too, at West Brynstan where the bend is.'

'Who's faster, you or Pete?' asked Corey,

'Oh Pete of course,' Max butted in. 'Pete's good at everything. You should see him curing lepers.' He sniggered and swigged at his bottle. I gave him the stink eye but he was ignoring *me* this time.

The air became colder as we reached the mouth of the tunnel; the smell of the limestone took me straight back in time. The slimy feel of the walls at the darkest point – the drip of rock water on my hair – all gave me a familiar thrill.

A little way along, Corey called out 'Oh my God' and it echoed around us. He'd seen a group of cats, all crowded around the carcass of a dead rabbit. As soon as they saw the torch, they began to scatter; some running back the way we'd come, others straight on into the tunnel.

'I told you there were cats down here,' said Fallon. 'Was any of them Mort, Corey?'

'No,' he called back, his voice sounding strangled.

'You really love Mort, don't you?'

Corey sniffed. 'He means a lot to me. I found him in a skip. He was only a few days old. I took him home and stayed up all night, giving him milk, keeping him warm. Granddad said I could only keep him if I laid out for all his food. So I did. He was my *reason*.'

None of us asked what Corey meant by that. I think we all just knew.

All of a sudden, there was chaos behind us. We looked

back into the darkness to see four figures on bikes, all hollering. As they got nearer, I realised they were just kids. But they were shouting abuse – mostly at Fallon.

I couldn't make out all of what they were shouting, but the odd phrase was clear. *All right, retard? How's your goats doing, Fallon? Hey, ugly girl! Butterface!* Two boys and two girls, all younger than us. The eldest boy, no more than twelve, waggled his tongue at her as his bike sailed past. It was all over in seconds.

'Who were *they*?' said Max as the whoops died away in the distance.

'Oh, just the Shaws. The boys go to that posh private school over in the next village. They're idiots. They shaved a couple of our goats over Easter. And they write things on the farmhouse walls sometimes. They think Mum's a witch who kills and skins people. You must have heard the rumours.'

None of us could deny it. We'd all heard the things people in Brynstan said about Rosie. The things *we* had all said. Things we'd laughed at.

'Can we go and see the Witch's Pool?' asked Corey. 'Just for old time's sake?'

'Uh yeah, if you like,' said Fallon. 'I doubt there will be any cats up there though. Never seen any animals round there at all.'

We were all looking at Max, as though it was up to him to decide whether or not we should go. He shrugged. So we carried on walking.

What had seemed like miles when I was a kid, actually took about ten minutes. Fallon suddenly veered off to the left where there was a weather-beaten sign saying *Wit Po* and she mounted the bank where some makeshift steps had been carved in the red earth. Max glanced at me then followed on behind her and Corey picked up the rear.

'Do people still come here?' I asked, as Fallon parted the overhanging branches to reveal a large overgrown meadow.

'I don't think so,' she said. 'The car park's just through those trees on the other side and it's all overgrown and people just tend to use it to dump old mattresses and oil drums. I don't even think the sign's on the main road any more. It's hardly a tourist attraction now.'

I felt uneasy as we walked through those long grasses. I wasn't actually scared – I guess it was a fear left over from childhood. A habit I hadn't grown out of. I had no reason to be afraid of it now. And once we had reached it, I could see the place for what it was – an algae-covered, pear-shaped lake with a small broken bridge at one end. The rockery, over which used to flow the fastest little waterfall, was now just a pile of slimy green rocks. But for the midges clouding over the surface, all was still.

'Is it really bottomless?' asked Corey, peering over the edge to look into the murk.

'Only one way to find out,' said Max, nudging him forwards, making him stumble and grab for the ground. I pulled Corey back up, throwing Max eye-daggers.

'No, it's not bottomless,' I said. 'It was just a story.'

'It's based on truth, Ella,' said Fallon. 'Don't you remember Jess telling us about it?'

'I do,' said Corey. 'Well, some of it. I remember it was Halloween and we were sorting out all our sweets in the shed at Max's.'

'Ahem, you mean my compact private members club pirate den?' Max corrected.

'Yeah, and Jessica came to the window and yelled boo!'

said Fallon. 'She couldn't get inside with us because she was too tall. Oh and something about some guy in a black hat?'

'I remember it,' said Max.

'So do I,' I said. 'Every word.'

*

BOO!

Jessica! Don't do that!

Come on then, share out your spoils. Whatcha get? Ooh, Scream Eggs, my favourite.

Where have you been? Mum said you were staying in tonight.

Dad made me work late at the garden centre. Did you have fun trick or treating? I love the outfits. What are you supposed to be?

I'm a Pirate Zombie, Ella's my Pirate Zombie Wife, Fallon's the witch from Wizard of Oz, *Zane's Thor and Corey's Hedwig.*

Oh you are a very cute Hedwig, Corey. Look at those little cheeks!

Can you tell us a story, Jess? A spooky one.

Another spooky one? You still haven't got over the last one, Zane. You just can't handle the scandal, baby.

Aww, please! Please, I promise I won't wet myself this time.

Yeah go on, Jess. Just a quick one. Tell us one about a witch!

A witch? Hmm, let me think. You live out near the Witch's Pool don't you, Fallon?

Yeah, but there aren't real witches there.

Oh but there were. A long time ago. See in the old days, like the mid-1600s, there used to be a Witchfinder who stalked through these parts looking for witches to put to trial and death.

Why?

Well people just didn't like witches. They thought they were evil. Any woman caught doing sorcery or something that couldn't be explained, it meant they were probably a witch. And so people like the Witchfinder General who was this big tall man in a wide black hat and cloak, used to round up these supposed witches, put them into cages on the back of his wagon, and take them out to places like the Witch's Pool at Cloud and test them in front of a crowd of witnesses, usually villagers and members of the church.

How did he test if they were witches?

He'd test their honesty. He'd tie a woman up inside a sack and attach a rope to it, then he'd throw her off the bridge into the water. If she bobbed back up to the surface, it meant she was a witch and so she was hauled out and burned alive or hanged. If she was struggling, he would realise she was telling the truth – she wasn't a witch so she could go free.

Didn't it just mean they were good swimmers if they came to the top?

Probably. Witchfinders didn't really bother with little things like common sense.

Did any of them just drown accidentally?

Oh yes. Lots of them did. The Witch's Pool is said to be bottomless, and many of the drowned ones were never found. That lake is said to be full of female skeletons. Their ghosts haunt it at night.

Zane's scared.

I'm not, Fallon. You're lying.

So if somebody's lying, does that mean they float on water?

So the Witchfinder said, yeah. Why, Ella? You're not lying about anything, are you?

No.

Are you sure?

Yeah. I always tell the truth.

Better not jump in the pool then or else we'll find out, won't we? Liars always float to the top.

*

It was a throwaway comment that hadn't meant anything, I realise that now. But I remember my face went bright red. And, after that, I never went swimming again, just in case.

It was magic hour by the time we'd walked the length and breadth of the old railway line, searching for Mort but there was no sign of him. We decided to head back to the farm and see if Rosie was home – our last hope was finding him in the day's truck haul of stray animals. My legs were tired as we crossed the last paddock and arrived back at the field with the trolleys at the entrance. The scorch had gone out of the day, and there was a warm, peachy sweep across the sky. The four of us walked in a line. And though Max hadn't reached for my hand all afternoon, I kind of didn't need him to with Corey and Fallon there. It felt like it used to.

I pulled my phone out of my pocket. 'What time was the second bus?'

'There isn't one,' said Corey.

Dread filled my chest. 'What? You said there were two buses a day. One at lunch and one at tea-time.'

'Yeah, but not on a Sunday. Reduced timetable.'

'How are we supposed to get back?' said Max. 'And we still haven't found his cat.'

'It's all right,' said Fallon. 'You can all stay at mine tonight.'

'No, it's OK,' I said. 'We'll get a taxi back.'

'It's fine,' said Fallon, flapping her hand. 'There's tons of sleeping bags and duvets. You don't have anything to get back for, do you?' She seemed slightly desperate.

We actually didn't. Corey's grandparents were still on holiday and my dad wouldn't be back for another couple of days.

'My parents will go spasmodic if they know I'm out here,' said Max, all twisty-face. 'I should get back.'

'Yeah,' I said, 'we don't have any of our stuff. Tooth-brushes. We need to go.'

'Oh please stay,' Fallon begged. 'We've got spare tooth-brushes somewhere. And blankets and sleeping bags. And more alcohol.'

'I could text them and say I'm staying at your house, Ells,' Max suggested.

'Yeah!' said Fallon. 'And we could get a takeaway too. I think the pizza place delivers out here, though I've never tried it. We get the leaflet though. We could have a picnic in the lounge and play Monopoly like we used to, what do you say?' Then she turned to me, all serious-faced for a moment. 'I'm *always* the boot though.'

'Very *Famous Five*,' I said. 'Apart from the booze.'

'Yeah! Do you remember Jessica reading the stories to us? She gave me all her books the last… time I saw her.'

Max smiled. 'She knew how much you loved them.'

'I always thought we were just like them,' she said with more than a note of sadness in her voice, 'the five of us. Max was like Julian, the eldest and wisest.'

I snorted. 'I didn't know Julian was a pot head.'

'Ella was George, the tomboy. Zane was Timmy the dog, strong and reliable. I was probably Anne.'

Max laughed. 'Yeah, and Corey must be Dick.'

If Corey was offended by Max's remark, he didn't say. 'Jessica called us the *Fearless* Five. That was our name.'

'Hey, he's right!' said Max. 'I'd forgotten that. Christ, that's a blast from the past.'

'Yeah well,' I said, 'we've all grown up a lot since then.' I almost felt insulted by it. We weren't little kids any more – we couldn't play those kinds of games now. She was dangling memories before my eyes like gold stars I couldn't reach.

'We could be the Fearless Five again, now,' said Fallon. 'Only we're four. We don't have Zane.' We looked at each other and smiled secretly, not knowing if she was joking.

'I know!' she cried. 'The baby can be Timmy! Then there's five of us again! Yay!'

'What baby?' said Corey.

'My baby,' she said. And that was the moment Fallon lifted up her vest to reveal a small, but definite, bump.

'So that's when you found out about Fallon being pregnant?'

8

Jolly Good Fun

'What?' we all cried. It was like in *Scooby Doo* when they see the monster for the first time; only we didn't yell *Zoinks!* and drop our sandwiches.

Fallon looked around at all of us. 'What?' The stretchy band of her denim shorts was holding her in at the waist, hiding much of her neat belly like the sea hides an iceberg. But, even in the dimming light, we could see she was *well* pregnant. She even had silvery stretch marks across her belly to prove it.

'Holy shit!' cried Corey.

'You're *pregnant*?' I said.

'Yeah. That's why I've got such a big tummy. I thought you all knew.'

'We just thought you were fat,' Max laughed.

I felt a rush of something weird – disgust? Jealousy? I didn't know. 'You're our age!'

'How far gone are you?' asked Max. 'I mean, how long till it comes out?'

'Four weeks yesterday, the doctor said.' We looked at each other in silence. 'It's all going well though, so don't worry. Mum's been to all my antenatal classes with me and got the nursery ready and everything. The heartbeat's been really strong on all my scans.'

'Whose is it?' asked Max.

'It's *mine*,' she said, wonderingly.

'No, I mean, who's its dad?'

'Oh!' She laughed, so much that we all laughed too. 'You don't know him. Come on, help me find the Monopoly board. I think I've still got all the pieces.'

Rosie wasn't home yet but she called while we were there. Fallon grabbed us some spare sleeping bags and duvets from the airing cupboard and told us her mum was going to be late – a baby giraffe had died suddenly at a zoo on the outskirts of Bristol. We wouldn't see her until nine at least. There were no cats on the lorry either.

Fallon brought down the light display from the nursery and put it in the middle of the lounge floor, to 'create an ambulance'. We all sat round it as it chirruped 'Twinkle Twinkle' while suns and moons danced around the dingy ceiling. Max fetched out his packet of weed, showing off now he didn't have to hide it from me any more. Mixing it up with his Golden Virginia, he showed Corey how to roll a spliff, and then offered it around. I refused, pointedly.

Eventually, fed up of being left out, I tried the Acid Rain. It was like strong lemonade tinged with spice and, as I drank, I started to feel warmer from the inside out. Soon we were all giggling.

Fallon wasn't drinking or smoking, but if she felt left out she didn't show it. Soon, Max, Corey and I were all in various states of undress from Strip Monopoly, and so pissed or stoned that none of us cared about anything. Corey had been to jail six times already, so he was sitting in just his pants. We'd eaten a feast of triangular cheese sandwiches, Wotsits, yoghurts, Cheesestrings, Maoams and Penguins on the rug in front of the fireplace.

Max shuffled up beside me on the carpet and put his chin on my shoulder. 'I've been a cock today, haven't I?'

I smelled the familiar scent of fuzzy peach shampoo on his hair. 'I guess that makes me Mrs Cock.' He laughed, toothy and exaggerated; the Acid Rain was beginning to reveal its full effects.

'I've never seen you this out of it,' I said, stroking his cheek.

He burped into my neck. Then he grasped my hand and put on an announcement voice. 'Fallon, Corneliusz, I want you both to know that I love this girl. I love this girl to Pluto and back again.'

'Oh God, here comes the speech,' I sighed.

'No, hear me out, I want everyone to know that one day, me and this beautiful girl are going to get married and live eppily aver rafter.' He burped again.

I chuckled. 'Don't give him any more alcohol, Fallon, for God's sake.'

She laughed. 'I didn't give him *that* lot! He helped himself.' Some sort of rat thing scurried across the carpet, into one of her discarded moon boots.

'It's true,' Max went on. 'I'd die for this girl. And we're going to make twenty babies together one day. Just got to work out all the sex stuff, and then we'll be off.' He started stroking my thigh, which felt suddenly sleazy. I felt myself sobering.

'Stop it!' I slapped him away. 'You're being embarrassing.'

'Aww, I think it's nice,' said Fallon, dreamily. 'It must be nice to be loved.'

I smiled. 'Sometimes.'

'I need a slash,' Max announced, staggering out to the lean-to.

'Whose go is it?' said Fallon, reaching across for the dice. 'Is it mine?'

'No, it's mine now,' said Corey, probably a lot louder than he meant to, and launching his dice across the board. He'd only thrown a three, but he leaned across and stamped his thimble twenty places to Pall Mall. Then he couldn't work out how to let the thimble go. Suddenly, his whole body dropped onto the board, scattering cards and houses all over the floor like confetti.

'Oh, Corey!' Fallon cried.

I couldn't see for laughing. 'Guess that's Monopoly over with then.' I began to tidy it all away, even though I could barely focus on what I was doing and my head was starting to go heavy.

'Guess so,' said Fallon, crawling across the carpet to put Corey in the recovery position so he didn't choke on the little green houses. 'He's a real sweetheart, isn't he? I'd forgotten how much I liked him.'

'Yeah. He's harmless.'

'Does your dad still write those romance novels about the buff guy in the kilt?'

'Yeah, I said. 'He's onto number thirty-eight now. Or is it eighty-three? No, it's thirty-eight.'

'I read the first series. They got a bit silly after that. Oh, sorry.'

'No, you're right. They're bloody awful. Even my dad says they're awful. But he gets amazing royalties from them so he's not complaining.'

'My mum's got all of them. Her favourite's *Call 999 For Doctor Delicious*. When Jock becomes...'

'...a doctor? Yeah. From the *Doc in the Trossachs* series.

God, that's the worst one. He's a haddock fisherman for God's sake. What's he doing taking out an appendix? Dad used to read passages out to me when I was ill. Just made me iller.'

Fallon smiled and looked down at Corey. 'Romance is nice. Being in love is nice, I imagine. I've never been in love.'

'What about the teaching assistant at school? What was his name?'

'Oh no, that wasn't love. He was just a quickie in the music room after clarinet practice.'

I tried hard to look unruffled but it was so difficult. I was so aware of every movement on my face.

'You and Max are in love, aren't you?' Fallon asked, stroking Corey's comatose head. He was still lying across the board, dribble pooling on the Community Chest space between Oxford Street and Piccadilly.

'Huh?' A blush crept slowly over my face. 'Yeah, of course. I love him to bits.'

'But... ?'

'I didn't say "but".'

'No, but... what did Max mean about the "sex stuff"?'

'Oh, nothing. Just something personal. He shouldn't have said it.' The blush deepened and started burning.

Fallon stacked the Chance cards. 'Is he too rough? Some boys are like that.'

'No,' I said, alarmed. 'We haven't. We just... haven't.'

Her eyes widened. 'You haven't had sex with him yet?'

'Why is it so shocking?' I said, exasperated. 'I'm only seventeen. It's not like I'm seventy.'

'I didn't mean it like that!'

'Sorry, it's just a bit – personal. Max thinks I've got this phobia about it.'

'That's understandable,' said Fallon, her voice dropping

to a whisper. 'You know, after what his dad did to you and everything.'

You know that feeling you get when the world just stops turning, just for a split second? Like that sick plunge of dread you get when you think your phone's been stolen, or you get a phone call so late at night that something bad must have happened? That's how I felt just then. Like the bottom had dropped out of my life. The top of my head had been opened like a sunroof, and my darkest secret had swarmed out into the open.

'Fallon, for Christ's sake!' I checked the doorway. Corey was still snoring £50 banknotes up in the air. 'Don't ever say that out loud again.'

'I'm sorry,' she whispered. 'I haven't told anyone, Ella, I promise. I just thought Max might know by now.'

My eyes couldn't get any wider. 'Do you think we'd still be together if he did? Do you think I'd still have to go round his bloody house once a month and eat roast beef at the same table as the man? Do you?'

'I'm sorry. I swear I haven't breathed a word to anyone. And I won't do. Ever.'

'Just keep it that way. All right?'

She nodded violently.

'Just change the subject.'

'OK.' But neither of us could think of another subject to change it to. It was too big a subject to manoeuvre round. My heart thumped. My brain swam. A cold sweat had washed over my body like I'd just walked through freezing fog. When Fallon hadn't been in my life, sometimes I could pretend it hadn't happened at all. That it was only my secret to know. My secret to stab me silently where no one could see the bruises.

'Corey seems to have perked up a bit,' said Fallon, eventually, after so much silence.

'He's not happy, he's drunk. They're not the same thing.'

'Oh.' Now it was awkward. Now I had to change the subject. We were turning in circles, like being back on the teacups at the Brynstan Fair. I'd felt sick then too.

'So, are you looking forward to being a mum then?' I said, my eyes still fixed on the money I was shuffling.

'I guess,' she said. 'It's a bit scary. I'm worrying about pooing, mostly. Mum says I came out when she was in the toilet. She said sometimes, in labour, you actually do a poo.'

I rammed the title deeds into a stack. 'I don't know what to say to that.'

'And if you have a baby in a water bath, you poo in the water and they make you get it out yourself, with a sieve. Mum says I can't take one of our sieves cos she needs it to strain the broccoli. I've got to eat a lot of greens at the moment.'

'Of course,' I said, numbly.

'But when the baby's here, it'll be nice to have someone who I can love and who will probably love me back.' A guinea pig crawled onto her lap and she began stroking it to sleep. 'These guys love me too, I know they do.'

A bubble of emotion surfaced in my chest. I stared at her belly. 'Thanks for not telling anyone, Fallon.'

She smiled. 'That's all right.'

I looked down at her bump. It seemed a lot more obvious now she was sitting down. 'Can I... touch it?'

'Of course you can!' She lifted up her top and presented her bump like a gift. I touched it with one finger. It was hard, like a basketball. I pressed three fingers against it. Then my whole palm, flat to the warm surface where her stretch marks shimmered in the firelight, like finger drawings on condensation. There was the faintest movement beneath my hand. And I just started crying, right there.

'Oh God I'm sorry.' I sniffed. I instinctively drew away, but she held my hand in place.

'You don't owe him, you know,' she said. 'Max, I mean. Don't ever feel bad about that.'

'Huh?' I said, wiping my eyes. 'I don't want him to see me crying.' I took my hand away again. 'Pete said the same thing when I told him.'

'Yeah and he's right. People might say I grew up with straw in my hair but I know some things about life, Ella. You should only do it with a guy when you're ready. If it's meant to be, he'll wait for you. If he doesn't, he's not the one.'

'What if he doesn't wait?'

She shrugged. 'That's his stupid fault then, isn't it?' She squeezed my hand and smiled as she let go. 'It is most definitely not yours.'

'You'll be a good mum, Fallon.'

'How can you tell?'

'Because you want to be.' She smiled even more at that. It felt good to give her a compliment.

Max appeared in the doorway, doing up his fly. 'I forgot where the toilet was, so I pissed in the road, that all right?'

'Yeah, whatever,' said Fallon. A one-eyed tabby cat wandered in and curled up on top of the broken piano in the corner.

Max grabbed an empty bottle from the sofa. 'Right, come on then,' he announced. 'Truth or Dare. We're all drunk and there's empty bottles about. We can't keep the cliché at bay any longer.'

Me and Fallon pulled Corey up into a sitting position, and set about getting him dressed again – like he was a doll.

'You playing, Core?' said Max, slapping his cheeks to wake him up.

'Yeah,' he said, eyes barely open. Fallon spun the bottle first – it pointed to Max.

'Truth or Dare?'

'Truth.' He smiled. My mouth went dry.

'Umm… tell us a secret.'

I could tell this wasn't going to end well. It never does in films.

'I don't have any secrets,' he said, looking at me. 'You know them all, anyway.'

'I didn't know about your drug addiction,' I said.

'I go in Jessica's bedroom sometimes. At night.'

We sat, silent, still like Stonehenge. Corey's eyes widened.

'I can't go in her room during the day cos my mum treats it like a shrine. No one but her is ever allowed in there. Even her pyjamas are still where she left them the morning she went. Her hairbrush has still got her hair in it. There's a pot of Nivea in there with her fingermarks in. It's like one of those rooms in a stately home that's roped off. Mum keeps a shoebox full of the newspaper cuttings from the accident as well.'

Fallon and I blinked at each other but said nothing.

'I look through the photo albums sometimes too. That's where I got the idea for your anniversary card.' He smiled at me. 'I found all these photos of her with us as kids. Trips to the beach. Trips into town. Trips out to the island. There's pictures of all of us, even Zane. She loved being with us. She taught me to ride a bike. I'd forgotten that till we saw those kids on the Strawberry Line today.'

Fallon smiled. 'She taught me how to spell "Mississippi". And she gave me all her old dolls' clothes. I've still got them.'

'She taught me to swim,' said Corey. 'Well, I can stay above water. And sort of move along. A bit.'

Max fumbled in his pocket and pulled out his wallet. From a secret pocket under the credit cards, he pulled out a folded photograph – *the* photograph of all of us that he'd copied for my card. He handed it to Fallon. Corey scurried over to her, looking at it over her shoulder.

'Wow,' said Fallon. 'I'd forgotten how beautiful she was, Max.'

'You've got the same eyes. The same smile actually as well,' I said.

'She looks like Jennifer Lawrence.' Corey hiccupped. We all looked at him. 'She does, though, doesn't she?'

'Yeah,' said Max. 'I guess there's some resemblance.'

'Did I do those plaits in your hair, Ella?'

'Yeah, most likely,' I said. 'My mum could never plait hair and I can't do them on myself.'

'God, look at Zane,' she said. 'Haha, look at his buck teeth! We're all so tanned.'

'Is that me?' asked Corey.

'Yeah,' said Max. 'In that bloody Ben 10 T-shirt. I was beginning to think it was a layer of your actual skin.'

'We lost touch just after she died, didn't we?' said Fallon, still gazing at the photo. 'We were all… ruined.'

None of us could say anything more. It was like someone had blown a huge bubble of truth and it had popped stickily in all our faces.

It was a heavy minute of silence until Max snapped his gaze away from the flickering flames and spun the bottle again, hard. It landed on Corey.

'Aha! Truth or Dare, my friend.'

'Truth,' said Corey, with a gassy burp.

Max thought for a second. 'Where's the weirdest place you've ever done it?'

'I haven't,' said Corey, as quick as a tick.

'What, never?'

'Is that such a major surprise?' said Corey, picking up a new bottle of Acid Rain. 'Who's gonna want to sleep with a guy who hasn't got the fine motor skills to undo a bra? I can barely tie my own shoelaces. As you can guess, my fingering game ain't so hot.'

Max shrieked with laughter, not for the first time that day, and doubled over in hysterics. So did Corey.

'Oh you poor sod,' Max breathed, wiping tears from his eyes. 'Bet your arm cardio game's amazing though, innit?'

'Oh yeah, I got that down, mate. I got that down. My right bicep's bigger than Thor's.'

They both rolled around in a hysterical embrace, like two kittens with a ball of wool. I couldn't help but smile.

'Corey, your turn to spin,' said Fallon, replacing the bottle. He and Max were still too out of control to concentrate, though, so she spun it instead. It landed on me. 'Truth or Dare, Ella?'

'Dare,' I said. She looked at me. 'What? It's boring if we keep saying Truth all the time. I'd prefer to do something.'

'But I can only think of a Truth. OK then, let me think.'

As Fallon pondered, Max levered himself up on his elbow. 'I dare you to text Hamlin something nasty.'

Fallon beckoned a small rat-type-thing to come out from behind the sofa cushion. 'Who's Hamlin?'

'Pete Hamlin,' I said. 'My running coach.'

'Oh,' she said. 'What do you mean, nasty? Something mean?'

'No,' said Max. 'Kinky stuff. Something like, *Hey Sexy,*

Thinking of you and me getting moist tomorrow at training.
Kiss kiss. Monkey face. Heart eyes emoji.'

'Max!' I said. 'That's ridic, he'll kill me.'

'No he won't. He can take a joke, can't he? He'll know it's just a laugh. Go on.'

'I'm not doing it. We should start tidying up anyway. Rosie will be back soon.'

'Ooh forfeit, forfeit!' said Corey.

'No, I'm not doing it. And I'm not doing a forfeit either.'

'*I'll* do it then,' said Max, and before I could stop him, he fished my mobile out of my hoody pocket, holding me at bay.

'Max, give me that phone! Max! Please! It's not funny.'

He was scrolling. He clicked on Pied Piper. He was texting. 'Please Max!'

He hit Send. 'Done!'

'I can't believe you!' I snatched the phone back from him and checked my sent messages. *Can't wait to get sweaty with u tomoz, Bae X*

'You bloody idiot!' I yelled. 'How could you do that?'

'Oh for God's sake, Ells. It's a joke. Be interesting to see what comes back, won't it?'

I didn't like the look on his face as he sat back down again – it was almost spiteful. 'What do you mean by that?'

'You never know, do you? Like, he could come back with something similar. Maybe you *hope* he does.'

'I don't think it's funny, suggesting my running coach is some kind of paedo.'

'Oh, come on, he must have tried it on with you at some point. You've been having one-to-ones with him for ages. And he's a hot guy.'

'So?' I shouted. 'I'm training for the Commonwealth

Sodding Games, Max. Newsflash: you need to train quite a bit for that.'

Max reached into his pocket and pulled out the little key bunch Pete had given me. I instinctively checked my own pockets – nothing.

'Fell out of your trackies earlier. There's a Brynstan Academy fob on there they only give to teachers. Why's he giving you his house keys?'

'So I can use his punchbag, all right? He's been teaching me how to box. Now give them back.' I grabbed the keys from Max and shoved them in my trouser pocket again, zipping it up this time.

The silence between me and Max at that moment would have frozen water. Fallon looked worried, like a child watching her parents argue. Then my phone beeped, and the screen lit up. Pied Piper had replied to the message. *You'll do anything to avoid cross-country, won't you? See you tomorrow. Don't be late, Bae* 😍

'See?' said Max. 'He can see it's just bants.'

'Bugger off,' I spat.

'You won't go home, will you?' said Fallon, a note of desperation in her voice.

'What?' said Max.

She looked hurt. 'You're going to argue and then you'll phone someone to pick you up and you'll go home, won't you? Can you stay – just for another hour? Please?'

We all looked at her. She was practically in tears.

'Why, Fallon?' asked Corey, sobering. 'Why's it so important to you?'

'The Shaws are coming. The ones we saw on the Strawberry Line, earlier. They've got into the habit lately of bothering me every night. I'd like a break.'

'Why?' I asked. 'What do they want?'

'Nothing. They just pester me, that's all. Stones at the window. Spooky noises through the letterbox. That kind of thing. They frighten me.'

'But nothing frightens you,' said Corey. 'Don't Dare Fallon, remember? I dare you not to be scared of them.'

She shook her head. 'It doesn't work with them. I still don't like them coming round. But if you're here...'

Max made a clicking noise with his tongue. 'Hang on a minute, those kids we saw on the Strawberry Line were, like, kids. Little kids. All of them under twelve at least.'

'I know,' she said. 'But I've told them so many times. Luke – the eldest – he winds the rest of them up and off they go. They never come in. But sometimes they've thrown stuff through the window. A brick. A bottle. Once they set light to a hay bale, out in the barn. If I hadn't seen them, the whole lot could have gone up. We had kittens in there at the time too, they could have been killed.'

I started folding up the Monopoly board. The game was clearly over.

'Little gits!' said Corey furiously. 'How dare they?'

Fallon nodded. 'The police won't do anything; I've rung them before. And they're too young for the courts to get involved. Mum says to ignore them; that they'll get bored soon. But I don't think they will. They know I'm scared. What can I do, Ella? What if they – try and do something to the baby when it's born?'

You know when you hear an annoying noise and it repeats on and on and on and on until you're so mad you could just kill whatever is making the noise? Like a banging door or a cough or a persistent fly that won't just find the damn window? That's how I felt right then – everything Fallon was saying about the Shaws just wound me up and up until I was raging inside so badly I wanted to break something.

'Ella, what are you doing?' said Fallon. I followed her gaze down to my hands.

Without even realising it, I had torn the Monopoly board right down the middle.

'So the rage took over?'

9

A Little Upset

Yeah, a bit. That horrible Acid Rain I drank just seemed to make it worse. I listened to more tales of the Shaws, and how they'd teased Fallon for so long now she was 'almost used to it'. But what I saw was emotional abuse. Physical abuse. Arson. Their latest trick was blackmail. They'd scammed over sixty quid off her, this summer alone. And they still kept coming back for more.

'Haven't you learned yet, Fallon, that paying them off doesn't work?'

'It does, though,' she said. 'They leave me alone for days when I pay them to.'

'Days?' I roared, flecks of spit landing on my knee. 'Days isn't good enough.' Corey was looking at me. Max fidgeted with his bootlace. 'What? Is no one else going to say anything?'

Max stopped fidgeting and shoved his hands behind his head. 'What do you want us to say? It's none of our business.'

'Of course it's our business.' I got to my feet. 'We need to do something.'

'Like what?' said Corey. 'It's, like, nine o'clock.' The little wig-shagging Jack Russell was curled up like an Artic fox in his lap. 'They'll all be in bed, won't they?'

Fallon was scattering some fish flakes into a murky green tank in the corner. 'No, they've gone to the Harvest Home tonight. They said they'll be round after it finished. That'll be about ten.'

'Right, then. We'll put a stop to it. Tonight.'

Max laughed. 'Hang on, Liam Neeson. You're not seriously suggesting we all lie in wait to kick seven sorts out of them, are you?'

'No, of course not,' I said, sitting back down. 'But we could still get our own back. Well, Fallon's own. We could do *something*.' I could feel my fists start to tingle.

At that moment, the lean-to door rattled outside, and heavy footsteps scuffed across the concrete floor. The caged birds and animals squeaked and cawed, and then settled again as Roadkill Rosie wobbled through the doorway of the kitchenette.

'Hi, Mum. You OK?' asked Fallon, struggling to her feet.

'Yeah,' came Rosie's gravelly reply. She hadn't changed one bit, but for a few grey streaks in her long black hair. Still short and squat, with a wide face and the same old wart tucked into the crease beside her nose. No wonder people thought she was a witch.

The moment she clocked us all in the lounge she thinned her eyes. 'What's all this, then? If you're them lot what keeps getting her to give you money, then you can piss off now or I'm calling the police!'

'No, no, Mum, they're not the Shaws. These are my friends,' said Fallon. 'This is Corey and Max and Ella. You remember them, don't you? From the old times?'

'Oh,' she said, looking directly at Max. 'You're the

Rittman boy. Surprised your dad let you come out here, what with all that business…'

'He doesn't know I'm here,' he replied, reaching into his jeans for his tobacco pouch.

'Just as well.' She sniffed. 'Have my guts for garters, he would, if he thought you were anywhere near here. If you've come to cause trouble—'

'He hasn't,' Fallon interrupted. 'Mum, they came over this morning, looking for Corey's cat. I asked you on the phone earlier if you've picked up any ginger toms today.'

'No, no toms. Couple more females but no toms.' I could hear her scratchy smoker's breath, even though I could barely see her in the gloom of the kitchen. 'You keep them out of the Skin Room, Fallon, you hear?'

'Yeah, I will, don't worry,' Fallon replied as Rosie went to the fridge to grab some food for her supper – a hunk of cheese, half a loaf of bread, three bottles of Acid Rain and a family pack of Penguins. She disappeared back through the door without another word.

When she'd gone, Fallon came to sit back down with us, smiling meekly. 'Sorry about that. She's a bit protective of me, what with the baby and that.'

We all nodded in understanding, and Fallon started tidying up our mess. None of us said anything for a little while.

But Corey could only hold himself back so long. It must have been killing him.

'Fallon, what's the Skin Room?'

*

When she was sure that Rosie had gone to bed, Fallon showed us the Skin Room. It came with a warning though.

'Look, are you squeamish?' she said, hand resting on the handle of the basement door. 'Because if you are…'

'I'm not,' said Corey.

'Depends what it is,' said Max. 'What's in there?'

'Well, you know what Mum does for a living now, yeah? And before she got busy, she used to do taxidermy as a hobby as well. You know the mounts on the kitchen shelves?'

'Taxidermy?' said Corey. 'Like, stuffing animals?'

'Yeah. She did a few pets for people we knew, sort of putting them into little poses. There's a budgie in a rocking chair reading a book and a dog playing snooker – they went a bit wrong and the families sent them back.'

'Oh, like Bad Taxidermy on Twitter, yeah?' laughed Max, swigging his bottle.

'Yeah,' she said, with a frown. 'Well, she still likes to do it sometimes, as a hobby. She calls it her 'art.''

'Riiiight…' I said.

Fallon looked sheepish. 'We just haven't got round to sorting out what's for burning and what's for keeping yet. So, until we know what to do with it all, it goes in here. In the Skin Room.'

'OK. Can we go in and have a look then?' said Corey, all but barging past her.

'We're all grown-ups here,' said Max. 'We can handle it.'

She nodded slowly, then turned the door handle and reached inside for the wall switch. The light didn't come on immediately. When it did, it revealed a rickety wooden staircase. The light blinked off, shrouding it in darkness again. Then on again, off again.

'It'll come on properly in a minute, just takes a little while,' she explained. 'Go on down, carefully. Mind the fourth step – it wobbles.'

Down we went, Corey first, followed by Max, then me

and finally Fallon, the tube light still blinking above the lower room. On and off. On. And off. On. And off.

We didn't need a steady light to get the picture though. If Fallon had told us twenty people had been shot dead down there, I wouldn't have been surprised. In fact, if she'd told us twenty people had full-on *exploded* down there, I would have believed that too. What I didn't expect was what I saw.

First thing I noticed was the blood; it was *everywhere*. Pools on the floor. Dry spatters and spray marks all up the whitewashed walls. A large wooden table in the centre, dyed red with it. And carcasses all over the place. On the side benches, on sheets of blue plastic on the floor, hanging from ceiling hooks. Hollowed out. Skins. Skulls. Ribcages.

'Jesus Christ,' I said. I just couldn't look away from it. The jar of eyes on the huge wooden table. The hollowed-out pig's head on a shelf in the corner. The three rabbits, gouged out, hanging from three rusty hooks by the door. The bucket full of dead piglets, in an old tin bucket on the floor.

The next thing I noticed was how cold it was. Cellar-cold.

Max was the first to turn around and walk back up the steps… I'd forgotten about his problem with blood. Corey was just staring at it all in wonder, like he'd walked into Wonka's factory. And me – little details kept screaming out at me.

The full bath of blood, slowly rocking in the room at the back.

'Don't worry, it's only pig's blood,' said Fallon brightly. 'We make black pudding out of it and sell it. Mum invented that structure it's on to keep it moving, else it clots.'

Corey nodded. 'I can see why your mum doesn't want anyone down here.'

'Yeah. A lot of this stuff is just waiting to go out to the

furnace. The ham's curing. And the pelts we sell to humane fur traders. Mum knows this guy down the market.'

'I'm just going to see if Max is OK,' I announced, leaving Corey investigating a barrel of dead rats on ice.

I went back up to the lean-to and into the lounge. Max was sitting on the sofa, clutching a bottle of Acid Rain and looking as white as the three-legged cat with the tiara, currently licking her own ass beside a stack of old *Hello!* magazines near the fireplace.

'You OK?' I said, sitting down beside him.

'Don't know what I expected.' He sniffed. 'I fainted when we watched *Twilight*.'

'Oh, yeah. I forgot.' I smiled.

'I think… No, forget it.'

'What? No, what were you going to say?'

He took a deep breath. 'I think about it sometimes. What Jess looked like. That night on the seafront.'

'Oh God, do you?'

He nodded. 'Can't help it. I remember the judge at the inquest, saying about all the blood on the front of the bus. And I can see it in my head, even though I wasn't there.'

'You shouldn't think about it. It doesn't help you.'

'Sometimes in the night, I'll be dreaming about something else and then I'll see the bus coming and I'll see it hitting her and… there's blood all over the place.' He looked at me. 'I saw them washing down the road the next day, Ells. She couldn't have meant that to happen, could she?'

'No, of course not. Don't think about it,' I said, lying back on the sofa, cuddling his head against mine. 'It was an accident.'

He took a deep breath and let it out slowly. 'She's never really gone, not to me. I haven't felt her leave. Do you know what I mean? I still feel like she's here sometimes. Is that weird?'

'No, it's not weird at all.' It was the drink talking now. Definitely the drink.

'But at night, all I can think about is the blood and the screeching of the brakes and the dent in that bus. It's a nightmare, Ells. It haunts me.'

It sounds sick, but that's what gave me the idea. The idea for the revenge on the Shaws. And as I sat there, holding Max against me, my brain went into overdrive, and a messy little snowball began to roll.

'So what did you do?'

10

A Horrid Shock

The lean-to door rattled first at 10.36 p.m. The sky was dark outside the farmhouse windows. A thrill ran right through me like a hot snake.

'OK, this is them now. Go go go!' I whispered, as each of us scattered to our positions. Fallon went to answer the door, but before she could get there, it rattled again. I watched from my spot behind the birdcage, coiling the string around my hand. The door creaked open.

'Oh. Hi,' said Fallon. I peeked around the side of the cage and caught my second glimpse of the four Shaw kids, standing in the glow of the security light. Straddling their bikes, they stood in the lane outside the farmhouse, threatening, like a dog-pack.

'All right, Fallon?' said the oldest, a chubby boy with zits marching down the length of both his cheeks and white flip-flops on. He had piggy blue eyes, and a blond buzz cut that could have grated cheese. I knew his name was Luke. 'Sorry we're late. We went over to the Harvest Home. How come you weren't there?'

'I didn't want to go,' said Fallon meekly, scuffing her

boot on the floor behind her. Her right hand was trembling behind her back.

'She was afraid to see us,' laughed the little blonde girl on the smallest bike. This was Luke's sister, Radclyffe; the most evil of the lot, apparently. Lighter of matches, thrower of bricks. She couldn't have been more than seven. Her two front teeth were missing, and she wore a white strappy sun dress and patent black Doc Martens. Her face looked sharp enough to slice Fallon in two. I could see why she was scared of them, though they didn't scare me.

'Let's have it, then.' The other boy, Alfie, lanky and black-haired, with a Mohican haircut, yawned.

His sister, Clem, who had a red bob, was on the bike just behind him, wearing a minty-green T-shirt bearing the slogan 'Butter Wouldn't Melt', with some cartoon character winking beside it. She didn't say a word, but her scowl was focused squarely on Fallon.

'I haven't got it,' said Fallon, a wobble in her voice. 'The money.'

'Oh dear,' said Luke, folding his arms. 'Well, that won't do at all, will it? You said you'd have it.'

'I mean, I do have it, but I don't have change. I've only got fifty pound notes.'

The four of them looked at one another like they'd just found pirate treasure. Alfie whooped manically, like a hyena, and Luke did some stupid hand-dance thing with him. God, did I hate bullies.

'That'll just have to do, won't it?' spat Radclyffe. She held out her hand flat, expecting her payment right that instant. Then they all did the same. Four outstretched palms.

'Come on,' said Clem. 'I'm tired. Hurry up and give us our money.'

'OK,' said Fallon, 'but you'll have to come in and get it.'

'No, we'll wait here, thanks,' said Luke with a laugh as he looked at Alfie. 'You don't give us orders, Hayes.'

'Are you afraid of my house or something?' asked Fallon.

Luke laughed again. 'Yeah right, I'm sooooo afraid of your weirdo farmhouse.'

'And your weirdo mum,' Clem added.

'Come in then,' she said, stepping aside.

Luke looked back at the others. No way were they going in. And no way was he going to look like some baby in front of them. He gave a long, dramatic sigh and threw his bike down. 'I'll do it then. You lot wait out here.'

'I wanna come, I wanna come,' said Radclyffe, dropping her bike and clinging on to her brother's hand.

'Christ's sake, come on then,' he snarled.

Fallon stood aside and allowed him to step over the threshold of the lean-to, closely followed by his little sister. They moved about the place like they were in a haunted house, staring at the cages, smelling the air, looking above them in case anything should fall from the plastic roof.

'Is Roadkill Rosie here?' asked Radclyffe, in a smaller voice.

'No, don't worry. She won't be back for ages. Uh, it's just through there,' said Fallon, allowing them to step in front of her towards the Skin Room. 'In our basement. It's through that door, just down the steps. After you.'

I thought we were home and dry then. But Luke stopped and looked at her. 'You go down and get it. We'll wait up here.'

'I can't,' said Fallon. 'I've hurt my ankle, so I can't make the stairs. Honestly, it won't take a moment. Just go on down the stairs and you'll find it in a pile on the table. There's a fifty pound note for each of you. I'll put the light on and wait here.'

That was amazingly quick thinking, I thought. And with that, Luke started towards the door, his sister following after him, like they were navigating through the rooms of some house of horrors. I guess, in their minds, that's exactly what it was. They'd heard all the stories. The rumours about Rosie. That was exactly why they picked on Fallon; it made her different. Vulnerable.

So, really, you could say we were giving them what they wanted. We were just illustrating the stories for them in black and white.

Or, rather, red.

Down the steps they went, creak, creak, creak, wobble.

'Where's the light?' called Luke.

Once Luke and his sister were both clear of the door, Fallon flicked up the light switch as I yanked on the string and…

SLAM!

Fallon lunged forwards and turned the key, trapping the Shaws inside the Skin Room. One of them – Luke – started banging and kicking on the door at once, shouting all sorts of things, too muffled to translate through the thickness of the wood. The other one – Radclyffe – just screamed and screamed and screamed.

'They're going to be traumatised for life if we leave them in there too long,' said Fallon, chewing on her thumbnail and looking across at me.

'Not nearly long enough yet. Give it a couple of minutes. Let that blinking light do its thing. Let them see that bath full of blood.'

'I wonder if the boys are ready?'

As if in answer, there came an enormous *SPLASH* from outside in the road, followed by two sets of shouts and another prolonged scream. I ran to the lean-to door and yanked it open to find the two other Shaw siblings lying in the road beside their bikes, soaked through with bright red blood.

'ARGH! AARGH! AARGH!' screeched Clem, over and over again. 'WHAT IS IT? ALFIE! ALFIEEEEE!'

Alfie shuddered and slipped as he tried to get to his feet, wiping his eyes on his sopping T-shirt. 'Oh my God, it's…'

He couldn't finish his sentence – he ran towards the hedge on the opposite side of the road and blew chunks of everything he'd eaten at Harvest Home into the dark ditch.

Clem was still a bloody mess, wailing like her bike had just given birth to her.

We looked up to the window above where Corey and Max were high-fiving and grinning like lunatics, their empty blood buckets dangling from their free hands.

I folded my arms and walked out into the blood-drenched road, towering over Clem. 'Now, that wasn't a very nice surprise, was it?'

'Who are you?' she whimpered, shivering in the cool night air.

Her brother returned from the hedge, pulling his bike up onto its wheels. 'You'll pay for that,' he threatened shakily, stabbing a finger at Fallon. 'Who's she?'

'Just a friend,' I said. 'And she won't pay for it, you're wrong about that.' I pushed him back down into the ditch, with his vomit. 'If you EVER come back here again, it'll be YOUR blood we're pouring from those buckets. Got it?'

Alfie scrabbled to his feet, but said nothing.

Clem rolled her bike to an upright position. 'I w-w-w-want to go home, Alfie.'

Her brother looked back at us. 'Where's Luke? Where's Raddy?'

Fallon looked at me, clearly not knowing what to say. This was my plan.

'They're inside. In the Skin Room,' I told them.

'What's that?' asked Clem.

'Where Roadkill Rosie skins her hides, of course. The ones she collects on the trucks. No one comes out of there alive. Sorry. Well, best be running along now then. Nighty night.'

'No, wait!' Alfie cried, grabbing my arm. I turned and looked at him, glaring like he'd just made the biggest mistake of his life. 'Please. We're sorry. Please, let them go.'

'No,' said Max, appearing in the doorway behind us, with Corey standing beside him. They looked like bouncers. Bespectacled, desperately-in-need-of-a-few-bench-presses bouncers, but still, there they were, looking mean, and I was glad of it. 'You'll just have to tell their mum and dad they're not coming back.'

Clem started crying harder. 'I want Mum, Alfie!'

'She's going to kill us when she hears we've been back here,' he muttered, wringing out his T-shirt on the roadside. 'You've got to let them go. Please, look, we're sorry.'

'No,' snapped Corey, shoving past Max and getting right in his face. 'You've asked for this, all of you. We know what you've done. And this is the price you're going to pay.'

They both just looked at us, all of us in turn, like we were the Avengers or something. They didn't know what to say, or what to do. I felt twelve feet tall.

Alfie scowled at Corey. 'What's wrong with him then?'

'What's wrong with you?' I said, stepping forward. 'That's what I want to know.' I pointed to the spot just in front of me where I wanted them both to stand. They came, both shivering and on the verge of tears.

'If you want your cousins out of that room, you better

be nice. You better give back ALL the money you've taken from Fallon over the summer. And you better promise her that you will never ride your bikes past here ever again.'

'What do we get in return?' asked Alfie.

'Your cousins don't get turned into meat pies. *That's* what you get.'

'We don't have the money.' Clem sniffled, her little body shivering in the night air. 'We spent it all on sweets.'

'We'll have the sweets then,' said Max, holding his hand out expectantly.

'We don't have them here,' said Alfie. 'They're at home. Under my bed.'

I looked at Fallon. She stepped in front of me. 'I'll let your cousins go. But first thing tomorrow morning, you better leave those sweets on the doormat with a little note apologising for what you've done. Otherwise…'

'Otherwise what?' sobbed Clem.

Fallon wasn't saying anything. Corey wasn't saying anything either. And Max was just staring at me. So I had to come up with the ultimate threat, right there and then.

'Otherwise, we'll be watching you. When you go to bed at night, when you're walking to school, when you're riding your bikes through the railway tunnel. We'll grab you when you least expect us, and we will put you into sacks. Then we'll sling you in Rosie's truck with all the other DEAD BODIES. She'll bring you back here. To the Skin Room. And she'll chop you up one by one and drop you in the Mincer. And then you'll probably end up inside a pie, which we'll leave on your parents' doorsteps. *That's* what we'll do.'

Both of the kids agreed to our demands on the spot. Without another word, Fallon went on inside, flanked by the two boys, and unlocked the basement door. The other two Shaws spilled out, running for the front door as fast as they could go. Neither of them said a word either – they just looked at both their blood-soaked cousins standing in the road, grabbed their bikes and then the four of them raced back up the lane, pedalling furiously and snivelling like idiots, leaving nothing but bloody tyre tracks behind them.

And the rest of us whooped and hollered, celebrating a truly good night of revenging. It felt like winning a race. Like punching that bag in Pete's garage. I imagined it was how proper sex felt. Glorious. Joyful. Just a giant, enveloping relief. Like an itch you finally scratched, or a huge, painful zit you finally popped. My tiny army had won.

'Ella, that was amazing!'

'Now *that* was payback!' said Corey.

'That was the best,' said Max, hugging Corey's head under his armpit. 'Legendary!'

'That was the most brilliant best thing ever,' Fallon squealed, hugging us in like we were her babies. 'I could never have done that by myself. We're the Fearless Five again!'

'Fearless?' said Corey.

'Yeah,' said Fallon. 'Don't you remember our gang name?' There was a satisfied little pause.

Then I realised something. 'I want to do it again,' I said.

'Yeah, so do I, actually,' said Corey with an impish grin.

'Yeah, I'm in,' said Max. 'That was epic.'

'Definitely!' said Fallon. 'Who else can we revenge on?'

'Zane?' suggested Corey.

'Of course!'

'No,' said Fallon.

'Come on,' I said. 'He's been after Corey for ages. It's payback time.'

'Yeah,' said Max. 'Yeah it's childish but so's he. Let's have one last summer of being Fearless Five.'

'There's only four of us?' I said.

'The baby makes five, dunnit?'

'We can't,' said Fallon. 'We can't do anything to Zane.'

'We ca-an,' I sang, high-fiving Max.

'No, I can't. It wouldn't be right.'

'Give me one good reason, Fallon.'

'Because he's my baby's daddy,' she said.

*

I think we were all too stunned to answer at first. Corey went even paler than he was already. After the initial shock, none of us said another word about it until we were under our sleeping bags and blankets in her bedroom. It felt cosy, us all sleeping in the same room again. Like it was before.

'Are you all shocked?' she said in the darkness. 'About me and Zane?'

Neither of the boys answered.

'A bit,' I said. 'I always thought he preferred playing the field. If I'd known you were his girlfriend...'

'Oh no, it's not like that,' she said. I could see her struggling to lever herself up in the thin shard of moonlight filtering through her Forever Friends curtains. 'No, we're not boyfriend and girlfriend. We stayed in touch, sort of. He came round one night, out of the blue really... He'd been drinking.'

I sat up. 'He forced you?'

'No, no, not at all. We just talked about the old times and school. And he dared me...'

'Oh God,' said Max. 'You screwed him for a *dare*?'

'Yeah, I kind of did,' she giggled. 'It was fun though. I enjoyed it. It was quite... quick.'

'I bet,' said Max. I noticed Corey was saying nothing at all. And I could see he wasn't asleep. His eyelids were flickering and his hands were twitching.

'He cried afterwards,' she said. 'I'd read in one of Mum's magazines that sometimes women cry after doing it because of all the emotion but I didn't realise guys cried too.'

'They don't,' said Max.

'How would you know?' I said, nudging him.

He shook his head. 'Well, they don't, do they? It's well known.'

'Well, Zane did anyway,' said Fallon. 'He got really weird about it. Said it had ruined our friendship. We've barely spoken since.'

'So he doesn't know?' said Corey for the first time. 'About the baby?'

'Yeah, I called and told him once I knew for definite.'

'And what did he say?'

'Nothing. He put the phone down on me.'

*

The next morning, we swapped numbers, and Fallon apologised again for not finding Mort. Rosie was nowhere to be seen, so we couldn't say goodbye to her.

It had rained in the night, and the rain had washed away most of the blood in the road. There was also a large carrier bag on the doorstep, full to the brim with every kind of sweet you can think of.

'Whoa, what a haul!' said Corey, whose face told the story of every Christmas morning he'd never had. 'There's money in here as well, Fallon.'

Fallon peered in, scooping out two twenty-pound notes and some random coins. 'So they didn't spend all of it then.'

She squeezed my hand as I got on the bus – a squeeze

that said 'Thanks,' and 'Your secret's still safe.' Then she kissed Corey. (The whole ride home he grinned like a jelly bean.) I felt a pang of gladness that we'd helped her, then a pang of sadness that I couldn't do more for Corey, to help him neutralise the threat of Zane. He didn't deserve to live in fear either.

'Someone's got an itty bitty cruuuuush,' Max sang, ruffling Corey's hair.

'Get off,' said Corey, beaming and going violently red again.

He might have been good-humoured with Corey, but Max didn't reach for my hand the whole ride back, not once. He hadn't touched me all night, either, even though we'd slept side by side on Fallon's sofa. And we hadn't spoken any more about what he'd said about Pete during Truth or Dare. Maybe he didn't remember saying it, or maybe he did, and was frightened a can of worms would explode in both our faces.

'I still can't believe it,' he said now. 'Who'd have thought *Zane* would have blown his beans up her pipe?'

I tutted my disgust. 'Max, for God's sake! Why do you have to put it like that? Gross!'

'Yeah, well. You think sex is gross anyway, Ella.'

I had no answer to that, so I changed the subject.

'It's weird, though, how she stayed friends with him.'

'Not that weird,' he said. 'Fallon said he just came round one night, out of the blue. It only happened the once.'

'God, one night and you spend the next eighteen years paying for it.'

He muttered something. It sounded suspiciously like 'Chance would be a fine thing.'

Aching and sick, we tried to doze, but none of us could manage it. Instead, I Googled the *Famous Five* on my phone, the Enid Blyton book series we had based our gang on when we were kids. Picnics. Islands. Mysteries. People up to no good. Saving the day over and over again. It was all so easy. It made me want to read the books again. To go back to the farm, too. I'd had a good time, despite the Truth or Dare thing.

As if he'd read my mind, Corey turned around in his seat. 'Do you think we could see Fallon again? All of us together, like before?'

Max yawned. 'Yeah, that'd be cool. There's a fair bit of alcohol out in that barn still, in't there?'

'You're such an alkie,' I said to him.

'Who needs two livers? There's always the other if this one packs in.'

Corey laughed. 'You don't have two livers, idiot. You have two *kidneys*.'

'Oh, is it?' Max laughed. 'I knew I had two of something.'

'How you got ten GCSEs I will never ever know,' I said as Corey and I shared a smile and the bus turned into Grange Close, coming to a sharp halt at the bus stop. We all got up and began trooping off the bus.

'I'm just going to walk to the shop and get some fresh milk. I fancy some Cheerios,' said Corey, jumping down to the pavement and hovering a bit, as if he was waiting for something.

'OK,' I said. 'Maybe see you later then?'

'Yeah, see you later, mate,' said Max.

We watched him amble down the rest of the hill towards his gate, head bowed. We'd already had a fry-up, cooked by Fallon herself, at her house.

'"*I fancy some Cheerios*",' mimicked Max, reaching an arm around me as we walked up the road.

'Yeah, what is he, some kind of multiple-breakfasting hobbit? I'm stuffed. Pete's going to kick my ass later.'

I could have kicked myself for mentioning Pete. There was a brief silence.

'I think Corey wanted to hang out with us,' said Max. I nuzzled into his shoulder, barely resisting the urge to fall asleep. The feeling of touching him again was like warm sun invading the shade.

'I've missed this,' I said, as we walked slowly towards my house.

'Missed what?'

'Being a gang. You, me, Corey, Fallon.'

'Beating up kids…'

'We didn't beat them up. Well, emotionally speaking, maybe. Poor Fallon. She hasn't had the easiest life.'

'Yeah,' said Max. 'And living in that hovel ain't making it any easier.'

'I knew Zane was a knob head before but putting the phone down on her when she told him she was pregnant? Ugh. He could at least have gone to a scan.'

'Well, he doesn't want to, does he? What did you expect? Him to suddenly come over all Super Dad just because he knocked up some chick?'

'"Some chick"?' I repeated. 'She's our friend, Max.'

'Yeah, but still.'

'I wonder how Corey feels about it? He always did have a bit of a crush on her.'

Max swung a kick at a stray can of Red Bull on the pavement, sending it flying over our neighbour's garden fence.

'Could we maybe hang out with him later? Just to keep him company?'

'Nothing else planned. I need to get some sleep first though. My eyes have rhinos sitting on them.'

'Sounds like a plan.'

He craned his neck and kissed me, and, for a split second, the world seemed right. Everything was in its place again, and there was nothing to worry about.

Then we heard a bone-rattling scream.

At first we couldn't work out where it was coming from. Then we figured out it was Corey's front garden, and we both sprinted down the close, the noise getting louder with each step. I reached the gate first. Corey was sitting on his front doorstep, just shrieking, his head in his hands. I followed Max's eye line to the lawn. In the centre of his front garden, hanging from the apple tree by its neck, dangled a cat. A scruffy orange cat with white feet.

Pinned to its back, a scrap of white paper fluttered on the breeze. I moved closer to the tree and read the note. It said just one word:

Gotcha

'Poor Corey.'

11

A Smashing Time and a Piece of Advice

'Cut him down, for God's sake!' I yelled at Max as I held Corey, trying to calm him.

'NO! NO! NO!' he kept yelling, on and on.

Neighbours had gathered at the gate now – I didn't know their names. The man with the solar panels, the woman whose recycling box was always full of wine bottles, and the couple with three Yorkshire terriers – they were just standing around in their slippers, gawping, arms folded. I felt my skin begin to burn.

'Do you all have to be here?' I shouted, striding towards them. 'Are any of you actually *doing* anything?'

'Ella, for God's sake!' said Max. I could see I was embarrassing him, but he started making excuses and ushering everyone back to their houses. I heard words – *bloody lunatic*, *bleeding row*, *spectrum*.

They left gradually, craning their necks to see the swinging cat in the tree, Corey breaking his heart on the doorstep. I helped Max drag Corey into his hall. Then we shut the door on the world.

'It's all right, mate,' said Max. 'It'll be all right.'

'No! No! Let go of me. I can't leave him there!' Corey sobbed, wriggling and wrenching himself out of our hands.

We didn't know what to say. Mort was Corey's best mate. And he'd just been murdered.

We sat him down on the sofa in his grandparents' beige living room, with its wood-framed pictures of dormice on the walls, a crystal cabinet full of corpse-like china dolls and sideboard piled high with bowling-club newsletters. There was a soft aroma of almond biscuits and Lily of the Valley about the place. Silently, Max grabbed a stack of old newspapers and went out to deal with Mort's body. I sat on the sofa beside Corey and reached for his hand.

'It's OK. It's going to be OK,' I kept saying. I didn't believe what I was saying though. How *could* it be OK? *What* was going to be OK? We'd just found his cat strung up by its neck in a tree. OK wasn't even in the building.

Corey squinched his eyes shut. Tears dripped down both his cheeks. 'It was him, wasn't it? He's done this.'

I couldn't deny it was Zane. I'd seen him yesterday underneath that lamp post, as plain as pickle in a Big Mac. This was payback for the Abominable Lunchman incident – I knew it as well as Corey did.

'It's cos of what *I* did,' I said, sagging. 'Isn't it?'

Corey shook his head. 'This is about him and me.'

We sat in silence for ages. I caught sight of Max walking through the hallway with a bundle of newspapers; then I heard the back door being unlocked.

Corey looked up. 'What's Max doing?'

'He's just taking Mort out the back. Putting him some-where safe.' I felt pathetic, saying that. What was safe? Safe was dead.

The kettle clicked on in the kitchen and, after much

clattering and clanking about, Max brought in a tray of hot black tea.

'There's no milk,' he said quietly, setting the mugs down in front of each of us, spooning sugar into two of them. They were all mismatched and hideous – a Milky Bar mug from some Easter egg set, a white Cornish Riviera one, and a chipped purple one with 'VOTE UKIP' written on it in big yellow letters. They had a pillar in their lounge, like ours. Bet no one ever had to wipe blood off that one.

'What did you do with him?' I asked quietly, like we were in a church.

'I've just put it – him – on one of the garden chairs. Wrapped up.' He looked at Corey. 'If it's any consolation, Cor, I don't think he died like that. I think he'd been run over first.'

Corey looked at Max. 'He didn't suffer, did he?'

I jumped in. 'No, I'm sure he didn't.' I looked at Max, telepathically urging him to lie his ass off.

Without too much hesitation, Max said 'No, he definitely didn't suffer, no.'

'I hate him,' said Corey through his teeth. 'I hate him, I hate him, I hate him.'

'Take it easy, Core.'

'Why should he?' I snapped. 'Are you seriously going to defend – this?'

'Hey, Snippy, no of course I'm not.'

'Right,' I said. 'Good. Because we need to do something.'

'Well we should call the cops then,' said Max. 'This is how serial killers get started. Before you know it, his neighbours'll be complaining about smells coming from their drains.'

'It's no use,' said Corey. 'The police won't do anything.

I've told teachers before. They never do anything. Zane just comes back at me harder next time.'

Max sipped his tea. 'Should we call your g-folks or summing? Maybe they should come back from their cruise.'

'No,' said Corey. 'I don't want them here.' His disability was so much more obvious when he was upset; the muscles in his face and arm seemed to spasm.

'You might not be safe here, on your own.'

'I don't care. Let him kill me. Let's see how far he'll go.'

'No,' I said. He looked at me – I'd said it firmer than I'd meant to. 'You can stay with us. In Ollie's room. I've got training later, but Max can stay with you till I come back. We've got Cheerios at home, I think. If not, Max'll pop out and get you some.'

'Yeah,' said Max, following my lead. 'You've got an Xbox, right? Bring that over. We'll play FIFA or summing.'

'I can't face work this afternoon,' said Corey softly.

Max got out his phone, Googled *Easy PC Electronics, Brynstan High Street*, and made the call to Corey's boss. Corey told him to 'play the cerebral palsy card' so he wouldn't ask any questions. It worked like a charm.

'Sorted,' he said, clicking off his phone. Then, without another word, Corey picked up the full UKIP mug of tea and lobbed it straight at the fireplace wall. It exploded in a dark brown sunburst.

I leaped up off the sofa. 'For God's sake! What was that?'

'I don't like tea,' he replied, quite calmly.

Max looked at him, his mouth open. Then he let out one of his chuckles. Corey started laughing, too.

'That felt good,' he said, picking up the Cornish Riviera mug and chucking that at the wall too. They both fell about laughing again.

Max handed him his mug, the Milky Bar one. 'Try that.'

Corey looked at him, then at the fireplace. Then he hoyed it against the wall behind his head, where it exploded into a satisfying shatter-splash of broken china and brown tea. Max started handing him ornaments from the sideboard – a china Little Boy Blue, a hideous Siamese cat musical thing and one that looked like a small yeti playing a flute. He was unstoppable. Both me and Max laughed harder and harder.

Then we stared around us, at the broken bits and wet living room carpet.

'Jeez,' Max whistled. 'What you gonna tell your g-folks?'

Corey shrugged. 'We had an earthquake?'

Max high-fived him hard. 'You are the man!'

Of course Corey needed to vent. He'd been name-called and laughed at and picked on and punched for practically as long as I'd known him. This smash fest had been good for him. It was a start. A step in the right direction.

And Zane had caused it. Zane 'Cat Killer' Walker. He'd made Corey feel as angry as I did on a regular basis. I could handle the rage, especially now I had the key to Pete's garage, but I knew Corey couldn't.

'I want to bury him,' said Corey, wiping a long snot trail all up his sleeve.

'Me too,' I said, with a smile that showed my teeth. 'We need to teach him a lesson.'

'No, I meant Mort,' he said. 'Under the pittosporum bush. He'd like that.'

*

It was raining hard when we went out to the back garden. I'd thought our garden was neat, but Corey's looked ready for Chelsea. The borders were overflowing with a rainbow of showy flowers, heads so big they were buckling their stems. Every leaf was polished green and the grass edges looked as though they'd been hand-trimmed with scissors. We wrapped Mort in a blanket that Corey swiped from the back of the sofa – he said he wanted him to be warm. I didn't see why a dead body had to be kept warm, but I said nothing.

At the top of the garden, near the brick barbecue, we found the pittosporum Mort liked to sleep under, and Max started to dig. Corey carefully laid his bundled friend down inside the hole, putting three plastic balls and a toy mouse beside him. We all cried; Max more than Corey, me more even than Max. I think it nudged the memory for all of us.

Max shovelled the earth back into the hole until the blanket was covered. He looked beautiful in the rain. I felt a familiar pang of sorrow as I watched him dig, his T-shirt getting wetter in the worsening downpour. When the grave was filled, the last thing to do was place a pencil cross on top of the mound and say some words. That was left to me.

'Please keep this animal safe and deliver him to the Lord with special blessings. And hope and love. And safety. Something about kingdoms and bread. We love thee, Mort, forevs and evs. Amen.' I had no idea what I was saying, but it sounded all right and Corey repeated the Amen. Max reached out for my hand and I took his.

'I saw him,' said Corey, out of nowhere. 'Kissing a lad from school behind the equipment shed. That's why he hates me.'

'Kissing a lad? You mean, Zane's gay?' said Max.

Corey nodded. 'He said if I told anyone what I saw, he'd kill me. He's ashamed of it. Like, *super* ashamed.'

'Oh God – is that his big secret?' I sighed. 'Is *that* it? That's nothing.'

'Not to Zane, it's not,' said Corey.

It did explain a lot, his secret and his shame. Why Zane always had to be the alpha male; why he worked out so much. Why he tweeted so often about which girls he'd 'knocked off' and hoped weren't 'knocked up'. Why he was always so angry.

'That's so messed up,' said Max. 'I mean, why did he sleep with Fallon if he's gay?'

I knew the answer to this one. 'Fallon told us last night, remember? She said he just came round, out of the blue, after months of not saying one word to her. How quick it was. How he cried afterwards. It was an experiment. Like he was just... making sure.'

'Still, it's majorly screwed up,' said Corey.

'There's nothing wrong with being gay,' I snapped, teetering on the edge of another bitchplosion. 'My brother's gay.'

'I didn't mean that being gay was screwed up. I meant Zane using Fallon to try and prove he wasn't.'

Corey sat down on the edge of the brick barbecue. 'I like Fallon,' he said. 'I like her more than just liking goes.' I sat down next to him. 'He used her. And he murdered Mort.' He looked down at the little pencil cross on Mort's grave. 'He's gone too far.' He dissolved slowly into tears again.

'So what are we going to do about it then?' I asked.

Max looked at me. 'There's a massive cake in the fridge.'

'What?'

Corey sniffed, wiping his eyes and replacing his glasses. 'That's my grandparents' anniversary cake. I picked it up for them yesterday. Lemon drizzle. It's a surprise.' Corey and Max exchanged a look, beginning to laugh. And then I caught on.

'You're not!'

*

The three of us demolished that cake watching mid-morning television. *Celebrity Sewer Hunt*. I'd never seen it before, but Max said he watched it all the time. The contestants were some woman who'd once shagged a footballer and a bloke who'd been in a coffee advert and been cleared of beating up a waitress. They were scrabbling around in a sewer for a five pound note. That was basically the premise of the whole show.

'Right, I better go home and get changed for training,' I said, groaning and stuffed. 'You two going to clear up and come over after?'

Max glanced briefly at the smashed china on the living room carpet, and the soaking wet wall, dripping with tea stains. Then he went back to the TV screen. 'Yeah, we'll just see the end of this.' Woman Who'd Slept With Footballer was leaning on a fatberg, her face running with mascara, so happy she'd won the money for her charity.

'OK.' I turned to Corey. He was equally transfixed. He also had a dab of royal icing on his ear. I flicked it away.

'You all right now?'

'Feel a bit sick.'

'So do I,' said Max, chucking his plate down on the cushion beside him.

'They're gonna kill me for eating it.'

Max shrugged. 'Well, if they do, we'll bury you next to the cat.'

I thought Corey was going to break into sobs again, but instead, he laughed.

'Right, well, I'm going jogging, so I'll probably be sick on the beach. Laters.'

'Laters.'

'See you later, Spinderella.'

*

I wasn't sick, but running with that belly bomb in my stomach was the last thing I felt like doing. I had a quick shower and brushed my teeth and Pete picked me up at one o'clock, with the teddy bear necklace that Max had given me.

'Thought you might have missed it,' he said, dangling it into my palm. 'You left it in the garage last time.'

'Oh God! Thanks,' I said, shoving it in the pocket of my trackies.

We ran down to the beach, where we did two miles of cross-country before stopping to stretch. Needless to say, my heart wasn't in it – I was still full up with cake and tetchy and tired. And annoyed when Pete sprinted past me on the long ramp down to the beach. I stopped first and sat down on the sea wall steps.

'You all right?' he puffed, still running on the spot.

'Just knackered,' I puffed back. 'I didn't sleep much last night. Or the night before.'

'Party, was it?' he guessed, sitting down next to me.

'Yeah. Sorry about the text. That was just Max winding me up.'

'I did guess,' he said, coming to a stop and stretching out his thigh muscle. 'Come on, eight seconds a leg. And one, two, three…'

I stood up, reluctantly and copied him on the wrong leg. 'I know what you're going to say. A good machine needs a full charge to run efficiently.'

'And?'

'And quality fuel.'

'Exactly. Is that icing around your mouth, Miss Newhall? And have you had—' *sniff sniff* '—alcohol?'

I blushed hotly, rubbing around my mouth. 'I only had a couple of slices. And, like, two bottles or something.' (It was more like six.) 'How can you still smell it? That was last night. I've brushed my teeth and everything.'

'I can always tell. What was it? Stella? Bud? Singha?'

'Home brew.'

He laughed. 'You might as well drink hand sanitiser! No wonder you're sluggish. How are things with Max? Switch legs and hold it one, two, three.'

I switched. 'I don't know. He seems different lately. I found out he's been smoking skunk.' Pete's face washed with alarm at that. 'I'm worried about him. I think he's getting hooked.'

'That doesn't sound good.'

'What can I do?'

'Nothing,' he said. 'Quad stretches for eight, go… It's his body, so it's his problem.'

I pulled my leg up for a quad stretch. 'He's not happy. Because of me.'

Pete switched quads. 'I highly doubt that.'

I stopped stretching and looked at him. 'Your keys fell out of my pocket last night – he guessed from the fob they were yours. He thinks there's something going on between us. Hence the text.'

Pete stopped stretching too. 'Ella, please tell me you put him right on the subject.'

'Yeah, I explained to him about the boxing.'

'You better hope he doesn't tell his father about that. Neil's not going to pay me to give you boxing lessons, is he?'

'He won't say a word, don't worry.'

'Let's hope not,' he said, going into lunges. I mirrored. 'So he's OK with me? He's not going to turn up on my doorstep to defend your honour is he?'

'Max? No way. He's not violent. He's just jealous, and he doesn't know how to handle it. He'll be OK.'

Pete didn't look totally satisfied, but he switched lunge legs without comment, then we went into squats for the count of four, and bicep curls for the count of six. My mind still wasn't on it though. It was reeling back over the night before.

Then when we were doing our cool down stretches, I told him about what Zane had done to Mort.

'Christ, that's sadistic,' said Pete. 'Did you call the police? It could just be a warning.'

'No. The police won't do anything. I think we should deal with it ourselves. You know, get our own revenge on him.'

'Well, just you be careful,' said Pete stopping and looking out towards the tide far out in the bay. 'You know what Confucius said about revenge, don't you?'

'Who's Confucius?'

He rolled his eyes, like I was such an ignoramus. '"Before you embark on a journey of revenge, prepare to dig two graves."' He brought his arm out in front and across to stretch his shoulder. 'Forgiveness is always better in the long run.'

'How?' I said, making a face. 'How can you just forgive someone who's done the worst thing in the world they could possibly do to hurt you?'

He lifted his eyebrows briefly, switching from shoulder to back stretches. 'Chances are, that person hates themselves far more deeply than they hate you.'

I didn't see it. Fallon had been wronged by the Shaws and we'd righted her. We'd made things better. Corey had been wronged and we were going to right him too. And I was hungry for it. Hungry for ideas on how we could get back at Zane. I kept hearing that hideous sad sound coming out of Corey. Seeing his shaking hands. Watching him throwing those ornaments against that wall and come alive with the relief it gave him.

I kept seeing Mort, swinging from that tree. The creaking of the branch. His fur fluttering on the breeze. Then, in an instant, I got the idea. Just thinking about it made our training session go quicker, made the adrenaline pump harder through my body and soon I was overtaking Pete on the race back home. I was charged up again. I had power. And the ideas began to flow like a river.

'So you had more revenge on your mind?'

12

Ella Thinks Up a Plan

At the start of the year, Dad was in hospital with an infection. He was in having IV antibiotics and sharing his room with a guy who had terminal bowel cancer; a gentle guy called Jim. Jim had four kids, seven grandchildren, had been married forty-five years, never smoked or drank, raised money for refugees and, judging by the amount of cards on the window sill, had hundreds of friends. As I sat there on the end of Dad's bed, watching him and his little bald roommate chatting about model boats, I thought, These are good people, so why is this happening to them? Why was Jim dying and my dad spending his forced retirement with needles in his veins and feeling tired all the time? Some days he didn't have the strength to press down the keys on his keyboard.

I asked Dad the same question. All he did was quote me some long spiel from this book he'd been reading.

'"Life is a storm,"' he said. '"You will bask in the sunlight one moment, be shattered on the rocks the next. What makes you a man is what you do when that storm comes. Look into that storm and shout 'Do your worst, for I will do mine.'"'

'What's that?' I said.

'It's from *The Count of Monte Cristo*. Alexandre Dumas. Wonderful story.'

He started telling me the plot with such fire in his eyes for this guy Dantes and his terrible betrayal and how he got his own back and all I remember is feeling annoyed. Annoyed that Dad didn't feel betrayed by life. Annoyed that he wasn't angry about the cards he'd been dealt. I was seething. I thought of Neil Rittman – the worst person in my world. Why wasn't he suffering? Why was he sitting up there at JoNeille in his golden bathtub, smoking cigars and laughing his head off with clear lungs and several thriving businesses while my poor dad was coughing up blood and sweating radiation? It should be the other way round. Bad people should be punished. Good people should have nice lives. I wanted to punish Neil like Dad and Jim were being punished. Only problem was I didn't know where to start.

For Zane Walker though, I did.

What we had done to the Shaws at Whitehouse Farm had been quite spur of the moment and childish; we'd got away with it because they were kids and, let's face it, stupid. We had to be cleverer with Zane, and I had an idea.

*

Fallon had a scan at the hospital a few mornings later at Brynstan General, just across the roundabout at the end of our road. Despite her baby-heavy state, she wanted us all to go on a picnic at the top of Brynstan Hill afterwards, like we used to. She said the exercise would do her good, and none of us had any argument ready. So Max picked her and Corey up from the hospital, and we drove to Church Lane where we could access the footpath through the churchyard.

'Show them the scan,' said Corey, nudging Fallon's arm.

He'd bunked off work again and gone with her that morning. Apparently, they'd spent most of last night checking out baby names on his computer and making a list of things she needed for her hospital bag. He seemed to be really into the whole baby thing.

I switched the picnic blanket into the crook of my left arm and took the little piece of paper Fallon held out to me. The photo had her name at the top of it – Hayes, Fallon Magenta – and the name of the hospital – Brynstan General.

'It's so clear, isn't it?' she said proudly as I stopped on the footpath to look at it properly. 'See, there's a leg. And another leg…'

'And another leg,' Max laughed.

'No, silly, she's only got two legs!'

I felt my heart tighten up, quite without warning. 'She?'

'Yeah,' said Fallon. 'There's no winky, so the doctor said it was most likely a girl.'

I swallowed down the lump in my throat. This grainy, big-headed alien with teeny tiny fingers and little ski-slopey nose was Fallon's little girl. And though Fallon looked delighted, and Corey was smiling like the proud dad he should have been, I couldn't help what I was feeling.

Jealousy.

'Corey's going to come to the birth with me, too.'

'Is he?' said Max, as we reached the top of the graveyard where the little wooden gate was. 'I can't even walk past the butcher's counter at Tesco. You're actually gonna go goal end while she's in labour?'

'Yeah,' said Corey. 'She needs someone there. In case her mum's not around.'

'Fair play,' said Max, switching the picnic bag from his left hand to his right. 'When are you due, Fal?'

'They said 10 September.'

The pain thickened my throat until it felt like my whole neck was swollen. 'That's not long.'

'I know,' said Fallon. 'I'm a bit scared about the pain, but Corey will be with me now, so it won't be so bad. I'm glad it's a girl, though, Ella. She'll have a foof, like us!'

I snorted with laughter at that, and my jealousy was gone in an instant, like she had pricked it with a pin.

We had to go super slowly for Fallon's sake. Halfway up the sloping churchyard that led to the turnstile and hill footpath, Max picked her up and carried her in his arms, and she giggled like a gurgling drain and he heaved like she was heavier than elephants but they went on ahead.

'Show-off!' I called out, but I smiled anyway – Corey was smiling, expecting me to do the same.

'I'm so glad we all hooked up again. All of us,' he said.

I nodded. 'It's fun, isn't it? But, just be careful, OK? I mean, don't go saying you'll be there for her if you're not. She's already had Zane let her down.'

'Oh, I'm not like him,' he said. 'I wouldn't do that. I just want to help her, that's all.'

I believed him. That was always the boy Corey was. He was our problem solver. If we were lost Corey would work out how to get home. If we were cold, Corey would get the fire going. Fallon was lost – he was going to light her way.

'Good,' I said. 'No, that's really great, Corey.'

He beamed.

At the top of the churchyard, Max and Fallon had stopped, right beside the gravestone. We never walked by it without saying something or laying something there, even if it was just a buttercup.

'Hi, Jess,' Max was saying as Corey and I joined them, staring down at the gold writing on the huge slab of black marble.

In Loving Memory of Jessica Joelle Rittman,
taken from us, 6 June Aged 18 years.
A precious daughter and big sister.
In our hearts forever and always.

'She'd have hated that headstone,' said Corey. Then he looked shocked by what he'd said. 'God, Max, I'm so sorry.'

'No, you're right,' said Max. 'Dad chose it. It was the most expensive one they had.' He clocked the bunch of pink roses beside the stone. 'Hey, who put them there?' He bent down to see if there was a card but there wasn't. We looked back at him blankly and shook our heads.

'Maybe it was your mum?' I said.

He shook his head. 'She wouldn't come up here.'

'Do you think we'll ever know – what actually happened?' said Fallon.

A silence followed her question. The air around us became thick and hot.

'As far my whole family's concerned, it was an unavoidable and tragic accident,' said Max. 'End of.'

'But what about you?' she persisted. 'What do you think happened, Max?'

He shrugged. 'Did you know they still use the same bus?'

'You're joking,' said Corey.

'No, I've seen it a few times. There's no dent in it any more, but I memorised the number plate. You've seen it, haven't you Ells?'

'Yeah,' I said, looking down at the pink roses. 'Come on. The Mini Magnums will be defrosting.'

Once we'd made the agonisingly slow, steep climb along the wildflower path, through the two gates and past clumps of bleating sheep, we reached the summit of Brynstan Hill at last. I always felt like it was the one place in the world

I could breathe to the bottom of my lungs. We could see all our houses from up there. The top was several football pitches' worth of uneven grass, and that day it was almost completely covered in buttercups. Out to the west ran the motorway and all the retails parks, where the cars glinted like little toys. To the east was the sea and sitting smack bang in the middle was the island, like a fat black rat in a bath. All I could hear was the wind.

We began to set out our picnic, Max wasting no time in doling out the Mini Magnums and the huge bag of candy we'd reclaimed from the Shaws.

'So, come on then,' he said, crunching down on his ice cream and slurping it up. 'What's this big plan?'

'Oh yeah, I still haven't told you, have I?' I said, peeling back the lid on my Tupperware box of mixed salad and low fat cheese. 'Well, I remembered this story Jess told us once, about a cat…'

I looked at all their faces in turn. They were all blank.

Then Fallon's eyes lit up. 'Oh, I know the one! We were having a midnight feast and we made a cave out of our sleeping bags, and the chairs in your dining room, Max.'

'Yeah,' I said, 'and we played on your Wii and your mum told us off for getting Ribena on the new cushion covers. Anyway, Jessica told us this horror story, about this alcoholic bloke who bullied his cat.'

'I don't remember it at all.' Max yawned, leaning back on his elbows and moving his aviators from his head to his eyes.

I started telling the story again. Pretty soon, Corey caught my drift.

'… then his house catches fire and he and his wife have to leg it. But when the man returns to the house the next day, what does he find? The charred image of a cat on one of the walls – a cat with a rope around its neck. Because that's how he killed it.'

Corey looked at me with a scared sort of wonder. 'I think I know where this is going.'

'I don't,' said Max. 'What happened then?'

'He starts seeing this new cat, another black one, large as life, hanging around his house. It's almost identical to his old cat, except this one has a white patch of fur on its chest – a patch in the shape of a gallows.'

'Ha, yeah, I remember it now,' said Max, blindly reaching for a Drumstick from the bag of sweets and lying back down. 'Not one of her best, but still cool.'

Corey grabbed another cheese and onion sandwich and started removing the onion. 'I think I've read the graphic novel. Who wrote the original story – was it Lovecraft? Or Poe?'

'Oh, I don't know; some old dead dude,' I said. 'It doesn't matter. The point is, there's this bit in the story when the man kills his wife in a fit of rage because he's so freaked out, and he buries her and the new cat behind the cellar wall. But then all these eerie, echoey meowing noises start in the walls, and everywhere he goes, he can hear it. It's the black cat, alerting everyone to the man's awful crimes.'

'OK, I get it,' said Max, levering himself up again onto his elbows with the Drumstick hanging limply over his bottom lip. 'Guy kills cat, guy gets plagued with guilt about killing cat. Zane killed cat, we plague Zane with cat stuff. Yeah?'

'Yeah,' I said. 'We keep reminding him of his terrible deed until he begs us for mercy.'

'Bit of a long shot, innit?' said Max. 'I mean, what did you have in mind? Setting his house on fire and shoving a cat behind his wardrobe?'

'Something along those lines,' I said, pulling at tufts of

dry grass at the side of the picnic blanket. Everyone was quiet for a bit.

'You're serious, aren't you?'

'Deadly,' I replied. 'Aren't you? Don't you want to get back at him? For what he's done to Corey and Fallon?'

'He hasn't hurt *me*, Ella,' Fallon jumped in.

'He's abandoned you. He used you and then dumped you and never called. He hasn't even asked about how *his* baby's doing, has he?'

'Well, no…'

'So that's asshole behaviour, isn't it?'

'Well… yeah.'

'Even assholes have a purpose,' said Corey. I looked at him. 'I'm just saying.'

'Well don't "just say". You want to get back at him too, I know you do.'

'Well yeah but Zane's a hard nut to crack. If we start chalking pictures of cats on the walls of his house, he's just gonna think it's stupid.'

'No, he won't,' I said. 'Because there's something about the night Jessica told us the story that you've all overlooked.'

Max was the first one to smile. 'The night Jess told this story… wasn't the night Zane wet himself, was it?'

'Exactly,' I said. 'He's terrified of horror stories. He always had to have the light on after she told one. He only listened to that one cos he was too scared to go in another room by himself.'

'I don't know,' said Corey slowly. 'Is it worth it? I mean, I'm grateful you're all willing to do stuff for me to get back at him and everything, but it seems like a lot of trouble to go to, starting a whole campaign of terror.'

'It's not just for you, Corey,' I said.

'Huh?'

'I want to do this. I *need* to do this. I think it'll help.'

'What do you mean, help?' said Max, levering himself up again. 'Help with what?'

I looked out towards the island. I held out my hands, palms down, showing them all my scabby knuckles. 'With this.'

Max looked at me.

'I lied to you. I didn't do this on the track. I've been punching the pillar in our lounge. I punch it until my hands bleed. And when the scabs come off, I go back and punch it some more.'

Max sat right up, and tore his aviators from his face, staring at me.

'I get so angry. Sometimes I need to lash out. Pound on something. It's just how I feel.' I looked at Max. 'That's why I've got Pete's keys. He lets me use his punchbag in his garage now. Every time I feel like punching the crap out of something, it's somewhere I can go and let off steam.'

'Why didn't you tell me this?' said Max, coming over to my side of the picnic blanket.

I shook my head. 'Because I can't explain why I do it. I just do. I feel… dangerous.'

'But why are you so angry?' asked Corey. A wind whipped up around us, blowing empty crisp packets across the grass. I got up and went to grab them, but when I came back they were all still waiting for my answer.

Fallon was staring at me. For a flicker, my heart plunged, thinking she might say something about Neil; but yet again, I had underestimated her. 'It's ever since your mum left, isn't it?'

Telepathically thanking her, I ran with the decoy. 'I guess I still resent her, yeah, for leaving Dad when he was going through his treatment and everything. And David moving away, as well – and Ollie never comes home now. Maybe it's all of it, or none of it, I don't know. But the other night, when we scared off the Shaws, it felt like it was going somewhere – the anger. It felt like it was being put to use. And the next morning, I didn't need to hit anything. I haven't felt like that in ages. That's why I want to do it again. I want to do something about what's making *you* angry, because I can't do anything about what's making *me* angry. Does that make any sense?'

Max didn't look sure at all, but Corey nodded.

'It does to me,' said Fallon, getting to her feet with Corey's help. 'Count me in. You helped me get rid of the Shaws – I'll do whatever you say.'

'Don't Dare Fallon.' Corey smiled.

She smiled back. 'I can't kill anything though. I couldn't kill an animal, unless it was already dead.' We all started laughing at that.

'I couldn't kill anything either,' said Corey, opening a pack of gummy snakes. 'But I'm down for anything else.'

'Good,' I said. 'How about you, Max?'

'You know I am.' He looked a bit sheepish.

'You sure?'

He nodded. 'Yeah, I'm down for whatever too. May as well.'

I put my hand over the centre of the picnic blanket. 'All for one, and all that.'

Corey put his hand on mine at once. Max mumbled about being childish, but covered Corey's hand with his own, too. As Fallon reached out, though, she suddenly shrieked out in agony.

'Ooooooohhhhh!'

The boys jumped back off the blanket.

'What?' I said. 'Oh God, Fallon, what is it?'

'The baby!' she said. 'It kicked! A massive kick! Oh! It's not ever done that before. I mean, it's moved and sort of slithered about a bit, but not a proper kick. Ooh, it just did it again! Feel it! Feel it!'

All together, we got up and put our hands on Fallon's belly. And, almost at once, a tiny but powerful *WHAM* hit all our palms.

'Bloody hell, what was that?!' cried Max, snatching his hand away.

'That was a foot!' Corey shrieked. 'That was definitely a little foot!'

'Actually, I think it was a fist,' said Fallon.

'Yeah, it was! A fist!' said Max.

'Like an *I'm in too* fist?' said Corey with a grin.

Max smiled despite himself. 'That was the baby saying, *Hell yeah, let's do this!*'

'So we *are* the Fearless Five after all.'

For the next two hours, the four of us – or five, counting an increasingly lively Bump – chitchatted and schemed on top of that hill like escaped prisoners planning a dash across the border. Before long, my tiny army had outlined its plan of action as though it were a military manoeuvre – and we were all equally excited to go to war.

*

I had a text from Dad, saying he was coming back in the morning, so to celebrate my last night of freedom, we decided to have a takeaway from the Taste of the Orient and sleep over in the motorhome on our drive – Corey and Fallon on the fold-out bed, me and Max at the other end on the mattress topper, with the curtain the only thing dividing us.

'Please don't have sex,' said Max, as he stood at the dividing curtain between the two ends of the caravan. Corey and

Fallon were snuggling in to watch old episodes of *Cash in the Attic* on Corey's iPad. 'Last thing we wanna hear are your squelching noises. Besides, the suspension ain't great on this thing.'

'Last thing on my mind,' said Fallon, as she glanced at Corey. His head was resting on her shoulder and he was already in an exhausted half-sleep, having blown his own mind with the amazingness of our Chinese takeaway. He'd spent the last hour alone talking about the marinade on the spare ribs.

''Night, Max. 'Night, Ella Bella Paella,' he called out dozily.

''Night, Corey.' I chuckled.

Max drew the curtain across and climbed into bed beside me. After a pause, he spooned against me and held me around my waist, sighing into my neck.

'He's brilliant, isn't he?' I whispered. 'So's Fallon, I really like her. They've got not sides to them at all, have they?'

'Yeah.' Max chuckled. 'Have you ever seen anyone so in love with a spring roll? And what's the matter with Fallon's doctor saying she was on the "autistic speculum". She's class.'

'Aw, don't take the piss out of her.'

'What? You started it.'

'Yeah, well, she's sweet. She's been a good friend to me.'

'So why'd you dump her at school then?'

'I didn't dump her. We just... grew apart. So did you and Corey. And Zane.'

'Well Zane brought that on himself.'

There was a nervous pause. I could feel Max building up to say something. At last, he opened his eyes and let out a long rattling breath. 'That was bullshit before, wasn't it? When you said you were still angry about your mum leaving. I know it was. You don't give a monkey's about her.'

I couldn't think what to say. So I just said, ''Night.'

''Night,' he returned, with a definite sigh.

*

The next time I opened my eyes, it was still dark outside the caravan and a light rain was pitter-pattering on the skylight. I looked across and Max was sitting bolt upright beside me, shivering. I reached out and pulled the curtain open a little way so I could see him more clearly in the light from the street lamp outside. He was running with sweat.

'Max? Are you all right?'

He shook his head. He looked too petrified to move. I'd never seen him like that. It was like he was in a trance. His eyes were wide and staring out into nothing, his pupils like full stops. I levered myself up and placed my hand on his back. He winced.

'Did you have a bad dream?'

He nodded. 'Same one.'

'What do you mean? Have you had it before?'

'A few times.' He rubbed his face all over on the sheet. 'Christ, I'm dripping. I need a smoke.' He made to get out of bed but I stopped him.

'What happens? In the dream?'

'I don't want to talk about it.'

'Is it Jessica?' Eventually, he nodded. 'The bus?' He nodded again.

I held him and rested my chin on his shoulder. 'You're OK now. It's all gone.'

'Tell me why you're angry,' he said.

'What?'

'Tell me why you punch walls and kick off at stuff all the time.'

'Max...'

'Tell me why you won't have sex with me.' I opened my mouth to speak, but no words escaped. 'It's driving me crazy, Ella. You leave me paranoid cos you won't say anything. And now all this stuff about you punching walls and using Hamlin's gym. Tell me.'

'Tell you what?'

'Is he... hurting you? Has he... raped you?'

I was a rabbit in the headlights, even though the caravan was dark. 'Pete? No. Why would you think that?'

There were snores on the other side of the curtain.

'Because Wikipedia says the main reason a person is genophobic is cos of sexual abuse. Rape. If he's grooming you I'll kill him, I swear. I'd die if I thought anything like that had happened and I wasn't there to stop it. Please tell me, Ella. I'm going out of my mind!'

'Of course it wasn't that,' I said, praying he wouldn't see my glowing red cheeks in the darkness. 'Pete's my friend, he wouldn't do that.'

His hand was shaking as he chewed a raggedy bit of skin on his thumb. 'You swear?'

'I don't know why I'm like this, Max. But it's not that. He hasn't laid a finger on me.'

A tiny part of me wanted to say it; to unload the sack of crap I carried around. I had thought that seeing Fallon again would force it out in the open so everyone would finally know. It would have been a relief, for a while. But however bad things were now, they didn't come close to how bad they *would* be if I told the truth. It was better left buried, inside me, where it couldn't hurt anyone else.

'I'm sorry you're worried about me. But there's nothing to worry about.'

'No, I'm sorry,' he said, kissing me gently on my mouth. I kissed him back and held the back of his neck with my fingertips. I could feel his body heat beneath his T-shirt. I wanted to take it off. Reading my mind, he ripped it off over his head and flung it across the floor.

'I love you so much, Ells,' he whispered.

'I love you too.'

Max pressed his whole body against mine and we lay down and stayed like that for the longest time, just kissing, just holding. Just being warm beneath the duvet together.

Then I felt him between my legs.

'NO,' I said. He rolled off and sighed, banging the mattress with his fist.

I felt around for his other hand and held it in the darkness. He was just lying there, eyes to the ceiling. He moved his head to look at me. 'Always something in the way, in't there?'

I couldn't look at him.

'Just Snuggly Duddlies then?' he said, at last.

'Yeah,' I replied, turning over so he could spoon me properly. Before he did, he put one of the small square sofa cushions between us. 'Just Duddlies.'

He planted a kiss on my neck.

'Are we OK, Max?'

'Yeah, I think so,' he whispered back. Moments later, his breaths become slower; I felt his body go heavy and I knew he was asleep.

Somewhere outside, the eerie trill of a cat's miaow echoed around the whole street.

'So even your dad didn't know?'

13

Up To Mischief

Tuesday, 4 August

Nobody knew, apart from Fallon. Dad would have made me go to the police. He would have made me talk about it. Gone round to JoNeille and... actually, I don't know *what* he'd have done. Dad wasn't like me. He never raged. Even when his cancer came back the second time, he just got on with it. He took his tablets, got nuked with chemicals every other fortnight until his hair fell out and his appetite never made it past crackers, but I never once heard him moan. Even when Mum ran off to Greece with the guy from the kebab shop. In fact, the day she left, I heard him wish her all the best on the driveway. I was the one in the hallway, holding the house brick I was about to launch through their windscreen. Dad paid for the new glass. He even *apologised*. I never did. I never would.

Looking Dad in the eye and saying those three words, saying what Neil had done to me, was impossible. How could I do that? If he missed an episode of *MasterChef* he went into shock. He wore half-moon glasses and hoarded all this junk in the garage, like he was storing breaths before going under water. No, it had to be kept locked in my head where only I had the key. I couldn't put him through any more. I wasn't her.

The next morning, while I went round to Pete's for training and a quick go on the bag, Fallon did the boys a fry up and then they went into town to get provisions for Operation: Zane. We made plans to meet outside Subway later on. Just as I was dozing off in front of *Loose Women*, I felt a breeze on my face. Dad was home.

'Hello, Sleepy Girl,' he said as I came to and stood up to greet him, nuzzling into his bobbly green jumper. 'Had a good time without me?'

I felt his warm hand on the back of my head and swallowed down the sob caught in my throat. 'Not really.'

'How come?'

'I just missed you, that's all,' I said.

'Aww, that's nice.'

'How's Matthew?' I said, still breathing in the familiar coffee scent of his jumper.

'Very cute, if noisy.' He chuckled. 'He's got Jack's big brown eyes too. They're both besotted. They want you to go and visit.' He pulled away and headed into the kitchen. 'Do you want a brew?'

'No, I'm supposed to be meeting Max in a bit in town. Oh… no.' I'd told Fallon I'd clear up the breakfast mess when I got back but I'd forgotten. Instead, Dad was faced with a bombsite of cracked eggs, greasy coils of kitchen roll, empty packets and toast crumbs. I followed him in. 'Sorry, I meant to clear it up after my shower.'

Dad filled the kettle. 'Have some friends over last night, did you?'

I busied about, clearing it all up. 'Yeah. Sorry.'

'It's all right.' He smiled. 'I'm glad. You *should* have

friends over. Leave it for now. Let's have coffee and chew the fat for a bit. I want to know your news.'

'I haven't got any news.' I slid up onto a stool at the breakfast bar as Dad pottered about, recycling used tea bags and putting tins in the yellow box and bottles in the green. 'How did your book signing go?'

'Oh all right. Sold about forty books in the end. Squeezed in some visits to a couple of local WI groups while I was up there and sold a few more. Did you do the cooking then?'

'No, Fallon did. She's a good cook.'

'Fallon. Fallon,' said Dad, pouring me out a coffee in my Regulators tour mug. 'I know that name. There was a Fallon at school, wasn't there?'

'It's the same one,' I said. 'We've got back in touch. And Corey from number three down the road. He's been going through a tough time. His cat went missing and we helped looked for it.' I saved him the details about Mort. He didn't need to know that. 'What are you smiling at?'

'I've missed my little girl, that's all.' It was a rare moment. He didn't smile that often but the break from me had obviously done him good. He looked proud and I smiled back at him, for once not wishing he was someone cooler or stronger like Chris Pratt or Tom Hardy.

I gulped down some hot coffee and let it burn the back of my throat. I couldn't say it back – *I missed you too* – it was a bridge too far. I knew I'd just blub all over him and he didn't need the stress.

'Did Max stay over last night?'

'Yes. They all did. We stayed in the caravan.'

He nodded. 'Has he started work at the garden centre yet?'

'No, he's having the summer off before he starts work, I've told you before.'

'Waste of a good brain there.'

I could almost recite his speech along with him, I'd heard it so many times. 'What can I do, Dad? Yes, so he got all As and Bs in his exams, and he's predicted all As in his A levels but he doesn't want to do anything else.'

'It's *Neil* who doesn't want him to do anything else,' said Dad. 'Max wanted to be a policeman for a bit, didn't he? What happened to all that?'

'Uh, he was eight?'

'You've got to ask yourself whether a boy like that with such low expectations of life, of *himself*, is worth the effort.'

I felt my grip on my temper slipping away from me.

'I hope you're both being careful.'

I gasped. 'Dad!'

'Well, it has to be said. Sex isn't something to take lightly, Ella. I don't want you wasting your own career because of a lazy mistake.'

I couldn't believe how frank he was being. He had never talked to me about it before. 'Where did this come from?'

'David asked about you and I said you and Max were still going strong.'

'*You* and David were talking about me and Max?'

'He's just worried, that's all. So am I. You're so close to a tremendous career and we don't want to see anything getting in the way of that...'

Before he could say another word, I had stomped up to my bedroom and slammed the door, as hard as the high carpet pile would let me. I only started crying when I saw a small Boots carrier bag on the end of my dressing table. Inside were a brand new tube of aloe vera gel, a box of non-drowsy antihistamines – and a box of fourteen latex-free Durex condoms. How crushingly embarrassing that he'd remembered I was allergic to latex.

How dare he talk to David about me? How dare he worry about me getting pregnant? I was so embarrassed, I wanted to bury myself in my duvet and suffocate. It was just like when he caught me sniffing one of Mum's scarves in his closet. I'd had a moment of weakness when I'd needed that sense of her around me. A hug. It was the nearest I could get to one – wrapping one of her old scarves around my neck. Taking in big nose-fuls of her perfume. And Dad sat me down and made me talk about how much I missed her. I hated that.

And I hated this. I wished he would bugger off to Manchester and live with David and Jack like they wanted him to. Or to Romania with that woman from cookery class I'd heard him on the phone to, giggling like a moron.

I sat on my bed and just let the tears come. He wasn't a moron. The last few days the house had been so empty without him, cooking up one of his curries from his class or the tapping of his keyboard in his study as he wrote. But him mentioning *that* was just so wrong. I remembered one time I'd flooded my bed with blood when I was thirteen. He bought me sanitary towels and sorted it all out but it was still mortifying, having to tell him. By the time I got home from school that afternoon, I had a fillet steak waiting for me – for the blood loss – and a brand new mattress. That's how we dealt with things. Stuff happened, he cleaned it up and we never mentioned it again.

I saw this quote posted on Flickr once – 'Do you realise there was a moment when your mum or dad put you down as a child and never picked you up again?' I thought about that quote a lot. I missed being held up off the ground where nothing could hurt me. I missed him reading me stories to get me to sleep. I missed him calling me Little Fish.

By the time I came back downstairs, he'd shut himself in

his study and I could hear the keys tapping out the latest instalment in his Jock of the Loch Chronicles, *The Lady of Glencoe's Lover.*

The kitchen was clear. We'd argued, he'd cleaned up and we'd never mention it again.

*

For the next few days, Operation: Zane was our main reason for being. In between lunches at Subway and jaunts down to the beach to drink Acid Rain in the sand dunes – well, the boys did; me and Fallon paddled in the surf – we plotted, planned and primed our target. Fallon and Corey were in charge of Stage One: Stalking. Working out Zane's movements, making sure exactly who was going to be at his house and when. As expected, he was a creature of habit. Every day was the same – an early shift at Lidl, then a cycle ride to the gym on the retail estate. After the gym, he went to The Wallflower – the same pub Max's dad Neil drank in, at the end of his terrace of houses on the seafront.

Zane's mum and sister weren't to be affected by what we were doing, which made things tricky but not impossible – and meant we had to work out their movements too. Zane's mum owned one of the hairdresser's in the High Street. Every day she left at eight and came back about six – later if she did Tesco. And his sister was only three, so she was in nursery.

Then we struck. Corey had read books on real crime and watched far too many episodes of *CSI* so he knew exactly how to get inside Zane's house. He's, like, a master at this kind of thing; he made sure we didn't leave any fingerprints or anything. A window at the back with a faulty catch was a big help too. Anyway, the idea was to make Zane think he was going mad, not to actually burgle him.

We started with stupid, annoying stuff. Max took all his left trainers. I was in charge of the remote controls for his speakers and his TV and DVD player – I had to hide them all – plus emptying all his aftershaves down the sink, and Corey hid an old cat alarm clock of his – which made a very spooky meowing sound – in Zane's room, programmed to go off every night at 3 a.m.

Then the best bit: Corey had this invisible ink that he got ages ago, from this spy mail order catalogue. It doesn't show up for forty-eight hours, so when Zane first got back home, his carpet would have looked the same as he left it. But first thing in the morning, all these weird black patches would have appeared all over it. Black patches that kind of look like cats.

We hadn't even ruined his carpet or anything; the ink disappears completely in seventy-two hours. It was developed by NASA, Corey said, although why they'd want invisible ink I didn't know. I hugged the knowledge of our secret to myself as I held the bag for Pete during our next sparring session; then as I punched it like nobody was watching me.

'Woah, you're getting stronger, girl. I pity the fool who finds themselves on the receiving end of those.'

I looked down at my shivering fists, water running down my forehead in little rivers.

At the end Pete undid his hand wraps, stepped away from the bag and walked to the mini fridge to grab us both an isotonic.

'Who are you thinking about when you're hitting that bag?'

I just smiled and hoped that was enough of an answer.

*

The plan for the masks was put into operation late that

afternoon, after training. This part of it was Corey's idea – he'd seen some animal masks in the big Hobbycraft store on the retail park when he and Fallon had been looking for a découpage set – they wanted to cover an old set of drawers at Fallon's house for the nursery. Anyway, we bought four plain white cat-shaped masks – not découpaged – and then we followed Zane. One by one.

In the Lidl car park, as Zane finished his shift, Fallon stood in the bushes as he walked towards his car. She was dressed in black and stock still, just the mask staring out at him.

'But he definitely saw you?' I asked her. 'Saw the mask?'

'Oh yeah,' she said. 'He did a proper double-take and everything.'

Later, when he was coming out of the pub and saying goodbye to his rugby mates, he crossed the road and there was Corey, sitting on the sea wall, wearing his cat mask. Zane tried to cross the road for a closer look but by the time the traffic had passed, Corey had simply disappeared.

On Friday morning, I appeared at the bus stop wearing my mask as he sailed past on his bike. He stared at me, clearly alarmed, and the bike swerved to avoid a pedestrian. I heard the screech of brakes as I nipped down a side alley and out of his sight.

Then, at 6 p.m. that Saturday evening, me and Corey followed him to Sweat Dreams Fitness Centre on the industrial estate by the garden centre, and found a spot in the flower bed beneath the two main windows. I crouched beneath one window, Corey beneath the other. Then we donned our masks. On the count of three, we slowly stood up, clocking Zane Walker on the other side of the room, pumping iron for all he was worth on the pull-down machine. He caught sight of me first. Then Corey. He lost his grip on the bar and it flew upwards, bringing the weights back down with a hard *CLANK* which we heard from outside.

He swore through the single-pane glass. Fear at last. He got up off the bench and ran as Corey and I escaped around the side of the gym and over the low wall. We ducked down, waiting breathlessly, hearing the front door creak and bang followed by quick footsteps on the tarmac. I peered over the wall. Zane was scanning the area like the Terminator, a dark patch of sweat blooming on his grey vest, murder in his eyes. He did a 360° then went over to the flower beds under the windows, frowning at the ground as though we'd melted into it.

'I'll have you!' he shouted out. Only his echo replied.

Corey nudged me. 'Get down. He'll see you!'

'I don't care,' I said, stifling the little giggle caught in my chest. 'He's bricking it, look!'

The adrenaline surging through my limbs was tremendous as I watched Zane trudge back inside the gym, still looking round.

'He's gone.'

We collapsed into laughter. We had got to him. We were David, beating the crap out of Goliath with our teeny tiny rocks. When we'd caught our breaths, we stood up, taking off the masks.

'Brilliant!' I cried. 'His face, Corey! You should have seen his face!'

'He's rattled, isn't he?'

'Don't mess with the Fearless Five,' I laughed, still panting furiously.

I wanted to cheer and whoop. I felt like I could run right the way up Brynstan Hill in one go then fling myself down the other side. I was volcanic in all the right ways. I didn't know if it was the revenge thing or the boxing or just the fact I was friends again with Corey and Fallon and they were my way back to who I really was.

Maybe it was all three.

Maybe the revenges were helping me come to terms with what had happened and that part of my brain was clearing out so that I could now invite other thoughts in. Like me and Max. Maybe I could start thinking of Max *that* way now too. Despite what Pete had said about revenge being bad in the long run, I couldn't deny this new power I felt. This new confidence. And if it was going to help me get over what I needed to get over, who knows what else it could do for me? For us.

'So, was that it for the revenge against Zane, then?'

14

A Shock for Max

Oh no, I didn't want to leave it there. I don't think the others did either, if they were being honest. We had to go further, push him to the edge. Dangle him over it, if we had to. Over the next week, we each saw Zane out and about at his usual haunts. His gym had a special offer on for new mums called the Postnatal Package, which included a crèche, discounted massage treatments and aqua aerobics, so Fallon arranged a trial.

'He just looked weirded out,' she said when we met up for double chocolate muffins and full cream lattes in Costa. Well, she had a muffin and a latte – I had no-added-sugar apple juice and a pot of chopped fruit. I'd been so bad with my eating lately, I knew needed to reel back on my bad sugar.

During the night, Corey drew a mahoosive chalk cat outside the entrance to Lidl. The next morning, Max spied on Zane from the car park opposite.

'He stopped, looked at it, side-stepped it and went inside the store.'

'How did he seem?'

'He didn't seem anything. Just kind of weirded out.'

One of Zane's every-so-often habits was to jog around the Saints – up St Mark's Road, into St John's, through the alley into St Matthew's Lane and then back towards home via St Luke's Avenue. But once he'd seen the cats Max and me had spray-painted on the fences along his route, he was spending less time there, and more time on the beach.

So I saw an opportunity.

I followed him one morning, watching him from the safety of the Esplanade. He was underneath the Pier, doing his warm-ups. I put up my hood, clamped the cat mask to my face and sprinted along to the steps, taking them two at a time down onto the beach. I found a large stick and drew the word MEOW in large scrawly letters, right on the tide-washed sand where he wouldn't miss it. I kept looking up, checking where he was. He was just lightly jogging. Kicking up his heels. I got to the 'O' and he saw me. He started sprinting towards me.

'Oi!' I heard in the distance. I looked up.

My breathing got heavier behind the mask.

'Oi, I'm gonna kill you!' I quickly scrawled the W then dropped the stick and raced back up the steps to the seafront, pumping my arms and sprinting the promenade towards Manor Gardens, ducking past the fish ponds and through the churchyard gates. I hid behind a huge weathered gravestone and waited. He appeared at the gates, doing his Terminator scanning thing again.

'Yeah. Definitely weirded out.'

Max had Googled 'How to Get Revenge', and an article had come up; how Sharon Osbourne once put a human turd in a Tiffany box and mailed it to a deadly enemy. None of us were willing to do that, however much we hated Zane, so we did the next best thing – we organised the delivery of a raw pig's heart, courtesy of Rosie. She didn't ask what

Fallon needed it for, just slapped it in her outstretched hand and continued butchering the corpse for their freezer.

'I wonder if it arrived on time?' she asked as we sat in the motorhome on the seafront that Saturday night. My dad had gone out to his cookery class, and then out for a drink with Celestina, so, with a bit of luck, he wouldn't even have noticed we'd borrowed it.

'Should have,' said Corey, still flicking through the pregnancy app he'd downloaded for Fallon earlier. 'They're a pretty reliable firm and he was definitely home when it came. I checked.'

'I'd love to have seen his face, wouldn't you, Ells? Ells? ELLA?'

'Yeah,' I said, barely listening. My itch was up on my neck and along both arms, and I didn't have my antihistamines with me, so I was prickly as a porcupine, pacing up and down to the steamed-up windscreen to see if Max was coming. He'd gone down to the Pier end to deliver a note through Zane's letterbox – it was only supposed to take ten minutes. He'd been gone for half an hour.

'This isn't good,' I said, getting up and pacing back down the other end to where they were sitting at the table.

I closed my eyes and sent my prayer up to whoever was listening. 'Come on, come back now. Please. Please God, make him come back.' The glow of the orange street lights along the seafront was the only thing keeping us from being in total darkness.

'Maybe he went to get fish and chips?' Fallon suggested. 'I'm pretty starving.'

'Yeah, me too,' said Corey.

'No, we were going to go for chips *after* this. He said he was coming straight back. He's taken a stupid risk, I bet. Goading him or something.'

'Why would he?' said Corey. 'He knows the plan. We went over it about eight times.'

'No, but he's different at the moment. All devil-may-care and acting tough. It's not like him. He's frustrated.'

'About your sex problem?' Fallon blurted out. 'Sorry.'

'Fallon!'

'It's OK, Corey knows. Just about the sex problem though. That's all though, I swear.'

I was too anxious even to get angry. 'What if Zane was waiting for him? What if he grabbed his hand as he put the note through the letterbox?'

'No way,' said Corey. 'Fallon's right, he probably went to get the fish and chips or something.'

I looked at him. 'You don't believe that, Corey, I know you don't.'

'Well what's the alternative?' he said, slamming down his phone. 'What if he *has* got him? We can't do anything. It'd be like fighting a Panzer.'

'I don't even know what that is but I'm scared,' said Fallon, her hands up to her mouth.

'I'm going down there,' I said, zipping up my hoody.

'No, Ella.'

'I'll come too,' said Fallon.

'No, you won't,' I told her.

'I can fight dirty when I need to.'

'You might be able to, but that baby can't, so you've both got to stay out of it.'

'I'll come,' said Corey.

'No, I don't need you to.'

'You're not going by yourself. I don't care if it's sexist or anti-feminist or whatever. I'm not letting you go down there on your own. No way.'

'Corey, if he hurts him, I don't know what I'll do.' Just

the thought of Zane's hands on Max was giving me heartburn. 'My dad'll be back from his class just after nine. He'll go ballistic if he sees the motorhome's missing. I said we should have taken the Audi!'

'Just hold your horses, OK? Let's give it another five minutes and if there's still no sign then we'll do something.'

'What?'

'I don't know what. Just come and sit down.'

In the next moment, we all heard fast footsteps padding up the pavement outside; then the door flew open and Max ran in, breathless, slamming the door behind him. He collapsed against a cupboard, his chest heaving and his cat mask shaking in his fist.

'Oh thank you, thank you God,' I cried, rushing towards him and wrapping myself around his heaving chest. His heart was thudding so hard.

'You've been ages,' said Corey.

'Sssh,' he whispered, almost completely breathless.

'What happened?' Fallon whispered, gingerly standing up from the banquette.

'He caught hold of me, that's what happened. Jesus. Check the window. Is he there?'

Corey crept towards the front of the van and looked through. 'Doesn't look like it. Did he actually see you?'

'Saw me?' Max wheezed. 'He had me in a bleedin' headlock at one point.'

'Oh God,' I said.

'I was going to put the note through the letterbox and I didn't hear him coming behind me up the path. He tackled me to the ground.'

We all gasped at the same time.

'I managed to get free, and I just kept running. I made it up the High Street. Round by Tesco, he got me again on the grass, slammed me down. Look at my jeans.' In the dim light, we could see his mud-caked knees. 'I just kept going round and round, like a knob, him grabbing me, me dodging him.'

'Oh you poor thing, Max,' said Fallon, kneeling down beside him and clutching his arm. She was out of breath herself now, despite the fact she hadn't run anywhere. 'Oh God, he knows who you are. He knows it's us!'

'I dunno. I had this on all the time until the elastic snapped on the back,' he said, holding up his creased white cat mask. 'He kept saying "Who are you? What do you want? Did you send me that thing in the box?" He's pissed off, man. Way *way* pissed off.'

'Did he hurt you?' I said, holding both his freezing cold hands.

'No not really,' he said, pulling me in again for a cuddle. His heartbeat had regulated a bit now, but his chest still heaved. In the orange glow, I could see the mud all over his Vans and grass stains on the elbows of his blue hoody. The side of his face was grazed with mud too.

'I was so scared, Max,' I said, nuzzling into his hot neck and keeping my face there.

'How did you get away?'

'Sheer luck. He nearly had me though.'

'That could have been bad. That could have been so bad,' said Fallon.'

'It was bad enough,' Max laughed, wiping the sweat from his top lip. 'It's getting dodgy. I say we don't do anything else for at least a couple of days. What do you think, Ells?'

I thought for a moment. I thought about how scared I'd been when Max was out. How close he'd come to being hurt or worse. I thought about Corey in that toilet cubicle when Zane had rearranged his face. He could have done that to Max, too. My beautiful Max. And then, all at once, I was angry. It spurted out of me before I could pour any cold thoughts on it.

'No,' I said. I pulled back from Max. 'We have to keep the pressure on. We just need to be more careful. Plan things better. Did you say you still had the note?'

'Yeah,' said Max, removing the crumpled page from his jacket pocket. 'But, Ella...'

'I'll do the note. He won't catch me.'

'I'm not letting you go anywhere near him when he's this riled. He's expecting stuff to happen so he's on hyper-alert now. You won't get away with it. He'll know it's you.'

'I think he already does,' I said.

'What?' said Corey, fiddling with his hearing aid.

'Oh, come on, guys. He must know it's us by now. He strung up your cat in your front garden, Corey. Even if he didn't see your face that time at the gym, or on the sea-front, he'll know you by your clothes. He'll know me by *my* clothes. I'm the only girl in the county who can outrun him, anyway. It doesn't matter if he sees our faces. He's rattled. And we want him to stay rattled. Don't we?'

'You're not doing it,' said Max. 'No way.'

'I'll do the note,' said Corey, standing up from the banquette. 'I'll do it tomorrow night. It's my revenge, so I should be the one to do the most dangerous task.'

'No,' I said firmly. 'I'm sorry, but you're just not as fast as me. It makes sense if I do it.' I turned to face Max again. He wasn't happy. 'We'll wait a couple of nights. At most. Let him stew in his own paranoia. Then I'll do the note.'

'Ella...'

'He won't catch me, Max. They don't call me Volcano Girl for nothing.'

*'So how did the revenge on Shelby come
into play?'*

15

A Rather Unpleasant Meeting

'*Come on, Jess; just one more, please!*'

'*Yeah, please, Jess. Tell us one of your stories.*'

'*One of mine?*'

'*Yeah!*'

'*I don't know. Zane got scared last time with my Black Cat story, didn't you, Zane?*'

'*I did not.*'

'*You so did, Zane.*'

'*I did NOT!*'

'*Liar. You wet your pants.*'

'*Hey, come on now, don't fight. Choose another story, not a scary one.*'

'*One about the island. Please?*'

'*Yeah! About the pirates. And the jewels they kept in the walls of the cave.*'

'*No, Corey, that's silly. Jess, tell us the one with the girl who wanted to wreak a terrible revenge on her whole family so she put this stuff in the Christmas turkey that made everyone need the toilet.*'

'*YEAH! Then she blocked up all the toilets so they had to poo their pants!*'

'*Please, Jess, that one please!*
'*Yeah, go on! "The Terrible Terrible Revenge"!*'
'*Pleeeeeease?*'
'*You've heard that one so many times, though. Ella, do you want to hear the one about the Terrible Terrible Christmas Revenge?*'
'*Yes, please, Jess.*'
'*OK. Are you all snuggled down comfortably? So, there was this girl who hated her family so much that she decided to wreak a terrible revenge on them. And one Christmas morning, she finally saw her chance. It would all start to happen as her family sat around the dinner table...*'

*

The last thing I needed that Sunday morning was lunch with the Rittmans, but I had no excuses. There was nothing I could say or do to get out of it. Max even picked me up. Door to door.

'Unaccustomed as I am to public speaking,' Neil began, standing up from his position at the top of the dining table ('*part of a limited edition set, carved from a now-extinct tree from the Amazon delta*'). There was the usual flurry of groans and scrunched-up napkins as he scratched the end of his nose to flash his watch ('*a Breitling Transocean Chronograph with gold face, diamond numerals and unidirectional bezel, £7,000*'). 'I'd just like to say a few words to the gathered throng, if I may.'

'Yeah, make it quick though, Neil. I wanna be back home for Christmas!' called out Auntie Manda, who was sitting on my left in a feathery jumper that made her boobs stick out like traffic cones. Her kids were sitting alongside her. The twins were in matching pink dresses, playing some iPad game where you had to tap the screen like a maniac, the baby was in her high chair, gnawing on a soggy Yorkshire, and Shelby was texting. By the look on her face, she hated this as much as I did, though I'd noticed a few smiles in Max's direction and a shared giggle as they brought out the condiments. He said they were laughing about Granny Ethel's back-to-front blouse. I didn't believe him.

'All right, all right,' said Neil, adjusting his Hugo Boss golfing trousers (*'£900'*) over his substantial gut. He picked up his red wine glass and held it aloft. 'I'd just like to thank my darling wife Joelle for this wonderful repast. You've outdone yourself again, my girl.' There was a round of applause. 'Shame about the roasters, but you can't expect miracles, can you?'

I'd seen that one coming. Neil rarely went too long after singing Jo's praises only before he cut her down again like a weed. Jo didn't help herself – she was constantly on mute when Neil was around, so small and mole-like, like she was apologising for being alive.

'I'd also like to thank my dear old mum for making it here all the way from Cobham today,' he droned on. 'I never thought the broomstick would make it this far.'

Sweat beaded my forehead; either the roast beef sweats or the closeness of all these hot bodies. The bay windows were steamed up, too – I could barely see the garden, just a vague blue blob where the pool was.

Neil's crooked nose glowed red with all the wine he'd drunk, 'just to bring out the taste of the beef (*'£90 a bottle'*)'.

'I'd like to thank Manda and Paul for coming along, despite all the highly stressful preparations for *somebody's* eighteenth birthday bash next Friday night.'

Everyone at the table looked at Shelby who dipped her head behind a curtain of bleached blonde hair and went astonishingly red.

'Yes, my beautiful niece Shelby turns eighteen next weekend; so the first of my toasts will be for you, my love. May your eighteenth year be full of cheer, and may you never turn out queer.'

The whole table – apart from me, Max and Shelby herself – roared with laughter like Neil was the funniest thing since Jesus. The kids, in their defence, didn't seem to know what was funny but the baby squealing away only made everyone else laugh even more because of it being oh-so-adorbs. I'd heard all of Neil's racist, sexist and homophobic jokes before, having been forced to go round for Sunday lunch at least once a month since childhood. The fact I never found him funny didn't stop him. It seemed to entertain him that I never laughed.

'Don't crack your face, Estella, will you?' he boomed.

'No, you're all right, I won't,' I said, swigging back my mineral water *('Ten pounds a bottle that. You can't buy it in supermarkets, you know.')* I looked at the clock, waiting for time to eat itself. I had the note for Zane Walker in my pocket and I was itching to stay true to my word and put it through his door. The dining room was so hot, I'd been concentrating on trying not to scratch my knees and forearms for the best part of an hour. To make matters worse, Granny Ethel had complained of being cold, so Jo turned up the thermostat. It was cramped in there too, filled to capacity with Max's relatives. Shelby looked stunning, as usual, in her pink jeans and wedges and tight T-shirt. Her face shimmered as mine sweated.

The table was littered with plates, glasses, baby bottles, dishes of cold vegetables and drips of horseradish and gravy. The knife block with the 'diamond-sharpening steel and ergonomic handles' was still sitting right in the middle of it all like some centrepiece, the largest knife was resting on the beef plate next to the carcass I'd sat looking at for most of the meal. Neil had carved, of course. Neil always carved. Why the whole knife block had to come out was obvious – so he could show off how much it cost. (*'Only twenty in the country. Seven hundred pounds, you know.'*)

Twat.

Uncle Alan and his wife Kathy were pretty harmless, if you didn't get too close to her breath or his BO. Their sons, Ben and Jack, were university geniuses, not easy to talk to: Ben was studying to be a petro-chemist, Jack, a doctor, and both were more boring even than Neil. Drunken Uncle Paul and Aunty 'Call Me Manda' were nice enough, too, though I found it hard not to look at his amputation – or her mahoosive cleavage.

'No seriously though,' Neil laughed, flicking back his not-at-all-Just-For-Menned-boyish bangs (*'Two hundred pounds and I didn't have to go on a waiting list either – this face opens any door'*), 'we don't get together that often as a family, being as far flung as we are, so I appreciate it all the more when we do. I look forward to occasions like this, and the big par-tay next Friday, when we can all let rip like we Rittmans and Gilmores do!'

Cue more cheers. *Just get on with it*, I mumbled under my breath. Max was checking his phone under the table but he'd heard me and looked up. 'You all right?' he mouthed.

'I'm boiling,' I replied, tugging my collar. If someone had handed me a noose right then, I'd have been tying it to the nearest chandelier (*'We've got five of them. Modelled on the ones at Versailles. Three grand's worth. You can't buy 'em over here'*).

'So we're all looking forward to a good old knees-up. And as I'm footing the bill, there's a free bar, and I want you all to get absolutely paralytic.' Another chorus of cheers rose up from the aunts and uncles as he explained about the under eighteens being taken care of by a qualified child-care team he'd laid on for the night (*'A few hundred quids' worth of childcare, mind'*). Neil's eyes drifted across the table to me. 'And our lovely Ella will be there as well, of course, as our guest – and the Honorary Rittman that she is. I don't know if many of you know, but Ella's on target now to be picked for the British Athletics team going to the Commonwealth Games in two years' time.'

There was more applause, entirely undeserved, and this time I went burning red.

Max leaned in to his dad. 'She's not been picked yet,' he muttered.

'I know, but she will be,' he said, smirking. 'She's my superstar, aren't you, Ella?'

I inhaled. I exhaled. It didn't matter. He didn't matter.

'And she's got the best trainer in the area, Pete Hamlin, coaching her privately to ensure the best possible results – so it shouldn't be too long now before we see her on that winners' podium, garlanded with medals. And she'll have the full Rittman team behind her the whole way. So a toast to our gorgeous Ella, if you will, everybody!'

Once again, the glasses were raised, and everyone looked at me, while I shrank in my seat and silently prayed for it to be over.

But Neil wasn't finished. 'Our baby boy, Max, has just finished his first year of A levels – and is predicted all A stars I might add…'

Everybody cheered. Everyone except Shelby. And me.

I was dying to chip in with: *It hardly matters what results he got if he's going to be stuck managing your stinking garden centre the rest of his life* but I held on to it tightly, like it was a child teetering on a cliff edge. The applause went on for ages. Then Neil started on about his football prowess and how he was even too good for the England team and Max was back slapped and high-fived and they were all oh so proud of him. All but me. And Shelby.

Then Drunken Uncle Paul piped up from nowhere. 'Shame our Shelbs couldn't manage her career prospects a bit better, n'all.'

'Leave it, Paul,' muttered Call Me Manda, who by this point had Soggy Yorkshire Baby clamped to her udder-like boob. (Granny Ethel was clutching her handbag to her lap and doing the sign of the cross.)

'No, they all deserve to know, Mand.'

Shelby looked up from her phone. 'Don't start, Dad, please. You said you wouldn't.'

'Go on – tell your auntie and uncle what you've gone and done.'

'I don't want to talk about it.' Her glossy pout shimmered and her cheeks glowed red.

'For God's sake!' said Manda.

But Paul wouldn't leave it alone. He turned to the table and counted them off on his fingers. 'Three Fs, four Gs and three Us at GCSE. And now, just yesterday, she announces she's dropping out of her college course and she's going to become a pop star. I mean, can you credit it? Pinning her future on bloody *X Factor*!'

Shelby, already at boiling point, slid back her chair and rushed from the room. The silence was punctuated by the baby banging her spoon on the edge of her tray.

'What did you have to go and say that for, then?' said Manda, whacking him on his meaty Burnley FC-tattooed forearm.

'What?' said Paul, oblivious. 'I only said the truth. She's

dropped out and she's applying for *The X Factor*. Couldn't hit a bloody note with a frying pan.'

'Never stopped anyone before.' Neil grinned, knocking back another glass of wine.

The baby started crying. Manda looked furious as she held her over her shoulder. 'I can't believe you did that. You know how funny she is.'

Jo got up with some empty glasses. 'Who's for crumble? The top should be browned by now.'

'I'll give you a hand,' said Manda, shoving the winded baby back in her high chair, where she started banging her spoon and roaring like a tiny crusty-faced MP.

'Oh, she needs that to chivvy her up a bit, she does,' said Paul, draping his arm across the back of my chair. 'Bloody wet blanket, she is. If she spent more time on her books and less time on her phone or lads or her bloody hair extensions, maybe she'd have some decent prospects to look forward to, instead of pinning all her hopes on bloody prancing round a stage. It's not going to happen, is it?' He turned to me, putting his hot, hairy arm around my shoulders. 'Well done, girl – well done you.'

'Can we go soon?' I whispered to Max, as he leaned across me to clear my plate, Paul's arm still around me like a blinged-up python.

'We haven't had crumble yet. Give it another half-hour, yeah? You haven't been out to see the Porsche yet, have you? Get Dad to show you.' Max disappeared out to the kitchen with a stack of plates, leaving me with heat exhaustion and a table-full of his relatives.

Neil butted in, reaching across me for the unopened bottle of Merlot. 'Yeah, you haven't seen my new motor, have you?'

Aunty Kathy leaned across Paul and touched my arm.

Her perfume was suffocating. 'Ella, remind me again what distance you are?'

'Estella's county champion in the 400 metres, aren't you?' Neil butted in again. I reddened, all down my sweaty itchy neck. 'Yeah,' said Neil, popping the cork on the bottle. 'Remember that face. That's who you're gonna be cheering for come the next Olympics.'

If I'd been any more embarrassed I'd have exploded and bits of me would have splashed all over the headache-white walls.

Kathy looked impressed. 'How thrilling. Going to be the next Mo Farah are you?'

'No, I'm middle distance.'

'Oh right. Usain Bolt then.'

'Well, he's more of a sprinter.'

'Oh right.'

I couldn't be bothered to explain any further. Her perfume had hit the back of my throat and I was suddenly nauseous.

'She's incredible. Like white lightning, she is. Did you know we sponsor her now? Yeah. Rittman Inc. on all her kit. She's known as Volcano Girl around here, cos she 'erupts right out of the blocks'. We'll keep sponsoring her until she loses – then she'll be out on her ear.' Neil winked at me, clearly thinking that was the funniest thing he'd ever heard.

'She knows I'm only kidding. We wouldn't do that, would we? She's our superstar.'

Finally at my limit with the heat and the tedium, I slid my chair back. 'Sorry, just need to pop to the loo,' I said.

To my horror, Neil got up at the same time. 'Come and see the car first.'

Taking some plates with me, I went into the kitchen, where Jo was getting the crumble out of the oven and Call

Me Manda had the Marigolds on. Then they started fighting over who was doing the washing up.

'No, Manda, you're a guest – I won't have it.'

'Jo, for goodness' sake, you've cooked, it's the least I can do.'

'We do have a dishwasher, you know.'

'I'll just leave these here,' I said, dumping the side plates on the draining board.

'Thanks, love,' said Jo. 'Are you staying for crumble?'

'Uh, yeah, I think so. Where's Max?'

'I don't know, love.'

I turned and walked right into Neil at full pelt. 'Come and see the Porsche,' he said, looking at Jo. 'Shan't be a minute. Custard on mine, please.'

I was practically frogmarched out of the kitchen, across the hallway and outside onto the double drive. Neil was right behind me the whole way. He was so close to me I could smell the gravy stain on his shirt.

The black Porsche was parked at an angle on the drive, taking up the space of about three cars and shining like polished coal. There wasn't a mark on it.

'What do you think?' he said, folding his arms and looking at the car like it was a brand new baby. 'Beautiful, isn't she? You should hear the engine. She purrs.'

I said nothing – I couldn't believe he'd infected my private space again, with his arrogance and fatness and general wank. I could hear him swallow. He started banging on about double exhausts, seven-speed gearboxes. I kept looking back through the kitchen window where I could still see Jo and Manda at the sink, gossiping and passing each other plates. He couldn't do anything with them there.

'You seem tense, Ella. You and Max haven't fallen out, have you?' I felt his hand on my shoulder and my entire body shook him away, like I'd stuck my wet fingers in a plug socket.

'All right, all right,' he said, looking around sheepishly. 'Take it easy.'

There were a billion words in my head, but none of them seemed powerful enough to tell him how much I hated the sight of him. The smell of him. How much I wanted to scratch and smash the wax out of that Porsche. How much I wanted revenge on him – this ugly, greedy, fat, old perv.

'Don't. Touch. Me,' was all I could manage.

He laughed, looking around again, his breath stale with red wine and roast meat. 'Whatever you say. Only that horse has kind of bolted now, don't you think?'

He left me there, standing on the driveway, all four of my limbs shaking with some weird adrenaline that had made my whole body go completely cold. Why could I stand there and let him say and do what he wanted? What was it that rooted me to the spot in terror about that one man? I could face down the Shaws, no problem. I could outrun a furiously angry Zane Walker, who could actually flatten me if he wanted to. I could even stare into the waters of the evil Witch's Pool and not give a crap about all the skeletons in its depths or the ghosts who lurked around it at night. But when it came to Neil Rittman, I turned to stone. I know it's there, waiting to come out. Waiting to erupt.

When I could summon the will to move, I walked back inside to the warm smell of baked rhubarb and custard and laughter floating along the hallway. Call Me Manda was bringing up the rear of the crumble dish with a box of vanilla ice cream and a handful of dessert spoons.

'Crumble's ready,' she said proudly. 'Go and round up the sulks, will you?'

I guessed that she meant Shelby. In the dining room, I

noticed Max wasn't back in his seat either. I think it was then that I knew.

I walked across the hallway towards Max's bedroom, knowing what I'd see through that slightly ajar door. Each footstep took me closer to a new level of pain. Sure enough, as I peered through the gap, I heard voices. Saw movement. Max lying on his bed. Him wriggling down his jeans. Him, fully excited. Her head in his lap.

'Quick, hurry up,' he whispered.

'All right, all right,' she said, giggling.

I wasn't repulsed that they were related. Or even angry, at that point. I was just sad, realising I had lost him. I didn't know him anymore. I knew he didn't want to hurt me but I also knew he needed sex. And that was something I just couldn't give him, no matter how much I wanted us to stay together.

I walked back towards the front door and stepped out onto the drive, the glossy black Porsche eyeballing me like a predator. I didn't stop to throw a stone at it, or scratch it or kick it like I'd wanted to, five minutes before. Instead, I broke into a run and sprinted back along the streets and roads and back alleys until I was at the roundabout to my house.

Then my phone rang in my pocket.

But it wasn't Max, like I was expecting. It was Corey.

'Ella? Ella? Are you there? It's me, Corey. Ella, I need help, quick. I'm at my house with Fallon. She's just bleeding everywhere. I don't know what to do.'

'Your head must have been all over the place.'

16

Junior Springs a Surprise!

I didn't have time to dwell on Max and Shelby right then. By the time I'd sprinted the mile or so to Brynstan General, I'd almost forgotten it. I was too worried about why Corey had said Fallon was bleeding. I didn't know much about childbirth, but I knew blood was a bad sign.

When I got to the hospital, I ran to the reception desk, sweating and breathless, and asked if she'd had been brought in. They sent me up to Maternity on the second floor. The lift took ages. When it opened again, I saw Corey, sitting on a chair in the corridor. His head was against the wall; his eyes wide open. Above him hung a notice board filled with leaflets on 'Coping with Miscarriage' and 'Common Birth Defects' and support groups.

'Corey?' I said.

He saw me and his face crumpled. I dashed straight to him and held him tightly.

'Is she OK? Corey, is she OK?' I felt him nod against my shoulder as he sobbed. 'Is the baby OK?'

He mumbled something. 'They said it might be – some long word.'

'What sort of long word?'

'Something about the thing detaching.'

'Umbilical cord?'

'No.'

'Placenta?'

'Yeah, it could be that. I didn't know what to do. I called the ambulance and they came quickly but what if I was too late, Ella? What if she dies because I was too late?'

'It's OK, it's OK,' I said.

He took off his glasses, wiping his eyes with his coat sleeve. 'We were sat down, looking at the plans I've made for the new chicken run...'

'What plans?'

'I've been doing some designs for the farm. Rose was talking about it and I offered. I'm going to help build a new coop and an extension to the goats' pen. I'm gonna set them up with a website too, so they can rehome the cats more quickly.'

'Corey, why didn't you go into work today?'

'Well, Fallon had a twinge and I was worried about her, so I called in sick.'

'They're going to fire you if you carry on like this.'

'They already have,' he said. 'I don't care. What if I *hadn't* been there for her, Ella? She could've ...'

'I know, I know.'

'We were gonna bring the cakes round to yours later. Fallon wanted to go to the beach for a picnic. All of a sudden she got this pain and had to sit down. And then all this stuff – blood and stuff – just started shooting out of her, right on my grandparents' kitchen lino.'

'You mean her waters broke?'

'I guess, yeah. All I could think was water and towels, cos you see it on the films, don't you? Water and towels. But when I *got* the water and towels, I didn't have a frigging clue what to do with them. So then I called Rosie and she told me where the overnight bag was and the money for the taxi and then I called you. I couldn't think what else to do.'

'You did good, Corey. Really good.'

He sat back down on the chairs but angled his head towards Room Five. 'What if I hadn't been there, Ella?'

'You *were* there,' I said, squeezing his hand. 'That's what you've got to think. If you want to go in with her now, I'll be OK here—'

'No,' he interrupted. 'It doesn't seem right. She's got her legs wide open and everything. And her mum's with her.' He looked quite faint. 'How do women do it? I mean, seriously? It looks very painful. And traumatic.'

'I think it is,' I said. 'Do you think we should call Zane?'

'Fallon said he won't give a crap.'

'Perhaps not, then.' I felt for the note in my pocket. It was still there, crumpled and creased and burning a hole.

Just then, the door to Room Five opened and out stepped Roadkill Rosie herself. Corey stood up, fiddling with the hem of his T-shirt. 'How is she?'

'About ready to pop. They're keeping an eye on her, don't worry. You can come and see her in a minute, all right, but let the midwives do their job. There's a waiting area just down there on the right. I'll come and tell you if there's news.'

I'd forgotten how nice she was, alongside her squat, witchy appearance and butcher's forearms. I remembered Rosie properly now. I remembered that I liked her. She'd been kind.

'Won't be long now.' Rosie patted Corey's forearm and smiled at us both before disappearing back into Room Five.

'Come on,' I said. 'I need something sweet.'

We made our way down to the waiting area and I headed straight for the vending machine. There was a circle of chairs around it, a table loaded with magazines, a box of Lego, a stack of colouring sheets and a pot plant that had grown to the ceiling. A bloke with sunken cheeks waited with one knee bouncing to the tune of 'Another One Bites the Dust', and an older woman in a furry cardigan and two kids were colouring in *The Gruffalo* on the table.

I checked the clock on the wall. It was 4.27 p.m.

By 5.19, we'd had another update from Rosie: labour was progressing normally, and Fallon had been given some drugs so she wasn't in so much pain. Every time we heard a scream, Corey had to cover his ears.

He sighed. 'Do you know what I bought myself at the start of the summer? A Marauders Map, a bottle of polyjuice potion and a wand. Over seventy quid I spent on all that. It would have been more if they had Golden Snitches in stock.'

'I thought you were over Harry Potter?' I said.

He glared at me. 'You don't ever "get over" Harry Potter, Ella. At best you just learn to live with the fact that fucking envelope's never going to arrive.'

'Well, whatever makes you happy.'

'Yeah, but I'm not a kid any more. I need to spend my money on things that matter. I want to be more independent. Nan and Granddad do everything for me – my washing, my meals, tidying my room. Nan even still buys my pants.'

'I know,' I said. 'I've seen her in Peacocks.'

He sighed. 'I just want to be useful. I wanna spend my money on useful things. I know I can be more than this, Ella. I can do most things. And yeah I'm a bit slow sometimes and I can't run fast but I know computers. And I can drive – sort of. I want to look after Fallon.'

'How are you going to support them with no job?' I asked.

'I'll get another one. The Costa in town is looking for a barista. You get free lattes and all the brownies you can eat. I've got some savings to be going on with anyway.'

'Are you sure you want to do that?'

'Yes. I've never wanted anything so much in my life.'

'Except a Golden Snitch.'

'Don't rub it in.'

I took my phone out. The screen was dead – I must have turned it off after I got Corey's call. I switched it back on. 'Then you *should* help her. You totally should.'

He smiled. 'Yeah?'

I could see it now. Corey wanted a family; people to worry about, to take care of, like his grandparents had always worried and taken care of him. He was dying to pay it back to someone. Mort had been enough for him, until now. He was growing up before my eyes.

'Yeah. I think it would be good for you. And you can pass on all your Harry Potter gear to the baby when it's older, can't you? Read the books to it and take it to the theme parks and stuff.'

He grinned. 'I'd really like that.'

My phone buzzed seven times in my hand. Missed calls. Messages. All from Max. Biting on my pride, I sent back;

At hospital with Fallon. Maternity level 2 main building. No kiss. Then I turned it off again.

When I put my phone back, I found a two pound coin, so I took it to the vending machine. Corey shook his head when I looked at him, but I got a bar of Dairy Milk and a Toffee Crisp as well, in case Corey changed his mind. Sitting back down, I ripped open the Dairy Milk and scrunched up the wrapper.

'Have you two had a row? Where is he?'

'I was round his house for Sunday lunch when I got your call. I came straight here.'

'I know it's none of my business, Ella, but if you want to talk, I'm here.'

'I saw him getting sucked off by his cousin, Shelby. He doesn't know I saw.'

Corey stared at me, his mouth hanging open. I closed it for him. 'We are not a codfish, Corneliusz.' I carried on eating the chocolate. It was only when I'd swallowed the last mouthful that I realised I hadn't actually tasted a single bite.

'Him and his...? You saw them? God, Ella.'

'I think I'm glad. He's getting what he wants – what he needs. He's not going to get it from me any time soon.'

'What about what *you* need?'

I picked up the Toffee Crisp and offered it to him. Again, he shook his head. I didn't taste that one either. I scrunched up the wrapper and dropped it in the bin.

'He's changed since I knew him last,' he said as I chewed my chocolate bar. 'I don't know what it is. He's just... different.'

'Skunk,' I blurted. He looked at me. 'I've noticed it too. He flies off the handle quicker. And he's got lazier. And he's been having these nightmares too, about Jessica. About me. He wakes up in a cold sweat and he shakes. I swear it's down to that. I wish he'd stop.'

'Have you tried asking him to stop? Max loves you so much. He told me he'd do anything for you.'

'Clearly, keeping his thing in his pants is the one exception.'

Corey started picking his thumbs, then shoved his fists under his armpits to stop himself. 'I don't know what to say. I don't know how to help.'

'You can't help,' I said. 'Not with this.'

'It couldn't be a mistake, could it? Like, you *thought* you saw her… giving him facetime but actually it was perfectly innocent?'

I laughed. 'What, that she was just using some new oral cleaning technique that dentists recommend? No, Corey. I know what I saw. I think they've been at it for months.'

The lift doors *bing*ed and there was Max, looking breathless.

'Don't say anything, Corey,' I said, as I waved to him. He began jogging up towards us, stopping briefly halfway along to sanitise his hands.

Corey had his arms folded, violence in his eyes. 'I don't know if I can hold it in.'

'Please, leave it. I don't want him knowing just yet.'

'Why not?'

'Just let me handle it.'

'I didn't know where you'd gone,' Max puffed. 'Why didn't you tell me? I looked everywhere for you. I called your phone like a million times.'

'Seven times,' I said. 'Sorry, I didn't think. I got the call from Corey and I must have switched my phone off. I just ran straight here.'

Max looked at Corey. 'How is she? How's Fallon?'

If Corey was a dragon, smoke would have billowed from both his nostrils, but he did as I'd asked him, and kept it to himself. 'They're both OK. I'm going to go and see if there's any more news.' He glanced at me. 'Will you be all right, Ella?'

I mouthed a 'thank you' to him as Max turned away. 'We'll wait here.'

Corey departed back up the corridor.

'You didn't try any of Mum's crumble,' said Max.

'Like I said, I didn't think.'

A nurse came to tell the family with the colouring kids that 'labour was progressing well and Mummy was comfortable, but not ready to push yet'.

'That's all right,' said Max, putting his arm across me, just like his lecherous uncle. 'I was just worried.' He kissed my cheek. I looked straight ahead at the vending machine. 'Do you wanna get a bottle of water or something?' He rooted in his pocket for loose change.

'No.'

'You OK?'

'YES.'

Some fury had leaked out. There was rage radiation in the air. Max could tell. I looked across at the man with the bouncing knee. I started bouncing my knee too. He was all 'Another One Bites the Dust' so I tried a bit of 'Radio Ga Ga'. We were practically in harmony.

'I'm just nervous. For Fallon. Do you want a cereal bar or summing?'

'No. Thanks.' I looked at him. 'I'm sorry I ran off. I just panicked.'

He seemed to sigh with relief. He reached across for my hand, and I let him hold it.

Two more bars of Dairy Milk, a shared pack of Smokey Bacon, a Go Ahead and a flick through two *OK!* magazines later, and Corey appeared again. I nudged Max next to me; he'd fallen asleep. Corey had plastic gloves on. There were streaks of blood on them.

Max and I both stood up and waited the agonising moments it took for him to reach us. He could barely speak. He could barely breathe.

'Fallon let me cut the cord. She's wonderful.'

*

Fallon looked knackered when we walked into Room Five; her hair was all electrocutey with sweat. Rosie was holding the baby, her face full of joy. When we came in, she handed her back to Fallon and went out, muttering about tea.

'Mum's a bit emotional,' said Fallon, cuddling the little girl close to her. 'What do you think of her then? She's not too ugly, is she?'

'I don't know how you did it. You were in so much pain,' said Corey, poking his finger inside the baby's fist. She clung on tightly.

'She's so cute,' said Max, peering over to look at her.

I went round the other side of the bed where there was more space.

'Yeah,' said Corey. 'She is. Fallon's, like, a warrior queen or something. I swear to God, I'll never know how you did that.' He was looking at Fallon in complete awe.

'Me either!' Her face brightened. 'Labour hurts a lot though. I thought I was coming apart at the seams at one point.' She looked at me. 'Do you want to hold her, Ella?'

'Me?' I said.

'Yes.' She smiled. 'Go on.' She began handing the baby over to me and I took her, worrying immediately that she might cry in my face. But she didn't.

'You don't have to ask to hold her, you know. You're practically her auntie now. And you two are her uncles, no question.'

'We're not related, Fallon,' said Corey. 'How can we all be aunties and uncles?'

'Because I said so.' None of us had any argument against that. 'Besides, she doesn't have anyone else. I don't have any brothers or sisters. I just have Mum. The baby needs a family.'

I understood now how new parents could spend hours

just looking at their babies. For what was basically just a pink blob with creases for eyes, she was fascinating. Every movement was delightful; every eyelid-flicker, every mouth-twitch was an event. Her little chest going up and down against the white blanket she was wrapped in. Her contented little mouth, like a sugarless Jelly Tot. The wisps of perfect brown hair, sprouting out all over her scalp. Suddenly, I was crying myself. I was crying more than Fallon.

'Aww, Ella.'

'You're so brave, Fallon. Look at her. She's great. And... Oh no.'

'What?' she said. 'Oh God, what is it? Is something wrong with her?'

'No, I've just noticed – she just looks like Zane.'

'Oh God, don't say that,' said Max, coming over to have a closer look at her. He could see it too then – the shape of her eyes, the colour of her hair. They even had the same nose.

Corey came round to look too. 'She does as well. Ella's right.'

'God, sorry,' I laughed, still crying freely. Unstoppably. 'I don't know what's come over me.'

'So this is Number Five, then?' said Max.

'Huh?' said Fallon, wiping her eyes.

'We're the Fearless Five, aren't we? Now we're complete.'

'Oh yeah,' said Fallon. 'I don't want to call her Timmy though. She doesn't look like a Timmy. I've no idea what to call her. We've looked through all the names, haven't we?' Corey nodded. 'I'd originally thought it was going to be something like Hermione or Ginny. But looking at her now, she doesn't suit those names.'

'Even though she is quite magical,' said Corey, beaming. Fallon nodded and let out a massive yawn.

'Aww you're knackered,' I said. 'We'll leave you for a bit to have a kip.'

'No, please don't,' she said, even though she was fighting against her eyelids. 'Just stay with me. I like you all being here.'

So we stayed. We sat around her room, taking turns to hold the baby and nip out to make hot drinks and phone calls. When Max had gone outside for a cigarette and Fallon was asleep, Corey turned to me.

'Do you know what you're going to do then? About Shelby?'

'Yeah,' I said, looking down at the sleeping baby in my arms. 'Yeah, I think so.'

'And what was that?'

17

Five Go Adventuring

I wanted to trash her birthday party; the big shindig Neil had paid for her at Michaelmas Manor that Saturday night. But this time, it wasn't going to be a Fearless Five thing. It was just a 'me' thing.

Days passed and I said nothing to the others about my plans. Fallon came out of hospital and Corey left home to go and stay with her for a bit, leaving a note for his soon-to-be-returning grandparents on their coffee table.

We carried on hanging out together, watching Netflix or playing video games. We ate out at Subway or Costa and took turns cuddling the baby. I trained with Pete and gave the punchbag a daily pounding. My body grew tighter with the effort and my arms stronger and harder at the top. And silently, I thought about my plan.

Operation Zane had been given a rest for a few days, so the man of the moment could freak out sufficiently, but I for one didn't want to wait any longer. One drizzly lunchtime I made Max drive us to the seafront. He parked up by the pavement opposite the jetty and they got three cod lots and curry sauce from Cod Save the Bream. The smell was glorious as they sat merrily stuffing their faces and making om nom noises as the baby snoozed soundly between Fallon and Corey in the back. I was too nervous to eat.

'Are you sure you don't want a chip, Ella?' Corey offered.

I bit my fingernails. 'No thanks. I'm fine.' Max was looking at me, his gaze unbroken by my staring back at him. 'What?'

'Are you gonna do it then or what?'

'I'm waiting for him to come back.' I took the note out of my pocket and smoothed it over my knee. 'I can't post it while he's out; what if his mum reads it?'

Max moved his chip bundle to the dashboard and started chewing his thumbnail. I could smell the shampoo on his still wet hair from football that morning.

I turned to face the two back-seaters, jaws chomping together. Corey sneezed and a little gust of chewed up fish-cake flew straight into the back of Max's headrest.

'God's sake!' he shouted, grabbing the tissue box from the footwell by my feet and chucking it into the back. 'Clean it off, now.' Fallon was wetting herself, probably literally thanks to her knackered fouf.

And while all that commotion was going on, I cleared the windscreen with the chamois leather and I saw a figure coming along the pavement.

'There he is!' I cried.

Zane was fumbling in his XXL Hollister coat pocket for his keys and unlocking the door of their flat. Max flicked the ignition over, releasing the windscreen wipers.

I started to open my door. It was raining blades outside so I hitched up my hood and tied it tight to my face.

Max leaned over my seat. 'He goes for you, just run and don't stop. We'll stay here with the engine running. All right?'

I nodded. I was shaking but determined. My fire in my

belly would help me, like it always had. I stood on the pavement, dazzled by the street lights and Amusements sign across the road. I made my way along the pavement towards Walker's place.

Over the sea wall, the tide was in and I could hear the waves crashing and retreating, crashing and retreating. It was a dark day and there were lights on the water, a couple of fishing boats. The Fun Pub was pulsing with some sad Eurotrash techno pop and a couple of Primark models were smoking cigarettes against a Postman Pat ride outside the arcades. I carried on walking and I didn't look back.

I stopped outside the gate. A light was on – it glowed either side of the thick curtains in what I assumed was the front room. I heard Max's engine revving down the road.

This was Walker. The Big Pig. Cat murderer extraordinaire. He was going to get his. The note would make sure of it.

Without another thought, I yanked open the gate, ran up the path and pushed the note through the brass letterbox, but the box was heavy and my hand got stuck. I yanked it back out so hard my scabby knuckles scraped against the metal and all the scabs tore off at once. I legged it back up the path as fast as my feet would take me. All I could hear was the clank of the letterbox behind me – the clank that said 'Job Done.'

As I was locking the gate, I looked up, I don't know why, and the bay window was different. The curtains were open. And Zane was standing there looking out. Standing there, looking at me. Not coming to get me. Not reacting at all.

I think I knew then that we'd broken him.

18

Curious Discoveries

'Need to talk about it?' asked Pete, letting go of the bag and sitting down on the bench. 'About what?' I said, concentrating on softer jabs.

'We're friends, aren't we?'

'Yeah.'

'Friends listen to each other's problems and help them find solutions.'

'I don't know what you're on about,' I said, even though I knew *exactly* what he was on about because it was cutting me to the bone.

'If your problem is the reason you run, if that's what's giving you the fire in those legs and those fists, then I'd rather you didn't run any more. I'd rather you stopped and faced it. I'd rather you were OK up here than fast down there.' He tapped the side of his head. He stood up and walked back to me, holding me on either side of my arms. His hands were warm. 'I just want you to be mended.'

I stared into his eyes. They were so kind. I stared at his lips. I had no words to answer him but I had the sudden urge to kiss him. So I did.

I put my hands either side of his neck and, before I could

think, I moved closer and pressed my mouth against his. I trusted him. I trusted him not to hurt me. I wanted him to love me and teach me to how be a lover without being afraid of it.

But he immediately pulled back.

'What the hell are you doing?' His face had changed, in an instant he was someone else. The kind understanding had gone, washed away by disgust and anxiety. He held me by my triceps again but this time firmly away. Arm's length.

'I don't know, I wanted to see what it was like.' The embarrassment was cocooning. I was covered by it. 'Oh God, I'm so sorry. Pete, I'm so sorry.' I fumbled out of my gloves and ran towards my bag on the floor by the door.

'Ella, stop.'

'I'm sorry,' I said again. 'I don't know why I did that. I'm messed up. My friend's just had a baby and, ugh, I'm sorry all right? I don't know why I did that.'

I fumbled my rucksack onto my back. My hands were shaking.

'Ella, look at me.' He came closer. 'Ella.'

'You must think I'm repulsive.'

'LOOK AT ME.' I turned to look at him. I couldn't meet his eye. 'Come here.' He held out his hands. 'Come on.' I shook my head. 'You are never going to feel any different until you confront that fire and put it out.'

Water filled my eyes and he became blurry. I turned away, fumbled with the catch on the garage door and yanked it up and over my head, emerging again into the dazzling sunlight, but, as I pulled it back down, I lost my grip and it banged down hard onto my face. I yowled and stumbled against the cottage wall, pain radiating out from my mouth, pulling down a clump of ivy and climbing roses. I sat on the path, blood dripping from my nose.

Pete came jogging out to me and started to help me up. 'Come here, let's have a look at it. It's all right, it's all right.' He led me back inside and guided me towards the kitchen, sitting me down at the breakfast table. 'Hold this against it.' He handed me a wad of kitchen roll.

'I want to go home,' I sobbed, snatching the wad from him and holding it to my mouth. I thought of Corey and me in the girls' toilets on the last day of term. What a mess he had looked. Now I was the mess.

'I can't let you go home like this. I need to check nothing's broken.'

After much coaxing, I took my hands away from my throbbing face and he held my head and looked at me, gently pressing against the side of my nose. He got up and went over to his fridge freezer, pulling out a new bag of frozen peppers and wrapping them in a clean tea towel. He left it to one side and came back over to look at me again.

'Is it still bleeding?' He guided my fingers to the part of my nose just above my nostrils and told me to pinch it. 'Lean your head forward. OK, stay like that, all right?'

I sat watching him, my hand cupped beneath my face as the blood *drip drip dripped* into my open palm. Salty tears had mingled with the blood in my mouth. *Drip drip.*

When the bleeding had finally stopped, he handed me the frozen tea towel. 'Hold this against it. It'll help with the swelling.'

I stupidly thought we were done talking. That this was our new focus. But he wouldn't put it down.

'You need to talk to someone, Ella. I don't care who. Whatever it is you're hiding can't be kept hidden any more. Look what it's doing to you. I don't care if it's me or your dad or a doctor. Just talk. Let me see.' I moved the frozen tea towel away from my face. 'That looks nasty. You're going to need a plaster on it. Stay right here, OK?'

As he vanished back out into the garage, I put down the tea towel on the sideboard, grabbed my bag and swung it onto my back, heading through the living room to the front door. I clicked the latch and sprinted back down the lane as fast as I've ever run before. I knew he couldn't catch me. Nobody could.

*

My face was a mess. I told the others I ran into a lamp post on my way home. Max was the only one who didn't believe me. He wanted to know why I'd been running full pelt from Pete's house in the first place and kept picking at the fact like a scab. I just kept changing the subject. Then Corey suggested a Call of Duty marathon and he seemed to forget about it for a bit.

'You're too slow, mate,' laughed Corey, pumping some virtual soldier full of virtual bullets. 'Admit it, I'm just better at this.'

'Yeah, well I still slay at FIFA.'

We'd met up at Max's house on Upper Dunes Close that Thursday morning. His mum was on a WI day trip and Neil and Drunken Uncle Paul had taken the Porsche out 'for a spin in the country' (aka a tour of local pubs) so it was quite safe for Fallon to be there, and no one was going to sling her out. We were all in Max's bedroom. The boys were in the gaming chairs in front of Max's TV while me and Fallon were cuddled up with the baby on his bed. I was in a terrible mood. Everything was cloudy in my head. I could smell Shelby's perfume on his duvet cover. There was a long blonde hair underneath his pillow. I needed the punchbag.

'Ooh yeah, feaky little snucker that one!'

'Yeah, he's the fast one. You gotta take him down first before all the others. There! Ten o'clock, on the tower.'

'Die you bastaaaaaard!'

Fallon stood up and went to the window, looking out across Brynstan Bay. 'See that over there, Baby Girl? That's the island. We're going to take you there for a picnic when you're all big and chong.'

'Big and chong?' Max chuckled. 'What the actual F is that?'

'Yes, big and chong. And on the island we'll play aaaall daaaaay long, just like we all used to. We'll do it all again for you. We'll have picnics and we'll play games and Corey will teach you how to fish and Max will teach you how to tie knots and Ella...'

'... won't be going,' I said, double-bagging the latest nappy and chucking it in Max's bin. Fallon turned and frowned at me. 'Sorry. I don't want to do that.'

'Ella, it was the best time of my life, when we were all kids. I want her to have that too.'

'Why bother? As soon as the picnics and the fishing are done, it's all exams, and jobs, and divorce and bullying and rejection and cancer. And death. Childhood's just one tiny little window of hope. Tell her, Fallon – once that's gone, there's nothing else.' As my throat clotted up and my voice started to break, I climbed off the bed and walked out. From the other side of the door, I heard Max's big sigh.

'Leave her, Fallon. She's just on one again. She's been like it for weeks.'

'No, she's upset.'

'I knew something was coming,' said Corey. *Bang bang bang bang.* 'Aha, got him!'

I moved away from the door and went outside to the back garden. I took off my shoes and socks and sat down on the edge of the pool, dangling my feet in. I looked down into the water for a long time. Then I felt the atmosphere change around me, and knew someone had come outside to see if I was OK. I didn't try to stop crying.

'I'm all right,' I said.

Fallon sat down beside me. She took her shoes off too and copied me with her feet in the water. 'No, you're not.'

I nodded, tears overwhelming me again. 'I'm so sick of it. It's like one day someone just said, "OK, you've had all the fun you're going to have. Now comes life."'

We dangled our feet in silence for a bit. The light from the pool beamed upwards underneath Fallon's chin as she looked back at the house.

'I never thought I'd come back here. Ever. And after the inquest, after everything my mum said, I didn't expect Max ever to speak to me again, either. Then, when you all showed up, it was like it had all gone away. I thought we could pick up where we left off, all be friends again. Do what we used to do.'

'But we can't.'

She looked at me. 'We can. Sort of. But it's still going to be there, isn't it? The things we don't talk about. And Zane won't be around.'

'Do you miss him?'

'What do you mean? As a friend? Yeah. I do. I've missed this. Us being a gang. I guess that's why I love being around animals. They're always there. There's always something to cuddle. And they love me.'

I nodded but didn't quite know what to say.

'Hey listen, I've been thinking of repeating Year 11 at Brynstan.'

I stopped swishing my feet through the water. 'Have you?'

'Yeah. I want to get some GCSEs and I want to get a qualification in something, like make-up or hairdressing. Something I enjoy. Like you with your running.' She pulled a small leaf from my hair and tossed it into the water where it floated off. 'I don't have any ambitions. Not like you. I guess you've inspired me.'

'Me? I've inspired *you*?'

'Yeah. You're driven and ambitious and stuff. You know what you want to do with your life. It was your idea to scare off the Shaws, to get back at Zane. You want to do something, you go out and do it. I want to be like that.'

I didn't have the heart to say anything to that.

'By the way, I saw Zane yesterday in town. Buying new trainers.'

'Did you?'

'Yeah. He looked bad, too. Like he hadn't slept much.'

I wiped my nose on my T-shirt hem. 'I wonder if the glitter bomb arrived safely.'

'Corey booked the delivery for twelve.' She looked at her Mickey Mouse watch. 'It should have got there by now.'

'What sort of a card did you pick?'

'A cat one.'

'Of course.'

'I might have found a name for the baby. What do you think of Polly?'

I screwed up my face. Her face fell.

'Oh.'

'Sorry.'

'Corey bought me this Baby Nirvana CD and I've been playing it to her to get her to sleep. There's this song on there called "Polly". I quite liked it.'

'That song's about a girl who gets raped.'

'Oh my goodness, it's not, is it?'

I nodded. We both said nothing for a while, just dangled our feet.

'I wish I could get in,' she said, kicking her feet gently through the water. 'Haven't been swimming for years. I've got this massive maternity pad on though so it'd probably drown me if it got wet.'

She looked at me. I knew she was waiting for me to smile so I did.

'I'm sorry I mentioned the island. I didn't mean anything by it, Ella.'

'No, no, it wasn't you. It used to be a happy place. You're right.'

'It could be again?' she said, eagerly. 'We could go for a picnic.'

'I don't want to.'

'What if just you and me went? We don't even have to take the baby. We could hire a boat and just go there for the afternoon or something?'

I looked at her. 'Why? What would be the point?'

She shrugged. 'Maybe if you went back there you could start to feel better? Me and Corey watched *Jeremy Kyle* the other day. It's this programme where this man…'

'I know who Jeremy Kyle is.'

'Oh. Well he was talking about this thing called "closure". Facing your problems so that you can move past them. He said it's the only way.'

I swished my feet through the warm water. 'I used to swim all the time.'

'Yeah. You were like a fish.'

'A little fish,' I muttered.

'We used to race up and down here. Making whirlpools. Playing pirates. Diving for coins. We had so much fun, every day.'

'Or did we?' I said. 'Maybe there were just one or two good days. Maybe the rest was just as bad as it is now, only we didn't see it then.'

All was silent around us. There was a pressure in my head that hadn't been there before. I thought I was going to cry, and I couldn't think of a way to stop it.

'I'd drown myself if I could,' I said.

Fallon frowned.

Suddenly, she reached out and pushed me down into the water. I stood up, gasping, bouncing up from the pool floor, and screamed, not in anger but in joy. I looked at her on the edge, spluttering and laughing.

'What did you do that for?'

'I thought you dared me to drown you.' She smiled. 'Do you mind?'

I treaded water. 'No. It's actually quite nice. It's warm.'

'I'd get in too if I didn't have this giant surfboard in my knickers.' We both giggled. 'You're right, Ella. Growing up does suck.'

'Let's not grow up then.' I smiled, and sent a tidal wave of water over her open-mouthed head.

Max was outraged when he saw us both standing at the back entrance to the garage, sopping wet, shivering and giggling uncontrollably.

'What the cocking hell… ?'

'Just had a swim,' I said. 'Could you grab us some towels, please? And Fallon's maternity bag.'

We dried off the worst of the water outside and Fallon started stripping off her clothes, bunching up her soaking wet top and wringing it out over the little drain under the back guttering. 'That was so much fun,' she said.

'Yeah,' I said, beginning to take my clothes off too. I wrapped a beach towel around me and dried my hair with a smaller one, all soft and snuggly from the airing cupboard.

Max came back out and smiled at us. 'What are you like? You can change in Jessica's room if you want. There's some dry clothes in her wardrobe.'

'Are you mad?' I said, squeezing water out of my pony-tail. 'Your mum'll hit the roof. Have you forgotten about the time I went in there to borrow a hairband and she went completely nuts at me?'

'She apologised for that and they upped her meds. Anyway, her coach doesn't leave Waltham Abbey till six. Bags of time. I'll shove your clothes in the tumble. It'll be sweet, don't worry. Go on. Just don't move anything around in there cos she'll know. She really will.'

*

It was eerie going back in there after all this time. Usually the door stayed shut, but for the rare times I'd been over there and Joelle had been in there vacuuming the carpet. The door was always closed again pretty quickly after she'd finished. It was just as it had always been. White bedspread with red poppies all over it, matching curtains. All white furniture. Crumpled pyjamas on the pillow. Duvet pulled back, looking like someone had just got out of bed. Battery-powered dancing flower on the windowsill. Two bookcases rammed with all kinds of books – poetry, novels, creative writing guides, horror novels. Horror short stories. 'How to Write Horror' guides. Stephen King. *Shockheaded Peter*. Edgar Allan Poe. Even some of my dad's Jock of the Loch novels. There were two shelves below filled just with notebooks.

Fallon felt all along the shelves. 'There's like, no dust at all. In four years?'

'Jo dusts it. Doesn't move anything, she just dusts and hoovers it. She's the only one allowed in here. Keeps it clean but she hasn't changed a single thing. Weird, isn't it?'

'I'll say.' She moved over to the dancing flower and started singing a Beyonce medley into the pot. The batteries were down so it didn't respond.

'Even her dolls house hasn't been altered,' I noticed, looking up at it on the shelf. 'It's all still as Jess left it.'

'Oh, hey look at this!' Fallon squealed, reaching up into the wardrobe for the Quality Street tin. Not just any old Quality Street tin – *the* Quality Street tin, that me and Fallon used to love playing with whenever we went round. And there was still that smell in the tin too; the sweet rubbery smell of a strawberry eraser.

'We shouldn't move it.'

'It's OK, we can put it straight back. Max'll never know.'

'Go on, then, quick.'

We opened the lid to a gorgeous waft of synthetic fruits and pencil shavings. It was all still there. Animal pencil toppers. Tiny trolls with mad luminous hair. Teeny panda notebooks with our childish scribbling in them. Crumpled Monopoly notes and title deeds drawn over with felt tip pen. Miniature packets of sparkly tissues. Little paints and paintbrushes. Rubbers shaped like little cupcakes and the pot of orange lip balm that tasted like medicine. Wind-up mice. Itty-bitty envelopes and Hello Kitty glitter pens and sushi-shaped ornaments and so much more, all small, all sweet and all kid-catnip.

'I'm going to have a tin like this for Bub,' Fallon announced. 'She'd love that, wouldn't she? Oh, I can't wait! I'm so excited.'

I left Fallon playing with the contents of the tin and went back over to the bookshelf.

'We can make her childhood wonderful, can't we, Ella? I know what you said about everything falling apart some-day, but we can make it fun for her for a good long time, can't we?'

'Yeah,' I said, pulling out one of the journals from the shelf. Scrawls. Stories. Film reviews. Book reviews. More stories. I pulled out another book from the shelf. And then another one that had diary entries in it. There was the Princess and the Rats story and a poem about the Witch's Pool.

'What's that?' Fallon whispered, getting up off the bed and scurrying over to me. 'Oh wow, that's Jessica's hand-writing. She had beautiful handwriting, didn't she?'

'Yeah, these are all her stories. Oh, look.' On the back page of the yellow composition notebook I was holding was a drawing scrawled in biro.

I sat down at the dressing table and stared at it – a large, fat rat wearing a suit. He had a noose around his neck and he was swinging from a tree branch. It had been drawn in red biro.

'Gosh, what a horrible picture,' said Fallon.

'Yeah.' I stared at the rat's face. Its tongue was hanging limp over its teeth and its eyes were bulging in pain. 'Look what it says.'

She read the red writing underneath the drawing. *Die Rat Man. Die.*

There were more too pictures too. Fallon took a different journal off the shelf to look through it. More stories. Half stories. More scribbles, word searches, torn-out magazine pages, more diary entries. Pages and pages and pages of notes. Ramblings. Sketches. Song lyrics that meant absolutely nothing to either of us. Drawings in blue biro. Black biro. Red biro. Green biro. And all the red stuff seemed to point to one thing.

Rat Man. And how much she hated him.

It didn't take either of us long to work out that Rat Man was code. For Rittman.

'Oh my God,' said Fallon, her hand to her mouth. 'He did it to Jessica as well.'

'You weren't to know.'

19

A Rather Splendid Party
Friday night, 21st August

I couldn't stop feeling guilty, or wondering when it had happened. Was it at the same time as he was doing it to me? Or earlier? We didn't have time to look through all the journals, but what we saw gave us enough. The odd phrase leaped out at us like grasshoppers.

Praying he won't come in tonight.

Turn to stone when he touches me.

Rat Man hit me today. I wouldn't touch him down there.

My eyes couldn't look away, and my hands kept reaching for more journals. In a terrible, awful way, it made me feel better. I wasn't the only one. I wasn't the freak I'd always thought I was.

I hugged the yellow composition notebook to my chest as Fallon sat back down on the bed. 'We have to tell Max.'

'No,' I said. 'No way.'

'But this is… his dad's a…'

'I know what his dad is. I know what this means. We say nothing.'

I thought she was going to shout, but her voice came out quieter than before. She pointed towards the door. 'He hates my mum. His whole family hates her, because of what she said at Jessica's inquest. She saw Jess step into the road in front of that bus. She wanted to die. And his dad's always denied it. This is *proof*, Ella.'

'This is nothing,' I spat. 'This proves nothing, and even if we did take it to the police, do you know what this would do to Max? It would be bad enough him finding out about me, but Jess too? No, we can't do anything.'

'That's why she gave me her *Famous Five* books the last time I saw her,' said Fallon, staring hard at the bookcase. 'She knew. She knew she was going to end it.'

I stood up off the stool and grabbed the other composition book Fallon was holding. 'That's not true. We just need to put these back on the shelf and—'

'NO! It is true! You know it, she was going to kill herself! She couldn't see any other way out! Ella, for God's sake!'

I glared, snatching the book back from her and waiting for a noise from outside.

Knock knock knock. 'Are you decent?' It was Max. 'Lasagne's ready.'

'Uh, OK, two minutes,' I called back, as we scrabbled away the books quickly, the aroma of home-made lasagne and garlic bread wafting under the door.

'We say nothing, OK? Nothing.'

Fallon helped me neaten the shelves and put the Quality Street tin back in the wardrobe. 'My mum was right. All this time. That's why Jess stepped in front of that bus. She couldn't take any more. Maybe she found out what he'd done to you as well and she…'

'If she found out what he did and she didn't say anything then I'm glad she's dead!'

I might as well have hit her across the face, from the look she gave me. I shoved on my trainers and walked to the door.

'Come on.'

'What if he's out there now, doing it to some other poor girl?'

'He's not,' I said weakly.

'How do you know that?' she sobbed. 'You didn't know about Jessica. Poor Jessica. You said Shelby had two little sisters. What about them? What if he hurts my baby?'

'Don't *ever* say that. Don't even think that. I won't let that happen.'

'How can you stop it? You couldn't stop him doing it to you. How old were you when it started?' She had a snot trail and grabbed a tissue from the nightstand to wipe it away, but I stopped her hand just in time.

'No, you can't.'

'We can't ignore this, Ella,' she said, cupping her nose. 'I can't.'

'If you say one word to him, I'll never speak to you again. I mean it.'

*

Max went to check the bedroom and make sure there was nothing out of place while we dished up. As far as Fallon and I were concerned, nothing was out of place, but over lunch he was definitely acting oddly. He was definitely fractious and all one-word answers. Corey didn't exactly help matters – he wouldn't stop crowing on about beating him at Call of Duty.

'Literally pulverised him. Like, you just couldn't catch a break could you? I've never beaten anyone as easily as that.'

'Yeah, stop going on and on about it,' Max spat. 'Well done, champion of the world. You whooped my ass. Gimme a minute and I'll whittle you a trophy from my awe.'

'Up for a rematch after lunch?' Corey grinned.

He shrugged. 'If you like.' A little while later, his fork clattered to his plate and he got up. 'I'm going out for a smoke.'

'I only beat him by one game,' said Corey. 'What can I say? I'm just gifted at digital warfare.'

'I don't think it's that, Corey,' I told him. 'I think he's just stressed at the moment.'

'Why?'

My brain fumbled for an explanation. The best it came up with was 'Oh just stuff.'

'Fair enough,' he said, gobbling up the last of his garlic bread.

When Max came back in, out of nothing, Fallon asked him, 'Did Jessica give you anything? Before she died?'

'What?' he said, mid-chew.

'She gave me her books, all her *Famous Five* books and a couple of *Secret Sevens*. Did she leave you with anything?'

'Fallon, don't ask things like that,' I started to say, but Max cut in.

'No, she didn't. Why do you ask?'

'I just wondered,' said Fallon, and I knew she was carefully avoiding my stare.

'She gave me something,' Corey piped up. 'Her Time-Turner necklace. I treasure it. It's in my mini safe at home. Max, you can have it back if you want.'

'No, no, it's fine,' said Max, a look of puzzled wonder on his face. 'She gave you it the last time you saw her?'

Corey nodded, his mouth full of pasta.

'She didn't give me anything,' I said, as though that would stop Max's thought train in its tracks. 'Or you.'

'No,' said Max, a little frown appearing above his searching eyes.

Thankfully, Corey changed the subject completely,

seemingly oblivious to the hideousness in the air above the dining table. 'Hey, why don't we go down to the beach after lunch? It's nice and sunny now. We could…'

'We have to go home,' said Fallon, who'd only eaten a quarter of her lasagne and none of her potato wedges. 'Mum wants to see the baby before she goes out.'

Corey didn't hide his disappointment. It was like the cheeky little boy inside him had been shot dead by the responsible adult. 'Yeah. We should go. I've got some ironing to do.'

'You don't have to go straight away, do you?' I said, looking at Fallon, my eyes pleading for some sign that she wasn't going to tell anyone what we had found out.

'I don't feel too well at all actually.' She semi-smiled, like she didn't want to worry us. 'Mum said I've been overdoing it lately. I think I just need to take it easy this afternoon.'

'You can take it easy here,' said Corey. 'We were only going to hang out, we weren't going to climb Brynstan Hill again or anything.'

'I just want to go home, Corey!' she said, standing up and throwing her napkin into her seat. And without another word, she marched out to the hallway to get their coats. Max paid for a taxi to take them back to Cloud.

'Maybe we'll meet you tomorrow lunch at Subway or something?' said Corey, folding himself inside the taxi, completely oblivious to Fallon's mood. 'Foot-long chicken and bacon ranch melts all round, on me.'

'Yeah, said Max, closing the door behind. 'Whatever. Text me later.'

The look Fallon gave me as the taxi drove away told me what I needed to know. We weren't going to see her tomorrow.

And the look Max gave me as we walked back inside told me we weren't right either.

*

I wore this dress for my older brother's wedding – a black satin fifties-style number with bronze flowers all over it. It was the only dress I had and the invite said to wear posh so I had to go with it. Half a ton of foundation, chemically straightened hair and a carefully hairsprayed fringe later, and I could pretend the girl in my dad's full-length mirror was someone half comfortable with wearing it, despite my miserable face. My body yearned to go back into my room and put my joggers on over my tights.

'Hey, look at you!' said a voice. I hadn't heard Dad's footsteps on the stairs.

Tears pricked my eyes. 'Yeah. Look at me.'

'Don't often see you in a dress. You look wonderful.'

'Despite my Avatar nose?' I said.

He'd swallowed my lamp-post story too. 'Of course. But then, you *are* my daughter, so you carry the Newhall gene for good looks.' I smiled at his Dad-joke. 'What's the occasion?'

'Max's cousin Shelby's eighteenth at Michaelmas Manor,' I said, redoing some grips in my hair. 'I don't want to go.'

'No, you've never been one for parties, have you. You take after me. Much rather stay home, have a nice meal and watch a bit of telly.' He held out both his fists in front of me. I tapped the left one, and that bloody teddy bear necklace fell out of it onto my palm. 'It's been through the wash, I'm afraid. Came out of your running trousers.'

'Oh right, yeah. Thanks,' I said, chucking it on my dressing table.

'Aren't you going to wear it?'

'Not tonight.'

'Everything all right with you and Max, is it?'

'Yeah,' I mewled. Nothing was right. He wasn't texting me as much as he used to and though he hadn't said as much, I had a horrible feeling he knew what was in those notebooks.

'Are Neil and Jo going as well?'

'Yeah,' I said again, with a sigh. 'His whole family are going. And a load of other people I've never even clapped eyes on.'

'I saw Neil in The Wallflower at lunchtime.'

'Oh?' Dad often ran into Neil at the pub when he was grabbing his pie and pint and a read of the paper on a Friday lunchtime. It was one of his 'Dad routines', along with tea and toast at the Porthole Café on a Monday, and Tesco and a stroll along the front on a Sunday.

'Yeah, Neil said he's so pleased with your progress in training, I think he'll be happy to sponsor you right the way through.'

'Thrills,' I said, and Dad's eyebrows jumped. 'I'm sorry, but I don't like the guy. I'll be polite, but don't expect me not to bitch behind his back. It's not going to happen.'

'All right, all right. Do you want me to call and say you're not coming?' He put his arm around my shoulder and looked at us both in the mirror. I was a clear half a foot taller than him in heels – it almost made me happy about wearing them. 'Perhaps you could stay home and help me chop the veg for my herb-crusted lamb cutlets with black olive and pine nut stuffing? And hey, *Foyle's War*'s on later. A whole two hours of wartime sleuthing.'

'No, you're all right,' I said. 'Maybe it won't be so bad after all.'

He winked as he grabbed his glasses from his bedside table. 'There you are, then.' He seemed happier than usual. I wondered if Celestina was coming round to gnaw on his cutlets.

I checked the contents of my bag, slipping the supersize bottle of Laxolot between the folds, like it was a gun and I was about to rob a bank. Not give one hundred and fifty people chronic diarrhoea.

At a quarter to seven, the Rittmans' shimmering black Porsche drew up outside, and I tottered downstairs to answer the door to Max who was wearing a tailored navy suit with brown brogues I hadn't seen him in before. Amazingly, it complemented the navy sheen in my dress. We looked perfect together. Like two pieces of a puzzle clicked into place. Appearances count for nothing sometimes.

'You look gorgeous,' he said, coming up the path to greet me. He cupped my cheek, kissing my mouth. He smelled of too-strong woody aftershave.

'What's that scent?'

'Dunno. It's one of Dad's.'

'It's vile.'

'Thanks.'

Neil was sitting in the front passenger seat, and me and Jo were squished into the back seat, which was just a grey-leather ledge. If I'd been any taller, my head would have been through the back windscreen; as it was, I had to tilt it slightly.

'Not an ideal family car, is it?' said Jo, fully penned in behind bunches of flowers, presents and cards.

I smiled non-committally. The music blasted out as Max switched on the ignition. 'But then we're not the ideal family, are we?' I muttered under my breath.

Both Max and Neil wearing that disgustingly spicy aftershave was nauseating in the close confines of the Porsche. I noted the cream and black-wrapped birthday present resting on Jo's lap. She stroked the soft ribbon between her finger and thumb.

'What did you get her?' I asked.

Jo was about to answer when Neil butted in. 'Some of that Jo Malone smelly stuff. Candles and perfume, you know.' I waited. 'Over three hundred quids' worth.'

'Of course,' I muttered, pulling a crushed birthday card out from under my thigh.

Neil pulled down his visor and looked at me in his mirror. 'What do you think of the wheels then? Ain't she a beauty? Rides like a dream. Top speed two hundred miles an hour.'

'Shame you can't do more than thirty miles an hour round here, isn't it?' I could have sworn I'd seen a smile creep onto Jo's face as she turned to look out her window.

'Ah, that's what *you* think,' said Neil. 'We'll get on the back roads in a minute. Then we can open her up. Camera's turned off around there. Ain't that right, son?'

'Yeah,' said Max, as he crunched through the gears. 'Hey, Ells, there's a chocolate fountain on every table tonight.'

'Cool,' I said, looking out my window at the green fields rolling by. Neil was egging Max on to speed up through the gears. There didn't seem to be a problem between them. Maybe Max hadn't read the notebooks, hadn't seen the drawing of Rat Man hanging. Maybe it was all in my mind him acting strangely over lunch. I wanted to believe it was anyway.

'Max, there's blind bends all along here,' Jo mewled, loud enough for me to hear but no one else. Neil just whooped encouragingly. I clung to my seat and closed my eyes until I felt us start to slow, eventually turning onto the sweeping gravel drive of Michaelmas Manor.

Max parked up on a grassy patch in front of a box hedge. I couldn't wait to get out into the cool evening air but Neil had to let me out and linger around the car as he did so; there were smokers outside watching and he wanted everyone to know whose car it was.

Michaelmas Manor was the dream place to have any sort of party. It was a sixteenth-century stately home and hotel complex on the eastern slope of Brynstan Hill, with acres of space – lawns, walled gardens, fishponds. There was even a flock of peacocks around, pecking at the gravel and making strange wailing noises every so often. There was something going on at Michaelmas most weekends. Weddings, proms, parties. I'd been a few times – first for Prom, then for Uncle Paul's 50th and again last Christmas. It was always the same. No expense spared. Superstar DJ. Ice sculptures. And Neil always footed the bill.

We walked through the main entrance and Neil presented the invite to the guy on the door who looked like a giraffe in a suit. 'The Rittmans and Estella Newhall, my good sir,' he said proudly. 'You'll know her as our Volcano Girl, of course.'

There was a horrible silence as the giraffe guy studied my face. Then he said, 'Oh yeah! I saw you in the papers.'

'You did indeed,' said Neil, his grin so Brie-sy I could have hit him. 'She's gonna be a big star one day. Blows Jessica Ennis out the water, she does.'

Oh God, kill me now, I thought, pretending to read the buffet menu by the door as Max headed straight for the food. Artisan pastries, breads and dipping oils, blocks of cheese, platters of sea bass, poached salmon, glazed hams and joints of pork so large they looked like they were on steroids. In a room to the right the walls were swathed with white silk so it looked like an igloo. There was a dance floor and all around were tables with complimentary wine and small chocolate fountains in the centres. The place was packed. Most were standing at the bar, around which hung silver and mauve banners and balloons.

'Do you wanna go and find our table, princess?' said Neil, his hand on my waist as he guided me towards the igloo room. Max didn't see me shrink away from his touch as he was already talking to a couple of his football mates – local hottie Craig Wilkins, whose sister had been on my relay team, and some knob head called Nick Parsons. Jo was talking to a woman by the buffet, so Neil went to join her. I walked into the function room alone.

Shelby herself was on the door to the main function room, welcoming people in and handing cards and gifts to two large suited minions, Uncle Paul and some starter-kit-boy-bander with almost-stubble and pure white trainers, their tongues sticking up over his black suit trousers. Parcels were stacking up on the table behind her (parcels that I was going to demolish during the superstar DJ's turn).

'Thanks so much! Aww, thanks for coming – I'm so glad you could make it!' she was saying to each person she greeted. 'We've arranged some entertainment in one of the other function rooms for the kids, a clown and a juggler and a bit of a disco, so we'll be taking them through in a minute. Aw, thanks so much, you're so kind! Lovely to see you!'

I stood watching her, kindling my own internal flame and looking for weak spots – praying for her to trip over her dress. Hoping a waiter would spill a whole tray of drinks down her. Boys flittered around her like moths. She was so beautiful, it almost hurt to look at her, with her long braided blonde hair draped over one shoulder and her halter-neck pearl-beaded dress skimming her curves and fanning out like a fishtail. That dress cost over £600 – Neil had mentioned it loudly during Sunday lunch. A 'pre-birthday present' he said. This was the dress I was going to drop invisible ink spots on when no one was looking.

She smiled across at me.

I had to smile back.

I *had* wanted to destroy her. I had wanted to destroy her party. She'd lured Max away from me with her big eyes, C-cup boobs and big lips. Big, red, wet lips. I reached into my handbag for the ink and held it tightly in my fist. I couldn't do it.

I headed for an empty table in the far corner of the room, beside a potted monkey puzzle. Everyone not dancing on the large hardwood floor to the deafening ABBA medley was either at the bar or at the buffet. The sign on the table said '*Neil, Jo and Max Rittman, plus Estella*'. I sat down, took the lid off the ink and poured it into the soil of the monkey puzzle. Then I reached for one of the complimentary bottles of white wine and a glass.

The lighting was low and had a purple tinge to match the balloons so not only could I not hear or talk properly, I couldn't see anything either. I needed to find the cake – this was the target for the liquid laxative, and then I needed to find the toilets – these I would block up once the speeches were underway. I was poised to do it – I could feel the super-size Laxolot bottle in my bag. I was going to do it. I just couldn't find the will to actually get up and start.

My problem was that this wasn't about Shelby. Shelby might have been a boyfriend-blowing bimbo, but she didn't deserve the humiliation I had planned. I watched Max at the bar. He was talking to his football team crowd, miming headers. He looked like a stranger.

Neil appeared through the tables like a shark cutting through murky water, bringing over a plate of chopped fruit on long cocktail sticks. He set them down on our table.

'Joelle's met up with some of her WI lot,' he said, with a smile. 'You OK over here?'

'Yeah,' I said.

He sat down and we both watched the dancing. 'You want anything from the buffet?'

'No,' I said.

'I brought you some fruit for the chocolate fountain.'

I necked my glass of wine in one go.

'Should you be drinking that? You've got training tomorrow, haven't you?'

'It's my night off.'

I stared at the dance floor. Shelby had been dragged up there for a smooch with some lad. I caught her eye and instinctively looked away. I waited for Neil to say something else. To make some spine-chilling comment like the one he'd made the other day. But he didn't. And when I looked back, he was gone, slinking into the crowd to play the benevolent host again.

'Prick,' I said, loudly. But no one heard me over the music. 'Pervert,' I said again. Still, no one looked. 'Paedophile.'

I poured myself another drink and sat there at that empty table, scratching a new patch of hives that had flared up on my upper thigh, my only companion the chocolate fountain bubbling in the centre of the table like an overflowing sewer pipe. I was forcing Fallon to stay silent when I knew she was right. We *should* tell everyone what Neil was like, what he'd done to us. We should light him up like a Christmas tree. We *should*.

But I couldn't.

I looked at the tray of fruit and swiped it to the floor. It landed everywhere.

The music pumped through my head. All around me were people who looked like they could just die laughing

cos their lives were so damn fun. I necked my wine. Then
two more. The effects were welcome. It coated my rage in a
cool, numbing blanket. I felt like laughing. I felt balanced.
Easy. My resentment began to fade until I felt deadened to
everything, even physical pain. I pinched the skin on top of
my hand. I couldn't even feel that. Every sip I took dragged
me a little bit further away from my scalding anger, until
my vision started to blur.

I carried on, listening to the music, watching people –
grinding on the dance floor, pulling purple and white crackers, stuffing forkfuls of sea bass and couscous salad into
their gobs. I listened in on conversations – women moaning
about their diets while troughing mountains of bread; men
chuntering out boring conversations about loft conversions
and how they would have got the sitter Jamie Hardy or Jack
Vardy missed and blah blah blah.

And all the while I sipped and I watched them.

Shelby Gilmore moseyed around the tables, making
sure everyone was having a good time, chomping on fruit
kebabs and flirting with the waiters. The table of presents
she'd been standing guard at was gone, and so had both her
henchmen. They'd been taken to a back room already. All
the guests must have arrived. I looked at her, waiting for
her to catch my eye. And she did. We held each other's gaze
for a few seconds before she looked away. Why was she so
damn interested in me? Maybe it was guilt.

As soon as she looked away, I stood up, afraid that if I
didn't I'd lose my nerve. I made my way through the maze
of white-clothed tables, past the buffet and through a long
corridor where waitresses were all bustling about with
trays of glasses and platters of sliced meat. Nobody noticed
me and, if they did, they didn't say anything. I clocked a

door at the end of another longer, quieter corridor marked 'Morning Room', and slipped quietly inside.

Presents for any occasion were always kept in here. I fumbled along the wall for a light switch until I found the panel and flicked them all on at once. It was a large lounge area, all yellow silk sofas and ugly chintz ornaments. There was a wide snooker table across the room and on top of it sat a mountain of wrapped boxes. I walked over and just sort of stared.

I reached for the biggest present on the pile, a large pink box with a thin shiny purple ribbon around its middle.

I shouldn't be here. I just shouldn't be here, I kept thinking. But the longer I stood there thinking about it, the quieter the voice became.

I swallowed once. And then I just sort of did it.

I trashed that room. All over the ornate wallpaper, the silk yellow sofas, the cushions, the rugs, the carpet. Three large vases. The big pile of presents. That room went from top end to dog end in about three minutes flat.

And do you want to know what I was thinking about the entire time? As I was tearing open gifts with someone else's name on them and snapping DVDs in half and smashing iPhones and laptops and watches?

As I squirted ink up and down that billiard table, soiling and tearing expensive gowns and shoes and cards full of money?

As I tore open boxes – hover boards, cameras, Nutribullets, make-up palettes, and perfumes, perfumes, perfumes, smashing the bottles and fouling up the room with their acrid, overpriced stenches?

Neil. That's who I was thinking of, not Shelby. Not Max. It was all about him.

I left the room in the dark, as quietly as I'd entered it. I headed back to the main function room. A stab of guilt hit my chest.

They weren't his presents.

People were still dancing. Eating. And I was still sitting on my own with only a chocolate fountain to talk to. I poured myself another wine, right to the top of the glass.

After a Maroon 5 medley and a truly toe-curling ten minutes of Dad Dancing when everyone got to their feet for 'YMCA', Max eventually appeared and took the seat next to me.

'Where've you been? I came over just now but you'd gone.' He was shouting over the music, looking at the mess of chopped fruit on the carpet. 'What's happened here?'

'Waiter dropped it.' I sipped my wine, concentrating on not looking as drunk as I was.

'What's up?'

'Nothing. I'm happy.'

'Ella – are you drunk?'

'Bit.' I sipped. 'It's all right. I don't even care about you and Shelby banging each other's brains out any more, I truly don't.'

I wanted to laugh so badly. His confused little face and big eyes were making me laugh. I was on the knife edge of hysterics for no reason at all.

Max sat down, going into lip-rub overdrive. 'What are you talking about?'

'I'm not stupid, Max. You should go and dance with her,' I leaned in to him and shouted. 'Grind on that. See how she likes it.'

'Ells, let me explain.'

I snorted, reaching past him for the bottle and filling my glass again. 'You don't have to. Honestly. I couldn't be more fine. I just want to sit here with my wine and not care. OK? I'm sick of feeling stuff, so I'm not going to. I don't want to think about you or Shelby or your dad. Or my mum. Or Zane. Or the Shaws. And this is helping a really lot.'

Max snatched my glass out of my hand. 'You're not having any more.'

'Yes, I am. You can't stop me. You're not my best friend any more. I'm going to find a new friend, OK?' I grabbed the other wine bottle on the table. 'Here she is. Here's my friend. She's called Blue Nun.' I laughed again. 'God, I'm so funny when I'm drunk.' I dropped the bottle on the floor. 'You should be writing some of this down.'

'I hate seeing you like this.'

'Like what? I thought you'd like me better like this – all loosened up and joining in?'

He watched me pour myself another glass. 'What about your training?'

'I don't care. I am fearless. I'm in the Fearless Five. I have no fear.'

'Ella, for Christ's sake, you're shouting!'

I glugged my wine and looked at him. His face whirled in and out of focus.

'We didn't have sex. Just – other stuff. We don't even kiss. I feel terrible, Ells.'

'You poor soul. I wonder if there's a helpline you can ring?'

I amazed myself with how calm I felt. I watched a tear fall onto his lapel and, for some reason, found it incredibly funny. I laughed in his face.

'Aww, Maxy. 'Why so sssssserious?' I pinched his cheek and he baulked away from me. 'So what's her blow job game like? Maybe she could give me some tips.'

'Stop it.'

'What? I'm interested. Does she spit or swallow? Do you finger-bang her at the dinner table while Neil's carving the roast?' I dissolved into giggles. 'Come on, gimme deets. Does she have that vibrator you wanted to get me from Ann Summers? The one that "goes from kitten lick to road drill at the touch of a button"?' I snorted like a pig. That made me laugh even more. I hadn't felt so happy in ages.

'It wasn't some long affair, Ella, I swear to you.'

'It's fine, Max. I don't feel bad you're having sex with your cousin. I don't feel anything. In fact, I feel so good, maybe *we* could try again now? Yeah, while I'm drunk! Let's go out to the car park and you can bend me over the Porsche. Your dad would love that, wouldn't he?' My hand crept to his crotch like a spider and started squeezing.

'Christ's sake stop it.' He gripped my wrist and shoved me away.

'I thought you wanted me to want this? Why are you acting like the Virgin Mary?'

Another tear fell down his cheek. 'I've never seen you like this. It's not you.'

'What – happy? I am funny when I'm drunk, aren't I? Go and ask the DJ to play a song for us. Maybe he's got that Taylor Swift one you pretend not to like.'

He blinked quickly. 'We need to dry you out and get you home.'

'Oh yeah, like *that's* a good idea.'

'Your dad's going to kill me.'

'I doubt it,' I said. 'He only wants me to be happy. And I am now. I feel, like, freeeeeee. All that stuff I used to cry about, s'all gone. I don't even care about my baby any more.'

'You don't have a baby. *Fallon* has a baby.'

'No, *my* baby,' I shouted over the music. 'My dead baby.'

Everything went to black. When I opened my eyes, I was

sitting on the floor, and my chair lay on the carpet beside me. 'Ooh, what happened then?'

I could hear his voice but I didn't know where he was. 'Why did you say that?'

'Max?'

The room was spinning around and around and around, and everything swam past my face so quickly. I couldn't focus on anything. Nothing would stay still.

'Why would you say that, Ella? Fallon's had a baby, not you.'

His face was spinning past me and coming back, spinning past and coming back. Something was bubbling up from deep inside. Something was going to happen.

'God, stay still already. Ooh, I need to be sick,' I said, getting to my heeled feet.

I headed out through a mass of laughing, sequinned people, towards the fuzzy doorway and into the brightly lit reception area. Outside it was dark and cool. Two peacocks were pecking about the front entrance and I barged straight through them, breathing in the cold night air, vision swimming, stomach lurching. My body convulsed with the urge to vomit. I tottered across the gravel as quickly as I could, past the parked-up cars, making it over to a topiary version of Mr Toad, behind which I vommed as though it was an Olympic sport.

When I was sure I was done, I sat down on the low wall and shivered. The lights at the entrance shone like dazzling balls of sunshine and the whole world looked like it had been put inside a salad spinner. Closing my eyes did little to stop it. I shivered.

'Ella, talk to me.' A voice somewhere above me. I opened my eyes.

'I'm going to be sick again. I need to stay here.'

A warm covering fell around my shoulders – Max's jacket. He crouched down in front of me, putting his hands on my knees.

'I don't know what I'm saying,' I cried. I puked again behind Mr Toad. I'd loved that book when my dad read it to me as a kid. My head banged like a church bell. 'My head hurts.'

'I know, but...'

'I want my dad,' I said, awash with sadness. 'Can you get my dad?'

'Ella.' He was sobbing. Someone was slapping my cheek. 'What baby?'

'Ssh,' I said. 'Get my dad. Please. I want my dad now.'

There was a long string of drool leading from my mouth to my hand. I needed to lie down. I lay on the cold wall, hitched my legs up and watched the world spin and spin and spin and go blacker before my eyes. I don't know what I said then. I don't know what else Max said, but I could still hear his voice. Then I must have passed out, because the next thing I knew, I was in someone's arms, being carried like a child. My right leg was freezing cold. I'd torn a big hole in my tights and I only had on one shoe. I heard a man shouting.

'Do something useful, Max, open the damn door.'

I knew that voice. Oh God, was it Neil? I couldn't move my body. If Neil was taking me somewhere there was nothing I could do. Nothing at all. I would be his all over again.

I opened my eyes and the world was still whizzing past at fifty miles an hour. But I looked up and saw my dad's stubbly chin, and smelled the coffee smell of his bobbly green jumper. And I knew it was all right to go to sleep.

'So that was when Max found out about your baby?'

20

A Mystery is Solved

Yeah. The baby I lost.

I remember it like it was yesterday. Fallon was sleeping over – we'd been to the carnival the night before. David and Ollie were living at home then, so she was in my room on the fold-out bed. I woke up with the worst tummy ache. And then I felt the wet between my legs and I panicked because I thought I'd come on in the night. I hadn't had a period for ages so I knew it would be a lot of blood. I was worried about how the hell I was going to get to the bathroom without her seeing me. I pulled my hand out from under the duvet and it was red. Cherry red. Then Fallon woke up, and I just started sobbing uncontrollably.

'Ella? Are you all right? What's that on your hand?'

And then I told her. I told her I'd come on and it was bad.

'It's OK, it's OK,' she kept saying.

She was amazing, I never realised how much at the time. She told me she had heavy periods too and she'd seen it all before. She helped me strip away the duvet and got me loads of wet wipes and flannels without anyone else seeing. She cleaned it all up. And it was all fine. Until she saw it in the bed. This little tiny jellified shape, like one of those jelly aliens we used to win on the grabbers at the Pier. It was about two inches long, almost see-through. Two stubby little arms. Legs like a baby bird's. A nub of a nose. Ears like the tiny Yorkshire puddings on my doll's house roast beef.

There were blood clots all around it on the bed but this was perfect.

'Oh my God, Ella.'

Fallon started crying, and I started shaking violently all over. But she didn't say anything else, she just sort of... tidied it up. I sat on a folded-up bath towel as she changed the bed, kept me warm and made me a mug of sweet tea. She wrapped the thing in a thick coil of toilet paper and asked me if I wanted to bury it. She even gave the heavy period excuse to Dad – we had to tell him something. My mattress was ruined. The most embarrassing part of the whole thing for me was that Fallon didn't ask me whose baby it was – she just guessed.

'It was Neil, wasn't it? That day we came to the island for Max's birthday. I knew you were weird that day. I knew he'd done something then.'

I didn't say a word. That way, it was still a secret. That way, I couldn't get into any trouble. But she just knew.

At school the following Monday, she sat beside me in English.

'I won't tell anyone. I promise,' she said.

'Do you swear?'

'Yes, I swear.'

'Let's not mention it again. Let's forget it ever happened. I don't want to think about it. It's gone. It won't happen again. I won't be so stupid.'

'OK.'

I wanted to know what she'd done with it but I never asked her. And she never told me. Because that was the end of it. The proof that anything had ever happened to me was dead. It didn't matter where it went. I assumed she'd flushed it down the toilet. That's what we'd always done with goldfish.

*

I opened my eyes to white light and clanking sounds. Blue curtains. People talking. Feet shuffling. Phones ringing. There was a strong stench of vomit and bleach. I definitely wasn't in my bedroom. I wasn't even at home. But Dad was sitting there beside me, looking at me the way he'd look at the mummified Stone Age baby in the museum.

'Dad?' My throat was sore and my voice came out croaky, as though it had been dragged out of my throat, sandpapered, then shoved back down again.

'Hello, darling,' he said. I felt his hand on my scalp, so gently. 'How are you feeling?'

That was when I felt a strong pull in my stomach. I ached all over. 'Horrible. Why am I at the hosp—' My voice broke in the middle of what I was saying. 'Why can't I speak? Why does everything hurt?'

'You've got alcohol poisoning,' said Dad. The words looked as though they hurt him to say them. 'They had to pump out your stomach.'

I went to lift my arm but it was attached to something. I was on a drip. 'Oh my God.' My legs were bare. My tights and shoes had gone. So had my dress. I was in a papery hospital gown. 'Where's my clothes?'

'They had to take them off. You wet yourself.'

'I *what*?'

I hadn't wet myself since I was about six. My system flushed clean of alcohol, I felt everything again – embarrassment, shame, anger, all screaming inside my head like a thousand clowns. How I'd acted. Falling off the chair. Puking behind the Mr Toad hedge. People all around watching and laughing. Max pleading. And what I'd said.

'The drip's just to rehydrate you,' said Dad. 'Nothing to worry about.'

I had a memory of Dad carrying me to the back seat of the car. He'd rested my head on the folded-up blanket we used to take on picnics when I was little. We'd taken it to the zoo the time Ollie had hidden a cricket in my pork pie. Why was I remembering that now?

'I wish I was dead.'

Dad stood up to begin the lecture. 'How could you be so silly? Why did you drink so much? Why were you drinking *at all*? What about your training?'

The stress vein had emerged on Dad's forehead. Oh God, I hated seeing him so worried about me. I coughed and then regretted it cos my throat was so raw. 'Owww.'

'It's all right, it's all right,' he said, but he kept rambling on about irresponsibility and why 'the Rittmans hadn't looked after me' and how Mum used to 'like a drink' so that must be where I got it from. I just lay there and looked at him through watery eyes.

'Dad?' I said.

'What?'

'Could you just give me a hug, please?'

He looked as though he was about to say something more, but stopped himself and stood up, lifting me until I was in a sitting position. I closed my arms around him and cried and cried into his bobbly green jumper.

He stroked my hair again. 'You worried me. We couldn't wake you up.'

'I wish I hadn't,' I mumbled.

'What was that?'

'Nothing,' I sniffed, wiping my nose on his shoulder.

'What's happened, eh? This isn't like you.'

Just then, the curtain rings clattered across the cubicle and a man nurse walked in, evidently in a great hurry. His badge said he was a staff nurse. His name was Jack.

'There's a lad outside waiting to see you. Matt Rickman or something.'

Dad turned to him. 'No, tell him to leave, please.'

'Uh, sir, I'm a bit busy at the moment, perhaps that's something you could do?'

'You either tell him to leave or I'll *make* him leave,' Dad shouted. I clung to him again as the nurse flounced back through the curtains with more than a hint of disgust.

Dad pulled away and looked at me. 'Has Max done something?'

I shook my head. 'No. I just drank too much, that's all.'

'I mean it, Ella, tell me what he's done. Something must have happened for you to let yourself get in this state, and I know it's something to do with Max. Answer me.'

'Dad, please just trust me. This isn't about Max, I swear.'

I heard Max's voice outside in the A & E. *I'm not going anywhere until I see her. You'll have to drag me out, mate.*

'Oh God,' I said.

'I'll get rid of him,' said Dad, peeling away from me and getting up off the bed.

'Dad, don't, please,' I croaked. 'It's OK.'

The sound of some classical symphony started up in the pocket of Dad's trousers. He pulled out his phone. 'Neil.' My heart squeezed. 'He was worried about you. I said I'd let them know how you were. I better take it outside.' He swept through the curtains.

I lay back on the bed. I couldn't hear anything else but the usual bustling and beeping and trolleys clattering past.

When the curtain opened again, Max appeared – his navy suit all creased, tie missing, his white shirt stained with blood spots, his hand bloody too.

'What the hell?'

'Uncle Paul,' he replied, all nasal, like both his nostrils were blocked. 'I kind of called Shelby a whore. It being her birthday and all that, he didn't take it too well.'

'She's not a whore, though, is she?' I coughed. My neck ached. 'Oww.'

He pulled the curtain across so we were semi-private, and sat down heavily on the chair. 'I wanted to lash out. She was nearest. She said you trashed the present room.'

'What...' It took me a second to realise what he was talking about and then I remembered what I had done. The red and brown sauce. The laptop smashing. The watches I'd stamped on. 'Oh God.' Everything seemed so loud to me, all of a sudden.

'I told her it was me.'

'Why did you do that, Max?'

He shrugged. 'I dunno. Just wanted to. I wanted to hurt her for hurting you.'

'She didn't hurt me. You did.'

'I know I did. We both did. Anyway, she slapped me. I said some nasty stuff, there was a big fight. Blah blah blah. Was it you who trashed Dad's Porsche too?'

'What?'

'The Porsche. All the windows are smashed. Bodywork's scratched to pieces, dented all over. There's even petrol on the seats. I think whoever did it was gonna set fire to it.'

'God,' I said. 'No, I didn't do that.' I silently thanked whoever it was who *had* done it though. 'You know what people are like though with expensive cars – they get jealous.'

'Yeah, I don't give a monkey's about any of that anyway. I just care about you.'

There was an elephant in the room and both of us were putting in Oscar-worthy performances to avoid it. He smiled sadly and looked around the cubicle, though there was nothing to see – the nightstand, the row of sockets above my head, a disposable glove dispenser and a hand sanitiser shackled to the end of the bed. I reached for his hand. One of us was cold – I couldn't tell if it was him or me. 'You really scared me, Ells.'

'Mind my wire thing,' I said, nodding at the drip. He released his grip, just slightly.

'Ella, please, just tell me. What were you talking about? What baby?'

There was nowhere else to go. I couldn't run away. I couldn't make any more excuses. Drunk people don't say that kind of thing out of nothing. So I threw it out there, quickly, like throwing breadcrumbs to birds in the middle of a main road.

'My baby. I had a miscarriage. When I was thirteen.'

I'd finally said the words I'd been holding so close to me for such a long time. Suddenly they were gone, untethered, like balloons floating above me and I couldn't grab them back now. Of course, he would want to know every detail. So I resorted to the plan B that I'd had in my head for the past four years – the substitute truth to be dragged out in case anyone found out about it.

'What?' A trickle of blood started down Max's nose towards his mouth. He wiped it away on his shirtsleeve. I kept on talking.

'Don't blame yourself for not knowing. I didn't want you to know.' A tear trickled down the side of my cheek to the crunchy white pillow under my head.

'But, you're a virgin.'

I shook my head. The pinch of dread in my chest that was always there had grown into a massive clenched fist, squeezing and releasing. Squeezing and releasing. But it was getting easier. 'Sadly not.'

'I knew it,' he said. 'I knew it was something like this.'

I knew what he was going to ask next. I answered him before he had to say it.

'You don't know him. He's moved out of the area. It was just some lad from school. It was only once and I hated it.'

Despite the tears, his face was like a stone. He wiped his cheek like his hand was slicing meat, quickly and cleanly. My lie seemed to have worked. He just swallowed it like a great big pill. Then the questions came.

'He forced you?'

'No.'

'Are you sure I don't know him?'

'Yes. Just some lad, like I said.'

'It wasn't one of your brothers, was it?'

'WHAT? No, Max, it was not! I told you, I didn't know him.'

'Or him. Your dad.'

'Of course it's not Dad. Dad's not a pervert. You're not listening to me, it was a boy my age from school.'

'Name?'

My brain fumbled for a name. 'I can't… Jack.'

'Jack?'

'Yeah.'

'Jack what?'

'IT DOESN'T MATTER,' I shouted, the force scraging my throat and making me cough. 'That's it, Max. I'm not telling you anything else.'

There was evil in his eyes. 'You're lying.'

'Max, stop it.'

'I know you're lying. I know you, Ella. It's Hamlin, isn't it? It's old Pied Piper himself.'

'What? I didn't even *know* Pete Hamlin when I was thirteen. Stop twisting things.'

'Yeah, you did. He taught at B.A. for years before he started coaching you privately. You *did* know him then, don't lie.'

'I'm not lying. We always had Miss Trentham for games until Year 11.'

'He's groomed you, and now you can't tell right from wrong. He raped you. I'll kill him.'

'No, you're wrong. You've always hated Pete. But he's not a bad man.' My throat was killing me.

He shook his head.

'I'm tired.' I turned over on my bed, facing the curtains.

'We can't go on like we are, can we?'

'I don't know,' I said, closing my eyes. 'You won't listen, so what can I do?'

I heard him get up. He came round to the other side of the bed and bent down beside me so his face was on the pillow next to mine. I opened my eyes. 'What about the baby?'

'What about it?'

'What happened to it?'

'I didn't keep it as a souvenir, if that's what you're asking. Fallon flushed it down the toilet. She was staying over when it happened.'

'Fallon knew?'

'No, yes, some of it. I made her promise... I'm tired. I can't handle this now, OK?'

'I love you so much, Ella.'

'I know you do.'

'Look at me.' His eyes weren't as warm and brown as they usually were. Something in them had died.

'I just want to sleep, Max.'

His face bunched into tears again. 'I don't have a single memory without you in it.'

I reached for his hand and he took it. 'I'm all right. It's over. It's all gone.'

'It's not, though, is it? It's always going to be there until something's done about it. It's still hurting you. What he did.'

'It wasn't him … Let me sleep.'

'Say we're going to be OK, Ella.'

'I can't.'

'Why not?'

'Because I don't think we are.'

'So you and Max split up that night?'

21

Mostly About Ella

I guess we did. I didn't see or hear from him for three whole days after that night. Even when we went on holidays with our families or school trips, we'd still emailed or texted or Skyped every day. Now there was just silence.

I didn't know myself for those three days. Normally, I'd be up at six for training, eating some carefully chosen sports cereal and chopping bananas before meeting Pete for a jog or a punch-up in his garage. But I still hadn't called Pete, and he hadn't called me. He was avoiding me too after our last disaster. I couldn't face him yet anyway. My nose still throbbed when I touched it.

I scoured the #Shelby18 hashtag and stalked a few of Max's mates who'd been at the party. The police were called about the Porsche wrecking and the 'break-in', and even though nothing was taken they were 'appealing for witnesses'. Just vandals, they said. Neil paid for all the damage. As he should.

The Rittmans sent me 'Get Well Soon' flowers, a big old bunch of lilies and violets. Dad insisted on putting them in the big vase right in front of the fireplace so we could look at them every time we watched TV or ate dinner. It was like Neil was watching me. The lilies stunk the house out.

I let laziness take me over for the first time in years. I lay in bed and ate whatever soup or sandwich Dad brought into me on a tray. I let patronising daytime TV people sell me houses and antiques, chefs teach me how to make Moroccan tagine and chocolate souffles, and watched couples staying in each other's B&Bs, then bitching about them behind their backs. I played a lot of Sims too; killed off a few maids, caught a few guppies at the Community Pond. I tried making my mum Sim get off with the bloke-maid, but he slapped her and quit to join the Army. Then she and her husband got depressed after the kids were taken in by social services for eating out of the bin, so I locked them both in the bathroom till they died of starvation. That cheered me up a bit.

I constantly refreshed Max's Facebook, Instagram and Twitter feeds. Not a word. No Favourites. No Likes. No pass-agg status updates about why women always lie to men. Refresh. Refresh. Refresh. He didn't even text me a goodnight kiss.

What made it worse was that Corey *was* texting and DMing me on Twitter, with all these little updates about him and Fallon. How the baby sneezed and it was so cute. How tiny her toes were. How he was living at the farm full-time now, in one of the spare bedrooms, and helping out with the animals as much as he could. How much they both missed me.

The last text I'd had from him made me feel sick with worry. And I was so sick of being worried.

Ella – Fallon told me about Rat Man. Please don't blame her. She really needed to talk to someone. I kept asking her what was wrong. I won't tell a soul. I think we should all talk though. We miss you. CM.

*

By Sunday, Dad had had enough. He came into my bedroom. I was sat up in bed snoozefeeding and watching YouTube on my phone.

'What are you doing?'

'Watching Hamlet.'

His face brightened. 'I didn't know you liked Shakespeare.'

'It's not Shakespeare. It's a video of a micro pig walking down the stairs.'

Dad sighed. 'Why don't you call up some friends, eh? Ask them round here, if you don't want to go out. I can make myself scarce. You can have the lounge and watch a video.'

'Might have to go back to the nineties first,' I told him flatly.

He sighed again and rubbed his chin. 'You know what I mean. Come to Tesco with me then. You can help me get the ingredients for this curry. You'll go stir-crazy if you spend much longer in the house.'

'What's "stir-crazy"?' I said, clicking off Hamlet and easing myself out of bed.

'It's what prisoners get when they've been incarcerated for a long time. They slowly start to lose their minds. Why don't you go up the park? There's always kids hanging round up there.'

I couldn't quite tell whether Dad was A) taking the piss or B) had no problem with me going up to a notorious dogging spot to drink cider out of the bottle, but either way I wasn't going. And I wasn't stir-crazy either. I wasn't like the random who used to walk up and down the High Street, jabbering about aliens anal probing him. Or the frizzy-haired woman who sits in Costa talking to her fist.

Despite my arguments, I went to Tesco, but I wasn't any

help. I hadn't been to a supermarket with Dad for ages. He had a firm routine and if he forgot anything from an aisle he'd already done, he wouldn't go back. He just put it on a new page of his little notepad for next time. I caught a glimpse of his list – it was all neat and each item had a poker-straight line through it as it went into the trolley. He had things on there like 'Shloer' and 'Meat free mince' and 'Tuck cupboard sundries.' Since when did he drink Shloer? And where the hell was our 'tuck cupboard'? It was a whole new experience.

When I had a go at the checkout woman – her double F cups were resting on the scale and she overcharged us for bananas – Dad shoved me out of there like we were on some kind of march. He hated supermarkets at the best of times. If it were up to Dad, we'd all have ration books and powdered cheese and friendly old grocers who weighed out your tea for you, and absolutely nowhere would have Wi-Fi.

That afternoon, after he'd had done his daily word count on his book and prepped the curry, he put on one of his favourite war films – the one where the guy gets his arse shot off. Despite the gunfire and cries of agony, I nestled into the warmth of the sofa blanket and fell into a deep sleep beside him.

On Monday, I didn't get out of bed until lunch. Dad was out in the garage, sorting through his nuts and bolts drawers, even though they were all immaculate. I lingered out there for a little while too, just sort of watching him. He was never happier than when he was doing little things. Reading one of his dusty old books, writing one of his crappy romance novels, making a model boat or aeroplane from one of his little kits. He didn't have my ambition, my need to do something extraordinary. He liked his little life.

'Your doll's house is there, look,' he said, pointing towards the middle shelf on the wall. I moved a stack of chunky leather-bound Shakespeares and there it was.

'Oh wow, I didn't know I still had this,' I said, opening the frontage. It was mostly knocked over and in need of a good dusting, but there all the same. Me and Corey spent a whole summer redecorating it once, laying new carpets, putting tiny posters up in the children's bedroom. I tried tidying everything up, putting Mum Raccoon on the sofa, reading *The Times*, Dort Raccoon sneaking in behind her to steal the biscuits from the coffee table. Dad Raccoon feeding the baby in the kitchen, and Son Raccoon lying on his bunk bed, reading the telephone directory. The dining table all laid up with the Sunday lunch – roast beef and the itty-bitty Yorkshire puddings. I used to imagine them getting up and moving around when I'd left them alone. But for the first time, I knew for absolute certain that they didn't. The paper wasn't being read. The telephone directory was a chunk of plastic. The TV scene never changed from that one still of Julie Andrews with her arms stretched wide open on the hilltop. I closed the frontage again. The dust mites were making me itch.

I popped a Piriteze and went for a shower. I was all set to go back to bed when the sound and smells of sizzling bacon climbed up the stairs. I only realised then how hungry I was, only having finished half of Dad's experimental prawn balti the night before. I wrapped myself in my dressing gown and slumped down the stairs. 'Thought that might do the trick,' he said, handing me a squashy new-bread sandwich on a plate. He'd scraped one side of each piece of bread with sauce – brown on one, ketchup on the other, just as I liked it.

'Thanks,' I said, saliva filling my mouth. I bit down into

the pillow of bread and a burst of sweet, savoury and salt sent my mouth into paradise.

'Any plans for today?' he said, flapping a tea towel over his shoulder.

'No,' I said.

'What's happening with training?'

'Pete's not very well,' I lied. 'He said he'd call me when he's better.'

Dad looked at me as though he was sucking on an unpleasant sweet. 'So what are you going to do in the meantime? Why don't you go for a jog? How about that gym next to the garden centre? It's Pay-as-you-Go, isn't it? You could join until Pete's better perhaps?'

'I dunno.' There was no way I was joining Sweat Dreams – I might run the risk of walking straight into Zane. But Dad clearly wanted me to go somewhere today.

'Why don't you go and see your friend with the baby? She's called twice. She's home from hospital now, isn't she?'

I carried on eating my sandwich, filling my mouth and chewing slower so I wouldn't have to answer.

He went back to his board and started dicing his peeled carrot. 'Talking of hospitals, you can take that off now, you know.'

He was looking at the white plastic bracelet they'd given me that had my name and date of birth on.

'Yeah, I know.' For some reason, it made me feel like something real had happened for once, rather than everything being in my own head. Proof I hadn't imagined everything I was feeling.

'That Malinowski boy keeps ringing as well. You know, Derek and Doreen's grandson from down the road? He came to the door while you were in the shower.'

'What did he want?'

'To see if you're all right. He said he's staying at the girl's house in Cloud to help her with the baby. Derek and Doreen are back from their cruise now.'

'Were they OK about him moving out?'

'Why don't you call him and find out?' *Chop chop chop.*

I purposely didn't look at him. I looked to the board where he'd been chopping prewashed veg – celery and onions. He started chopping up a leek. 'Are you making soup?'

'No, I'm trying that rabbit ragu from the Jamie Oliver book. The one you got me last Christmas. Thought I'd give it a whirl.'

'You can't stand Jamie Oliver. You always say he's an overconfident barrow boy who needs to run a comb through his hair.'

'Well, he might be, but I like the look of this recipe.' He scraped the diced vegetables into a large saucepan and moved it to the draining board. 'His fish pie looks good as well. Thought I might try that tomorrow. Will you have some?'

'If you take the poo pipes out of the prawns this time, yeah.' I offered him a brief eyebrow raise before going back to my sandwich, disappointed to see I'd only got one corner left. 'Celestina's coming over for dinner, isn't she?'

He didn't answer immediately. He was concentrating too much on washing his hands and washing them again, just to be sure they were un-oniony. 'I thought she might like to come over and try this. We're doing Italian cookery in the next couple of weeks.'

'That's why you want me out of the house, is it?' I smiled.

'No, of course not. You're more than welcome to join us. I just don't know if it's too soon. After your mum, I mean.'

'Dad, it's been five years. You're entitled to fall in love

again.' He actually reddened, and couldn't look at me. 'Aww, Dad.'

'I think you'll like her, Estella. She's got a good heart.'

'You mean she's completely different to Mum?'

He started to protest, but that was all I needed to know. My dad was going to be OK. As for me…

He kissed my head and smiled, one of his toothy ones. 'Thanks, Little Fish.'

And those two words seemed to make everything a little bit more all right. Dad hadn't called me Little Fish for ages. When I was tiny and I'd fallen over, Dad was the one I always run to and he always called me Little Fish and it somehow managed to sprinkle magic on any wound.

'I'm going to get dressed,' I said.

'And then?' said Dad.

'And then I'll go for a walk. Maybe a jog.'

Dad winked at me and scraped his peelings into the food bin. 'That's my girl.'

*

I jogged all the way to the seafront and sat on the sea wall with my water bottle, just staring out to sea and breathing in. I did feel a bit better. I felt a buzz in my pocket.

A text from Corey.

I had a letter. From Zane.

Zane Walker? I text back.

Well, yeah, it wouldn't be Zayn Malik, would it?

What sort of letter?

I'll ping it over to you. Hang on.

Within seconds, a picture message flashed up. It was of a handwritten note, scrawly handwriting, badly spelled. It was Zane's handwriting. It hadn't changed since he was a kid.

Corey,

I want to call a truss with whatever it is ur doing with this cats thing. I'm sorry 4 evrything. You don't diserve it, ur right. I need to sort myself out. U won't hear from me again.

Zane

I didn't feel as euphoric as I'd felt after we'd done the whole Skin Room thing to the Shaws. Don't ask me why but I felt bad.

How awesome is that? came the next note.

I didn't really know what to say. It didn't feel awesome. It felt a little sad. Like we'd toppled Nelson's Column or something.

So I just put *Yeah, that's awesome. So glad it worked.*

Are you better now? he asked.

I didn't answer him that time. I didn't want to tell another lie. I jumped down off the sea wall and began walking back towards the Pier. I thought about jogging to Max's. I thought about getting an ice cream. I petted a couple of frisky Jack Russells being walked by a kind old lady who stopped and chatted about the new colour tarmac they're putting in the High Street. The residents were planning a protest, apparently.

I was dead opposite Zane's house when an Easy Riders taxi pulled up to the kerb by his gate. A chunky woman, wearing a psychedelic pink cardigan, leopard-print leggings and gold sandals got out and tottered round to the other side. Zane's mum, Zelda. She opened the door and out stepped Zane himself, wearing a T-shirt and board shorts and trainers with no socks.

I stood by the sea wall, flicked up my hood and watched. The taxi sped off down the road and Zelda teetered up their garden path to unlock the door. Zane stood at the end of the path, looking round, like he was expecting someone to be there. He looked awful. Paler, thinner. Still big, still angry-looking, still ready for a fight, but changed. Brutalised. Hollow.

Then I noticed his wrists. And the clean white bandages that covered them.

I looked both ways to cross the road and walked along the pavement to the gate of number thirty-one. All along the path were little sun-bleached gnomes, sitting on mushrooms with fishing rods. He saw me through the front bay window, just as I saw him. Neither of us moved. Moments later, he vanished.

The front door opened and there he stood. He had on a hospital bracelet too, over one of his bandages. I rolled up my sleeve to show him mine.

'Snap,' I said.

His eyes were watering. I didn't know if it was the breeze off the sea or if he was crying. Either way, he looked like something was going to burst out of him.

'Want to talk about it?'

He sniffed. 'No. I want to scream.'

'Come on, then,' I said, opening the gate. 'We can scream together.'

He looked unsure and, for a moment, I thought he was going to slam the door on me. Instead, he turned around, grabbed a white hoody from the banister, and called out to his mum that he was going for a walk. Somewhere in the distance, she shouted out instructions peppered with angry swearwords. He slammed the door on her, mid-flow, and came down the path towards me. 'Where?'

'The island,' I said, closing the gate behind him. 'Tide's

not in till late tonight – we can walk over. It's the one place in Brynstan you can scream and no one will hear you.'

'How do you know?' he said curiously as we walked, side by side.

'Cos no one heard me.'

'So you and Zane talked?'

22

Back to the Island

We walked across the sand in silence. Words were kind of unnecessary. We were both walking in the same direction, and, in a way, that was enough. I noticed he had flecks of purple glitter in his eyebrows and behind his ears, but I didn't mention it.

'When was the last time you were here?' I asked, when we were halfway there.

'Dunno. Years. You're not gonna pull some cat move on me when we get there, are you? Cos if you are…'

'I'm not, I promise. We're done with that.'

He nodded warily and we walked the rest of the way in total silence. It took us about twenty minutes to reach it – it would have taken five, in a boat. It was sunny, for a while, but by the time we'd got to the little pebble beach on the east side, it had started to rain. The amount of litter on the shore was depressing. Not just driftwood and plastic bags, but bottles, cans, tyres, rusted bits of metal, plastic buckets, broken car parts, fag butts; you name it. OK, I hadn't been out here for a few years, but there never used to be so much rubbish around.

It wasn't that bad being back there, though. I'd had so

many nightmares about it, but, as it turned out, the fear had been worse than the reality. There was no one threatening here. Just Zane. And he was no one to be afraid of any more.

The rain was coming down harder by the second.

'Quick,' I said, pulling up my hoody and running into the thicket of trees until we were deep enough inside Mushroom Woods to be sheltered from it. We found a little copse of felled logs and sat down. I wondered if he'd remember the den we built there once. The sound of rain battering the leaves above us almost drowned our voices.

'We were lucky,' I said. 'Just made it.'

'What if the tide back comes in?' said Zane, shivering inside his hoody.

'It won't. It's not due in till later tonight,' I replied. 'We've got plenty of time.'

'How do you know?'

'I run on the beach. I have to keep an eye on the tides.'

He looked around us, rain beading his face. He was afraid.

'There's no one else here, I promise, Zane. No one comes out here any more. It's not on the tourist trail, and no one would hire a boat if they didn't know the tides.'

The air was actually warm, despite the fact it was tipping down. The trees were our umbrella.

'This is them woods where I found the mushroom,' he said. 'We had a den here.'

I smiled. 'That's right. This is Mushroom Woods. You named Jewel Creek. Max named the Pirate Graveyard. Like we discovered them.'

He suddenly put both his hands up to his face. It was like he'd been bottling his tears for a lifetime. As the rain came down around us, so they flooded down his cheeks.

'... and Jewel Creek. I thought the walls were covered in jewels. But they weren't. It was just where the sun caught the wet rock. We could go and see it when the rain clears?'

'Why did you bring me out here?' he said, wiping his nose on his hoody.

'Were you there when we played Robin Hood at Bucket Bay, with bows and arrows made out of branches and bits of string? And when I lost my Polly Pockets in Jewel Creek and me and Fallon spent ages looking for them? I used to go down to the shore all the time, thinking they might wash up, but they never did.'

'What are you going on about?'

'Making dens. Eating picnics. Police stakeouts inside the ruin. Always having picnics. You miss those days too, don't you?'

Zane pulled up his knees and rested his face on them. Then he began unravelling the bandage on his left wrist. I felt my legs go weak at the thought of what was underneath, but when he got to it, there was barely anything there. Just a few little scabby red cuts, like a tally.

'Turns out Gillette ain't the best a man can get.'

I looked at the tally in silence.

'What a pussy, eh? Wanted to die, but didn't want it to hurt.'

'What about the other one?' I said. He did the same again, unravelled the bandage, and showed me. Fewer tally marks this time, but these ones were deeper.

'There was a load of blood,' he said. 'Mum took me down to A & E.'

'Was she worried about you?'

He scowled at me and started wrapping one of his wrists again, all ham-fisted. 'Of course she was, Estella.'

'So she didn't want you to die?'

He scowled again, like I'd just smeared dog muck on his jeans. 'I'm her son, for Christ's sake. Her *only* son.'

'So why can't you just tell her you're gay?'

Zane seemed to shrink. 'I ain't. I *ain't*, all right?' He went so much more Essex when he shouted.

'There's no one here, Zane. No one can hear you.'

'I. AIN'T. GAY. There, you hear that, do ya?"

'To thine own self be true, Zane,' I muttered. I didn't think he'd heard me.

'What?'

'It's this quote my dad's got up in his office. He's got loads of book quotes in frames all over the walls. It's from Hamlet It's good advice.'

'I'm not …'

'You like kissing boys. Corey saw you.'

'I knew that prick couldn't keep his mouth shut.' He tried wrapping up his other wrist again, but he was getting it all wrong. I stopped his hands and pulled them towards me. He snatched them away.

'Come here, I'll do them.'

He let me, but he wouldn't look at me.

'My older brother David's gay,' I told him.

'So? *I* ain't.'

'Yeah, you said. David didn't come out to my dad for ages, but when he did, it didn't matter. It was no big deal. And my dad loves him just as much as he loves me and Ollie. Him and his husband have just had a baby.'

He glared at me. 'I don't care about your brother, right?'

'Yeah, you do,' I said, beginning to wrap up the other wrist, exactly as I'd done the left one. Just like Pete showed me for before I put my gloves on. 'You care quite a lot, actually.'

He laughed. 'You don't change.'

'Don't I?'

'Nah. You were like this when we was kids. Always the first in the Wendy house to ask what's wrong if one of us were in there sulking. Interfering little sod.' He knuckled his eyes. 'I thought in time it'd go away. I'd meet a girl I fancied, and that'd be that. I'd stop thinking about him.'

'Who? The boy Corey saw you with?' I finished the bandaging and sat back on the log.

He nodded. 'Mark Figges. Football captain.'

'Yeah, I remember. His parents moved to Whitstable, just before our mocks.'

'Sometimes it *is* a phase, isn't it? I didn't have no trouble with Fallon, you know. Doing it. We'd stayed in touch, sort of. Texting and that. I went round there…'

'She told us.'

'I got hard when we was kissing. She said I could do the business. So what the hell's *that* about?'

'Maybe you're bisexual?'

He shook his head, looking at the ground. 'I dunno what I am. I can't be a dad to that kid, Ella. I don't have a clue about kids.'

'Well, you can't put her back where she came from, Zane. She's here now. She looks like you as well.'

'Does she?'

I nodded. 'She's got your nose. She's got your smile too as well actually.'

He smiled briefly at that. I saw him swallow. 'She won't want a poof for a dad.'

'Don't say that. Don't talk about yourself like that. Did you know Corey is living with Fallon now? He's helping her with the baby.'

'She'll be better off with him as her dad. I sent him a note.'

'I know,' I said. 'He texted me.'

'Right. So, that's that then, innit? I ain't gonna bother with him again.'

'Not really,' I said. 'You're not fixed, are you?'

He snorted. 'I knew what you were doing, you know. The second I heard that meowing sound in the wall. I punched a hole trying to get to that thing.'

'Did you?'

'Yeah. And then the masks and the ink on the floor. I remembered that story Max's sister told us.'

'I didn't think you would.'

'I remember a lot of 'em. That one about the kid who trashed all the Christmas presents and put laxatives in the turkey and gave her family diarrhoea. "The Boy Called Moses With Sixteen Noses Who Liked Pinkish Roses"...'

Something clicked in my memory. 'It was you who put those roses on her grave, wasn't it?'

He nodded. 'She was like a big sister to me, n'all. She knew about – me, you know. She talked to me about it. Last time I saw her. When she died, I thought it had died as well. I tried to bury it, but it wouldn't go away.'

'Yeah, Stuff in shallow graves has a habit of digging its way out again.'

'That another of your dad's quotes?' he smirked.

I shook my head. 'No. Just sort of came to me. It doesn't need to be us against you, you know, Zane. We used to be good friends. How did you go from being that boy who helped Corey write his name with a sparkler on Bonfire Night to beating him up and killing his cat? He's bloody disabled...'

'I took the whole rap for that at school, you know? I didn't drag him into it when the teachers asked what had happened. Or you. And I didn't kill Lord Voldemort.'

'Uh, yeah you did.'

'No, I only went round there to put the frighteners on him again. Cat was already dead, under a hedge. Been run over, by the looks. Someone must've left it there. I just saw it and strung it up in the tree as a warning.'

'Some warning,' I said. 'Zane, he was heartbroken. What were you even doing there?'

'I was gonna piss through his letterbox or summing. Nothin' major'

'Oh. Nice.'

A silence descended again. We spent whole minutes just listening to the rain.

'I don't wanna be different, Ella. I just wanna fit in.'

'Tough,' I said. Zane glared at me, but let me carry on. 'Why do you want to be like everyone else? Different is *good*. But you're not even that different. Jesus, look at us. You're the "normal" one out of us lot. Fallon's a single mum and lives in a zoo with a witch who collects roadkill and stuffs dead dogs to look like snooker players. Corey's a disabled orphan with dead junkie parents and a cat fixation; Max is shagging his cousin and doing so many drugs he's got Wiz Khalifa on speed dial. And as for me...'

I ran out of steam at that point.

'. . . but you – you're fine the way you are. You know – when you're not being a bullying psychopath, that is.'

Zane took a deep breath, then let it out high above, into the trees. He looked around again. 'My mates'll tear me apart.'

'Find new mates then. Things could be worse, Zane. At least you want to have sex with *someone*.'

'Eh?'

'Me and Max don't do it.' I surprised myself, saying that to Zane of all people.

'Why not?'

'Cos it brings back memories. To me, sex means pain, embarrassment. Wishing I was dead. And I think I need to face up to that, or else nothing will ever get better. That's why I suggested we come out here.'

'Is it something to do with Neil Rittman?'

I gasped, like he'd dropped an ice cube down my back. 'Why would you say that?'

My phone buzzed in my pocket – a text from Max. *Where are you? I need to see you* – and I posted it back inside my hoody.

'I saw summing once. At Max's house, when we were all round there. Saw him... kiss you. In the kitchen. It was summer, and we were all outside in the pool. You'd gone to get a drink or summing. He was touching you. And you were just standing there, letting him. You had your eyes closed. I started to hate you then, cos I thought you were having an affair. My dad ran off, about the same time, you see. Didn't realise till later that this was totally different.'

'You never told anyone what you saw?'

He bowed his head. 'I told Jessica. The day before she died.'

*

The rain was easing off by the time we left the wood, and there were more scraps of blue tearing through the clouds. Hoods still up, we walked across the heath and climbed the rocky ground up to the Pirate Graveyard. I was bizarrely calm.

'When it started happening, I was about nine. Maybe ten. It was just the odd kiss. Or touch. Sometimes he'd pat my bum. I thought it was just something adults did. When it got worse, I tried to avoid it. I tried just not being in places 'where he was. But he'd always find a way. Sitting down on the sofa next to me and… I didn't know it was wrong. I just knew I didn't like it. So I'd pretend I was frozen. Like in Narnia, when the queen freezes people. Ironic, considering I'm supposed to be "Volcano Girl". But I couldn't do anything else.'

Zane sat down on top of one of the graves.

'Sometimes it was easy to avoid. I'd just stay right out of Neil's way, or I made sure that whenever I went round their house, Max or Jo or Jessica was there too. Or I'd call round to Corey's, or meet you and walk round?'

He nodded, but said nothing.

'But once, there was a whole house full of people. Jo's 50th, it was. Everyone was there, even you guys. We were all outside watching the fireworks on the hill. I'd gone inside to the loo and, when I came out, he was there. He pushed me into their bedroom. I could hear the party going on, the music thumping through the walls, the fireworks. He kissed me on the mouth. He was all cigar stink and his tongue was hard and slimy and his hands were everywhere.

'He said it was my fault for showing my legs. And that I shouldn't wear dresses cos they "fired him up". He called me a deviant. He said I pretended to be all innocent but really, I wanted it. And he said if I told anyone, I'd be in big trouble. So I kept my mouth shut. And I stopped wearing dresses. And I stopped showing my legs. I stopped trying to be pretty.'

Zane stared across the bay, towards the hillside, where JoNeille House was, looking like he was trying to burn it down with his eyes. I could have told him not to bother. I'd tried that a million times and it had never worked.

'Nothing else happened for about two years. In the meantime, he was over-nice to me. Kept giving me presents, through Max – jewellery, iPhones, money no object. Fifty quid for my birthday; a hundred quid for Christmas. When I started running, and getting good at it, he started sponsoring me, telling me what a big star I was going to be. At first, I thought it was an apology. Then on *EastEnders* one night they had a storyline about grooming. And I realised that's what he was doing. He was buying my silence. Owning me. Like he owns everything else.'

There was another buzz in my pocket. *Ella, where are you?* M. No kiss.

'Sorry,' I said, getting my phone out and replying to the message. *Will text u later.* Then I turned it off. 'The thing… the rape, it only happened once. Right here.'

Zane looked up, his eyes dark and dead. 'Here? On the island?'

'I thought it was all over. I thought he'd realised what he'd done wasn't right, and that he'd stopped it all. I thought not wearing dresses and not wearing make up had worked. That I'd won. But then it was Max's birthday. Remember, we all came out here for a picnic? Disposable barbecues, blankets, all his family, all of us lot? It was a scorching hot day. When I got to the house, no one else was there, but Neil made me think everything was OK, that Max and Jo and everyone had gone on ahead to the island. So me and him were supposed to take the rest of the furniture over in the speedboat.'

Zane cleared his throat. 'But no one was here.'

I shook my head. 'He said he'd got it wrong. But never mind because he was sure they'd be here soon. Then he said we should get on with setting up the furniture anyway, and then go back and pick them all up. And I believed him.

'The tide was in, so it wasn't like I could just run back to the house. I was trapped. And I knew what was going to happen. He said we should go for a walk in the woods, and he kept asking me stuff, private stuff. He asked if I had a bikini on under my clothes. I said no. He asked if I'd started my period. I said yes. He asked if I was having my period right then. I said no. Then he started kissing me, but I didn't kiss back. He told me to touch him. He forced my hands down... then he pinned me to the ground in the woods.

'I tried so hard to make it difficult. I screamed at one point, but he held my neck. He said if I'd just lie there and let it happen it would be so much easier. Cos if I struggled, it would hurt more. And then Max would see the marks. And my dad would see them. And they'd both worry. So I stopped struggling and just let it happen. I let him hurt me in the most painful embarrassing way anyone can hurt another person. And afterwards, I kept it all inside me where it couldn't hurt anyone else.'

'You never told no one?'

I shook my head. 'I tried telling Jess a few times but I always stopped myself. I didn't want her to think badly of me.' I looked out, across the water towards Brynstan Hill. 'I've hated the sight of that hill ever since. Afterwards, Neil said he'd done me a favour. I'd got it "out of the way". "No girl wants to be a virgin." And again, he said if I told anyone about it, I'd be in big trouble. I thought he meant he'd find a way of stopping my dad's cancer treatment. I don't know how I got that into my head, but I did and it wouldn't budge. Telling people about it meant losing Dad. It meant losing Max. It meant I was on my own. I changed that day. Something in me got cold. He did that. Just him.'

Zane looked down at the damp logs. 'He did it to Jessica as well, didn't he?'

I nodded. 'I think Rosie Hayes was telling the truth at Jessica's inquest. I'm sure she took her own life. I think she

could handle what he was doing to her, but when she knew
he was doing it to me too, she just...'

'... couldn't.'

I nodded. Zane came over to me and stood beside me at
the little white stone.

'Did Jess give you anything, the last time you saw her?'
I asked him.

'No,' he said.

'Oh.'

'I've never forgotten what she said to me though. She
told me to be strong, whatever happens. No one can mess
with you if you're stronger than they are.'

A pain rattled deep inside my chest.

'What about you?'

I shook my head. 'No, she didn't say anything. You think
I should have told someone sooner, about what Neil was
doing. Don't you?'

He shook his head. 'I don't think anything.'

Before I knew it, he had his arms out to me and I walked
into them and he embraced me in the tightest, safest hug
I'd ever known. And the wind took away the sounds of our
crying, so no one else would hear them.

*

It was dark by the time I got back home. On the walk
back I'd got several things straight in my head. Now I'd
told Zane, I knew it would be easier to tell others. Maybe
even the police. Maybe they would look into it. Zane said
I could trust him to back me up if no one else did. Telling
Max would be a different story. What if he didn't believe
me? I'd already spun him a line about having sex at some
imaginary sleepover. What if he told me I was disgusting
and never wanted to see me again? These were all thoughts

I'd had before. But I knew the time for bottling things up had ended. The volcano had to erupt.

There was a note from Dad in the kitchen saying he'd gone to swing dance class with Celestina. I didn't even know he'd signed up for swing dance classes. There were twelve messages on our answerphone. I switched on my mobile to see twenty-three missed calls, all from callers various. The first voicemail I picked up told me all I needed to know. It was Fallon.

'Ella, please pick up. It's an emergency. Max is here. He's got Pete Hamlin tied up in the boot of his car. I think he wants us to kill him.'

'In the boot of his car?'

23

A Nasty Surprise

It didn't make sense to me either just then, but I knew I had to get to the farm somehow and find out what the hell was happening. I scrolled through my numbers for the local cab firm and booked a taxi, grabbing all the loose change in the housekeeping tin for the fare. Then I paced the house, top and bottom, while I waited, thinking and overthinking. Maybe it was a prank. Maybe he'd got Fallon to mess with me? No. Fallon wouldn't do that. And Max wasn't a pranker. This was happening.

The taxi arrived. On the way there he tried to make small talk about the tourist trade in Brynstan, but all my replies were one-word answers. I couldn't get Corey or Max to answer their phones – both kept going to voicemail. What if I didn't get there in time? What was Max going to do? What had Pete done to deserve this? I had a horrible feeling and the feeling wouldn't shake.

A part of me knew – had known all along. Max was jealous of Pete, always had been. I'd tried and tried to convince him there was nothing between us, but he didn't believe me. Why would he believe me anyway? I'd kissed Pete, hadn't I? I'd done this. I'd caused it.

When I got there, the sky was darkening – it was just after 7 p.m. The taxi dropped me off on the road outside Whitehouse Farm and zoomed back up Long Lane.

The lane was quiet. The house was quiet, too. I knocked on the door of the lean-to, and the security light blinked on above my head. But apart from the usual barking and meowing and squawking hullaballoo inside, nothing else happened. I couldn't see Max's car, or any sign of a struggle. Quiet wasn't good. The security light blinked off again.

My phone buzzed. A text from Corey.

We're at Witch's Pool. Hurry.

And I just took off then, sprinting through the damp fields, into the woods and down the dry tracks onto the Strawberry Line, pelting along the road through the long dark tunnel, not stopping until I'd reached the section of embankment we'd climbed up a million times and the sign for 'Wit Po'.

I scrabbled through the long grasses until I saw a movement. Heard a noise. A baby was crying. I ran closer, into the clearing, and saw Fallon first, standing back from the pond. Corey was in front of her, shielding her it seemed. They both saw me at the same time. Then their eyes darted back across the pond.

There on the rickety bridge stood Max. And at his feet was a large, long bundle with a bag over its head. A wriggling bundle. A wriggling man. I got closer. It was a pillowcase over his head. The pillowcase was tied around his neck. The bundle was Pete.

'Is he dead?' I whispered. I don't know why I whispered. It was as though any sudden noise and Max would kick forwards and Pete would roll into the pond and disappear.

'No,' said Fallon, her voice soft, quivering like feathers.

'But he says this will get the truth out of him. Ella, he won't listen to us.'

'He said he wants us here as witnesses,' said Corey. 'He's hit the green stuff hard tonight, Ella. He's not thinking straight at all. He's out of his mind.'

I turned back to the pond. 'Max,' I said, as calmly as I could. 'If he goes in there, he'll drown. You don't want to kill him.'

'I want him to tell the truth,' said Max. I started moving around the edge of the water, getting closer to Max. His cheeks were tear-tracked and he looked shabby. Dirty, even. There was stubble on his chin and his hair was as greasy as I'd ever seen it. His pale green T-shirt had a couple of stains down the front. Oil-dark. Blood-dark.

'I want to hear him say it.' Max pulled on the pillowcase and it flew off Pete's face and he was yanked into a sitting position. One of Pete's eyes was puffy and his nose was bleeding. His skin was sweating and his T-shirt was wet through. When he saw me, his good eye opened wider, and he garbled behind his gag. 'I want to hear him say he raped you. Then I'm gonna kick him in. Let them deal with him.'

My mouth dropped open. 'Max, no,' was all I could say. 'No. No. No.'

I looked across at Fallon and Corey, who were shivering like two puppies left out in the cold. Let who deal with him? I wondered. And then I got it – he meant the witches. The women who'd drowned, the ones who haunted the pool.

'It's just a bloody story for God's sake, it isn't real. It's something they made up for tourists,' said Corey, wrapping his arm around Fallon's shoulder. She was shaking so hard, even though it wasn't a cold evening. It was only then that I noticed Fallon had the baby in her arms, wrapped in her coat.

'Why are Fallon and Corey here, Max? They've got the baby. It's not fair…'

'I need witnesses,' he gabbled. 'People to testify whether or not he sinks or swims. Otherwise it won't work.'

'The baby doesn't need to be here though.'

'Yes, she does. She's in the Five.'

'Jesus, Max, this isn't a game any more. This isn't a Fearless Five thing. You've got to see that. You've got to untie him.'

'No.' And he yanked him closer to the edge of the pond and balanced his foot sole on top of his thigh. 'Not gonna happen.'

'Max, Pete hasn't done anything to me,' I said slowly, moving closer to the bridge. 'He really hasn't, I promise you. You need to untie him now.'

'Don't touch him. He's mine.'

'OK. I'm staying here. It's all right.'

His chipmunk smile had been replaced by a thin, closed mouth, like his teeth were caged just inside, frightened to be seen. 'I'm teach-ing the tea-cher a les-son,' he sing-songed.

'A lesson in what?' I said, breathlessly, desperately trying to keep the panic at bay.

Max laughed, the candles all around him flickering. 'A lesson in revenge, of course.'

'But Pete hasn't done anything! Listen to what I'm saying. He's innocent.'

'I don't believe you, any more than I believe him. So we'll let the water decide,' he said. 'I figured it out, Ells. Why you hate running. Why you're always angry. Always moaning about Pete. Why you've been coming back injured from training. Why you never *ever* wanna talk about it. And why you won't let me touch you *there*.'

His eyes dropped to my thighs and my cheeks flamed instantly.

'He's gonna pay for what he's done to you, at least. Just like the Shaws paid for what they did. Just like Zane paid. Just like Shelby paid. Only much worse.'

'I told you at the hospital he's never laid a finger on me. It wasn't him, I swear.'

'He said you kissed him.'

I looked at Pete, then back at Max. I could smell rotting vegetation at the edge of the pond where it had all silted up. The water looked black in the early evening light. Oily and thick with weed. 'That was all me, Max. And it was only a few days ago and my head was all over the place. Seriously, that was nothing...'

'He did it to Jessica, as well. I know he did.'

'What? No, he didn't. Jess didn't even go to our school.'

Max nodded slowly. I didn't know what he was nodding at but he rolled Pete closer to the edge of the pond. I couldn't figure out why Pete wasn't fighting back and then I realised his feet and hands were tied together. And he was right on the water's edge now.

'I swear to you, this is a massive mistake. He didn't even know Jess.'

'They do this, you know. I Googled it,' he said. 'They groom their victims until they can't even admit what's happened to themselves.' He looked up at me. 'You and Fallon – when you changed in Jess's room the other day, at my house. You looked in her journals.'

'I...'

'We put them back after,' Fallon called out. 'All of them.'

'One was out of place,' said Max. He fumbled behind him and pulled out the yellow Composition notebook that had been tucked into the back of his jeans. 'This one,' he announced to the meadow.

I could feel Fallon's eyes on me, and I glanced at her. I could hear her quiet sobs on the warm summer air.

'You left it sticking out. Only slightly, but it had definitely been moved. I would know, see, because I have to make sure everything's back the way it was for when Mum goes in there. She doesn't like anyone touching Jess's stuff, even me. She still thinks one day Jess is going to come home. You were both acting weird over lunch.'

'So were you,' I said.

'Yeah well I'd seen it, hadn't I?' he shouted. 'I'd seen this.' He opened up the book and held up the white page but the writing was too fine to see.

'I think we should take the baby back to the house now,' said Corey quietly, moving himself and Fallon away from the water's edge.

Max heard him. 'Stay where you are. I need you here. All of you.' He started thumbing through the pages. 'Stories. Drawings. Little thoughts Jess had over the years. Some of it I didn't get at first. It confused me. But some of it was clear enough. About wishing kids never had to grow up. About this older guy taking advantage. Kissing her when she didn't want him to. Forcing her to do stuff. She never said who. I could only read so much of it.' He held the same page aloft again and I moved close enough that I could read it.

The page was turned to the drawing of the rat with the noose around his neck, swinging from a tree branch.

'Ring any bells?' he said. 'Rat Man. Now who could Rat Man be, I wondered.'

'Max…'

'And then I got it. The Pied Piper. He was the Rat Man,

wasn't he? The Pied Piper took the children, and they never came back. I cracked her code. And I cracked yours too.'

'You're wrong, Max. Pete *hasn't* been molesting me, and he *didn't* hurt Jessica.'

'What does he call it then? Love? Your little special little secret?'

I'd never seen Max's eyes so black. He was submerged in the lust for revenge, so much so I didn't think I could reach him. Not just because he had the wrong man – but because I was so afraid of what he'd do when he found out who the *right* man was. He grabbed hold of Pete's hair and yanked his head back. The baby grizzled in Fallon's arms.

Pete looked at me and his eyes started to water.

'Ella, tell him,' said Corey. By this time the baby was wailing.

'So you say you didn't rape Ella,' said Max. 'And you didn't touch my sister.'

Pete sighed. 'For the hundredth time, I didn't even KNOW your sister.'

'Max, don't do this,' I said, making plans to grab Pete the second Max pushed him forwards. I inched closer still.

'What, this?' he replied, punching Hamlin in the side of his face.

'Stop it!' squawked Fallon. 'Please!'

Pete spat out a glob of blood onto the wooden floor of the bridge. He looked up at me. I heard a creak. How it was holding both their weights I didn't know. They could both go in, at any second. I would lose them both.

The baby was screaming now. 'He's not saying anything, Max,' said Corey, gently. 'He's telling the truth.'

'The water has to decide. Then we'll all know for sure.'

And still Pete looked at me. And still the baby screamed into the hot summer air.

'Shut that kid up, Fallon!' Max yelled.

'Tell him, Ella. Please tell him!'

'I didn't do anything to her, I swear!'

'Is that your final word?' Max got squarely behind him.

'NO. NO!'

'What's the matter, didn't she love you back? How old was she when you raped her and got her pregnant and left her to deal with it, huh? THIRTEEN.' He pushed Pete to the bridge and held him there with his boot, ready to roll him off.

'Ella – *please*,' Corey screamed.

'Ella, stop him!' Pete shouted. 'For Christ's sake, please, please say something! I thought you were my friend.'

'He'd going to drown in there!' Fallon cried, echoed by her baby.

'Max,' I said, walking onto the bridge. There was another creak, louder. 'Max, I'll tell you who it was. OK? I'll tell you what you want to know. Let him go.'

He wasn't listening. His boot was still poised.

'I SAID LET HIM GO!'

Max looked up at me.

'Pete is not Rat Man. Rat Man is someone else.'

It was so quiet when it came out it was almost a whisper. But it did come out. And Max heard me. They all did, then.

'It wasn't Pete who raped me *or* Jessica.'

'You're protecting him. If it wasn't him, then who was it? Cos you know. I *know* you know who it was.'

I walked forwards, stroked his quivering eyebrow with my thumb. I put my sweating forehead to his and I kissed his lips. And then I let go completely.

'It was Neil. Rat Man is Rittman. It was your dad.'

'How did he take it?'

24

Discoveries at the Witch's Pool

Sucker-punched. It sounds stupid, but from that moment on, Max looked different. He dropped the book and just stared down at the water. Pete was lying still, all out of breath on the bridge, sweating and breathing like crazy. Corey and Fallon were as still as statues. The only sound was the baby's crying but the air had somehow muted it.

'She's hungry. I need to take her back,' said Fallon, though she didn't move.

'Yeah, we need to go,' said Corey, but he didn't move either.

I knelt down beside Pete and began freeing his hands. Max didn't try to stop me. He was still looking down at the water. The book, lying open, fluttered on a breeze I hadn't felt until that moment.

This was my eruption, and there was no way of stopping it. I told him everything I'd told Zane hours before. About the touching, how it had started, *when* it had started. About his mum's 50th. About the island. About Neil blaming me and calling me a deviant because I'd led him on, wearing dresses and swimming costumes. And about the miscarriage. Every word that came out of my mouth was a relief, an ache that didn't ache any more.

But now the ache was where I always feared it would go – it was all on Max.

He sat down on the bridge, holding the post close to his face like a teddy bear. 'He called her a deviant too,' he said. 'She wrote it about a thousand times on one of the pages in that book. All over it – Deviant Deviant Deviant.'

Without any warning, he got to his feet and ran down the other side of the bridge, pelting over to a thicket of trees where he threw up.

I left Pete untying his ankles and ran after Max. He was bent over, cowering in the long grass, retching and spitting.

'I didn't lead him on, Max. I promise you.'

'You didn't need to,' he said, spitting. 'He worships you. Why didn't I see it?'

'Because you didn't want to see it. And I didn't want you to, either.'

'I always thought he wanted you, like, as a *daughter*.' He threw up again, then again, letting out a long groan afterwards like it was a relief. When he was done, his whole body hardened and he stood up but his knees buckled and he went down hard onto them, holding his head in his hands.

He wiped his mouth. 'Did he… to Fallon?'

'No.'

He looked as though he was going to hit me for a moment. As though he was seeing everything I'd told him, replaying in his mind like it had played again and again in mine for so long now. The rooms in his house where Neil had touched me or kissed me, for ever infected. In a way, I wanted him to hit me. He needed to take it out on someone. All my own lava-hot anger had left me now. I was hollow. There were only all the little fires to put out.

Or so I thought.

'Fearless Five screwed this one right up, didn't they?' I said, attempting a laugh.

He shook his head. He looked like a little boy again in the early evening light. The boy who didn't want to leave Disneyland. The boy who ate too many sweets and threw up over the edge of the Pier. The little boy forced to sit at the dinner table until he'd eaten all his runner beans. I didn't know how to pull him back from this.

'All this time... you've sat there, Sunday after Sunday, eating lunch at the same table. Sitting next to him. Christmas dinners. Parties. Barbecues. I made you go to... everything. I guilt-tripped you.'

'I wanted to protect you from it. But I can't any more. Come on, Max. Let's go back to the farm. Let's go and talk it all through. Please.'

'What are we gonna do, sit around and drink tea? I nearly killed a man tonight.'

'Ssh, you didn't.'

He stopped. He seemed to be choking on his words. He just kept saying again and again, 'Not my Ella. Not my Ella.'

'Max, don't. It's OK, I'm here, I'm here now, it's over.'

'No, it's not! I wanna kill him! Look what he did to you. He's my *dad*. Oh-fuuuuuuck!' He slammed his head into his palms again and again.

'Come on,' I said, reaching for his hand. And eventually, in his own time, when his breathing was under control, he took it, and we got up and started to walk.

*

Corey drove Max's car back to the farmhouse – he'd parked it at an angle in the old dumping ground through the trees that had once been for tourist parking. None of us said one word the whole journey – even the baby was quiet.

The farmhouse had changed since we were last there. It was much tidier – a few of the animal cages had been cleared out so there was a clear run to the lean-to door now. All the old broken buckets and watering cans and empty paint tins had gone and, in the kitchen, the corners were cobweb free and all the cupboards had been scrubbed clean. Where the stacks of old newspapers used to be were now clear stacking boxes of baby equipment and drawers labelled 'Sterilising Fluid', 'Dummies' and 'Muslin Cloths'. There were a couple of new rugs on the living room carpet and a clean white throw on the back of the sofa. There was even a vase of fresh flowers on the end of the kitchen counter.

As we sat in the farmhouse living room, waiting for the new kettle to boil, an image of meek little Jo Rittman flashed into my mind. How quiet she was when Neil was around. How she always looked as though she was on the verge of tears whenever she said anything. Max always said the permanent shadow in her eyes was grief. Now we knew it was guilt.

'God, what a night,' said Pete, shoving a tabby out of the armchair so he could sit down.

'Are you OK?' I asked him, shivering. I'd given Pete my hoody to warm him up. It turned out Max had pounced on him while he was out jogging, bundling him into the back of his car before driving him to the Witch's Pond. It had been a warm day, but it was turning into a cool and blustery night.

'Who wants coffee, who wants tea?' Corey called out from the kitchenette.

'Just do four mugs of hot and sweet,' said Pete, getting

up and going to the sideboard. 'I need something stronger.' He pulled out a bottle of Acid Rain and undid the cap, knocking it back. His face was a picture.

I asked him again. 'Are you sure you're all right though?'

He looked across at Max. 'I have no idea, Ella. I don't know whether to punch him or hug him. Apart from that, tickety-boo.'

Max was sitting on the sofa, looking into nothing. He has tears in his eyes but he wasn't speaking, his mind obviously playing a rerun of the evening's events. I wanted to hold him but I thought he wouldn't want me to, so I stayed where I was on the footstool.

Upstairs with Fallon, the baby was still crying too. We heard the baby Nirvana CD go on in the distance, and eventually she stopped.

'She knows something's wrong,' said Corey, sitting on a space beside the fireplace. 'She knows we're not happy.' The kettle started boiling then clicked off.

'She's probably hungry, isn't she?' I said.

'Oh yeah, that too,' he said, his face reddening. He got up to finish the tea.

I couldn't even guess at what was going through Pete's head.

'You can go Pete, if you want,' I said to him, quietly, like I was in a library. 'We can call you a taxi or something.'

Pete laughed, although his face didn't join in. 'Grand. I can be home just in time for the *EastEnders* repeat.'

'Are you going to go to the police?' asked Fallon, appearing in the doorway.

'God knows.' He looked across at Max again. 'I don't *think* he's psychopathic, but I dread to think how tonight could have ended up.' He looked across at me. 'Secrets, Ella. This is what secrets do.'

Corey brought over the teas on a tin tray, which turned out to be an upturned hubcap. He settled it down on the hearth and offered us one each.

'I'm sorry,' said Max, his whole body trembling.

'Sorry?' Pete laughed. 'You knock me out, tie me up, lock me in the boot of a car, drag me to a remote lake and tell me you're going to drown me and you're *sorry*?'

'I don't know what else to say.'

Fallon had found Pete a checked shirt from the clothes horse in the outhouse. She gave it to him, and Pete put it on over his T-shirt.

'I'll start a fire,' said Corey, reaching for one of the brass pokers and the box of matches, and started stoking it up. 'Warm us all up a bit.'

'Good idea,' said Fallon, spooning sugars into each mug. 'The wood's in the basket there, and you can shred some of that newspaper.'

The whole atmosphere of the room felt like we'd all just watched someone die. No one knew what to say next. It was all mugs of tea and uneasy glances. Apart from the crackling fire, the only other sound in the room was Max's occasional sobs or Pete's lips smacking against the lip of his bottle.

We heard the heavy grinding sound of a truck in the lane outside the window.

'That'll be Mum,' said Fallon.

The cut on Pete's eyebrow was bleeding again where Max had whacked him. He dabbed at it with the sleeve of the shirt. 'I don't suppose you have a first aid kit, do you?'

She pointed towards the door. 'Downstairs cloakroom. Straight across the yard, green door. There's plasters and cotton wool in the cabinet.'

Max looked up at Pete as he crossed the room in front of

him. 'If you wanna go to the police, I'll take whatever you wanna throw at me. I don't care.'

Pete turned to him. 'I think you've got enough to deal with at the moment, don't you?' And he left.

'I'll just go and see Mum and check on the baby,' said Fallon. She left too, leaving just the three of us.

'So what are we going to do now?' asked Corey.

My tea was too hot and kept burning my mouth. 'What do you want to do, Max?'

He shook his head.

'I think we should just go straight to the police,' said Corey. 'Tell them everything we know about Neil. We'll all back each other up, won't we? I mean, we've got evidence now. They're not going to be able to ignore that, are they?'

'It's not that easy,' I said. 'This is going to change everything. Especially for Max.'

'Don't worry about me,' said Max. 'This isn't about me, it's about you. And Jess.'

'It's your name though, Max. Everything that happens to him will ricochet back at you. I don't want that to happen.'

'Can't see how you're gonna stop it,' he mumbled. 'I can't handle this.' He got up from the sofa and started walking out of the room, just as Fallon returned, yawning.

'Where are you going?' she asked.

'A smoke,' he snapped. 'Don't follow me.' He vanished through the wooden door, slamming it behind him and making the menagerie out in the lean-to squawk and flutter.

Fallon sat down gingerly on the sofa next to Corey. 'He's not doing very well, is he?'

Pete returned from the cloakroom, a small wodge of tissue clumped against his eyebrow. He picked up a brass poker and started stoking the fire. 'Where's he gone?'

'For a cigarette,' said Corey. 'I think he just needed to get out of here for a bit.'

'He's seriously lost it. What the hell is that kid on?'

'Skunk,' said Corey. 'He never used to get this angry about anything.'

'What did you expect?' I said bitterly. 'How did you expect him to be? This is why I've kept it in for so long – I knew he wouldn't be able to handle it. He *worships* that man.'

'He worships you too,' said Corey. He blinked across at Pete. 'How would *you* feel?'

Pete drained the dregs of the Acid Rain bottle without answering. Fallon got up to get him another one, but he shook his head.

'How's the baby?' Corey asked.

'She's fine. Mum's doing "Lithium" with her,' said Fallon.

'What?' said Pete.

'It's a song,' I said quietly. Pete rolled his eyes and shook his head, like he was hoping to wake up at any second.

Max was gone ages. It didn't occur to me until Corey had poured us all out another mug of tea, and I noticed Max hadn't touched his original mug.

'He said he's going to kill his dad,' I said. 'His eyes were all dark.'

'That's just something people say though, isn't it?' said Corey.

'Usually,' said Fallon, holding my stare.

'I'm going to see where he is,' I announced, getting up and making for the door. 'Max?' I nudged the front door slightly and opened it. The security light *ping*ed on.

'Max?' I called out again. Nothing, and no one in either direction.

I ran back into the lounge.

'Did he come back in?' I said, breathlessly. 'Did Max come back in?'

'No,' said Pete, getting up. 'Why?'

'He's not outside. And his car's gone.'

*'How did you get back to the house with
Max's car gone?'*

25

Several Things Happen

Rosie had a Jeep in the garage next door, caked in mud and badly rusted up all over – but, by some miracle, it still went. Pete drove. I told Fallon and Corey to wait at the farm, but neither of them would listen. Fallon had expressed milk earlier so the baby would be all right without her for an hour or so and Rosie was staying with her, so they were coming with us – end of story.

I don't remember much about the journey, other than the fact that the floor of the Jeep was thick with hay and clumps of dry mud, and every so often it buckarooed for no apparent reason. I was terrified the Jeep would break down. That was my biggest fear – that we wouldn't get there in time. That we wouldn't reach Max, and he'd lose the last rag of control and do to his dad what he would have done to Pete. It was unthinkable.

As we turned into Upper Dunes Close, I could see the lights were on in JoNeille, and that the gates were open. Pete parked up outside, and I jumped out and ran to the front door. A warm, sandy wind blew against my face as I looked for signs of movement behind the kitchen blind.

'I can't see anyone moving about,' I called back.

'Maybe he's done it?' said Corey. 'Maybe it's already happened?'

'Corey, for God's sake!'

'That's not helping, OK?' said Pete, shoving the keys to the Jeep in his pocket. 'Why don't you two go back and wait in the car? We'll go and see what's happening.'

'No,' said Fallon. 'We're a team, aren't we? Fearless Five, remember?' She looked at Pete, and frowned. 'Technically, you're not in the Fearless Five though. Sorry.'

'I'm sure I'll cope,' he said.

'Ssh,' I said. I could hear something going on inside – a noise I couldn't identify. I rang the doorbell. A light came on in the hallway and a red shape appeared through the frosted glass of the front door. It was Jo – I recognised her red dressing gown.

It was clear that *something* had happened the moment she opened the front door. Her hair was scruffy and her eyes were bloodshot; behind her on the carpet lay the potted plant and the telephone table, upturned and smashed. There was scattered earth everywhere. Her cheeks were wet, and she looked through me like I wasn't even there.

'Jo? What's happened? Has Max been here?'

Before any of us knew what was happening, she fell forwards and collapsed against the door frame. Pete caught her just in time to stop her hitting the step face first.

'Jo? Jo?' He started lightly slapping her cheek; then he laid her out flat on the floor, half on the hallway carpet, and half hanging outside the front door. He knelt down and put his ear to her mouth to listen for breathing. 'She's all right. She's had a lot to drink, though.'

Jo was gabbling, gibberish and sobbing noises that none of us could decode. It was the most I'd ever heard her speak.

'She stinks of whiskey,' said Fallon. Pete lifted her to a sitting position and she started sobbing into his neck.

'Help me lift her, guys,' he said. 'Corey, take one of her arms with me. On the count of three, one, two…'

'Thank God you're here!' Jo wept, suddenly. 'Thank God. Thank God. Thank God. Got to go after him. Please Estella, please.'

We lowered her again.

'Is it Max?' I said. 'Or Neil? Where are they?'

The front door was wide open – I only realised then how loud our voices had been. A neighbour from across the road was walking towards us in his silk robe and slippers. Fallon headed him off on the gravel drive, doing her best to assure him that everything was fine.

'Is Neil here?' asked Pete.

'Max. He's g-going to kill him,' Jo stammered as we dragged her into the kitchen. 'Oh God. Oh GOD. Oh GOD!' She was screeching like an owl, clutching Pete's shirt to the point of ripping it (again). We managed to get her to her feet and guided her towards the nearest stool at the copper-covered breakfast bar (which, as Neil liked to remind everyone, had cost over £3,000 to install).

'Please. He's going to kill him. He's going to kill his father,' Jo kept on burbling.

She looked straight at me, didn't even blink. When I moved, she kept looking straight past me to the sink, her sobbing broken up by quick hysterical breaths and hiccups. 'H-he was h-here. H-he shouted at me. He's s-so angry. He thinks it's my f-f-fault! Oh God. Oh God. My Max. My Max!'

Corey looked at me.

'Where's Neil?' I asked her. She didn't make eye contact,

just clung on tighter to Pete, and kept sobbing. 'Jo? You need to tell us where Neil is.'

Jo shook her head. 'This isn't happening.'

I lost all my patience then. 'You knew, didn't you? You *knew* what Neil did to me.'

'No, no! I wasn't sure.'

'Did you know what he did to Jessica? And you didn't do anything? You still let me come here. You still left me alone with him. Why didn't you *do* something?'

'I didn't know for sure, I swear I didn't! Ella…'

'Why didn't you protect us?' I pushed Pete out of the way and got right into her face.

'I couldn't. I didn't.'

'Ella,' said Pete. 'Not now.'

I was shouting 'Tell me where Neil is. Tell me where Max went.'

'He'll kill him. Then we'll all be free of him, won't we?' She said it like it made good sense, like it was a logical solution. Max would kill him and that would be that.

'No, Max isn't killing anybody. I'm not going to let Neil ruin anyone else's life. Just tell us where Max went!'

'W-wallflower,' she sobbed. 'The p-p-p-p-pub. Seafront. Ella, he took it.'

'Took what? Make sense, you stupid bitch!'

With a quivering finger, she pointed towards the kitchen counter. There beside the draining board was the £700 knife block, with the knives made of 'diamond-sharpening steel'. It had been knocked onto its side. And the biggest blade of the bunch was missing.

26

One Goes Down to the Sea

I didn't think, I just ran. Out of the kitchen, across the hallway, through the office to the conservatory and out into the back garden. I could hear them all behind me, shouting.

Ella, no!

It's too dark.

Where's she going?

You'll never make it! We'll take the Jeep.

I'm gonna call the police.

Moonlight was my only friend as I wrenched myself over the back fence and scrambled through the sand dunes, stumbling and tumbling through the collapsing mounds of sand and long grasses and forging on down towards the beach. The tide was coming in, like a billion angry tigers storming the beach with snarls, eating up the sand by the second. I didn't have long – only minutes – before it swallowed everything, but I'd run the beach a million times before with Pete in training, and I knew this was the quickest way to the pubs-and-clubs end of the seafront where Max had gone. It was exactly eight minutes to the jetty directly opposite The Wallflower if I sprinted.

And so I ran. I tore across the wet sand faster than I'd

ever run it before, my arms pumping against the wind, the
tide biting at my trainers all the way. The salt was in my
throat, but Max was the only thing in my mind. He'd never
had to handle anything hard before – his parents had always
bailed him out, or shielded him from any sort of harm. If he
was going to fall, I had to be there to catch him.

As I rounded the headland, I could see the lights on the
seafront – I could just make out the sign of The Wallflower,
swinging in the wind. I prayed to God that the police were
there before me but as I got closer I couldn't hear any sirens
– just the bassy thud of the music from the Fun Pub next
door. I could smell the burgers frying in the van opposite
Tesco. Behind me, the stretch of sand I had run had already
been swallowed by the tide. I could feel water through my
shoes but I just kept going. It was already up as far as the
second lot of stilts on the jetty. I was about two minutes
away when I saw the two silhouetted figures halfway down
the boardwalk. I knew it was them.

I heard their raised voices on the wind as I hoisted myself
up onto the dry boardwalk. They both turned to face me.
Still catching my breath, I looked for the knife.

Neil glanced from me to Max and back again. We were
either side of him, trapping him like a wild animal. Then
I saw the blade in Max's right hand, as the light from the
street lamps bounced off the metal. He was nudging his
father along the jetty with it, making him walk the plank.

'What the hell have you told him, you lying bitch?' Neil
shouted. I was instantly shocked – he'd never shouted at
me, never even raised his voice to me before. I had a split
second of feeling ashamed. And then there was no feeling
at all.

Max looked at me, desperate. 'He's just denying it.'

'If someone has been making up vicious lies about me, I

want to know why,' Neil spat. He glanced at me and back to Max. Then me. Then the knife. 'Max, come on, son. Come on. Give it to me. We can sort this.'

'You're a nonce,' Max wailed, crumpling down to the boardwalk, toppled by the weight of what he was realising. 'You're disgusting!'

'I haven't done anything, I told you! Jesus Christ, you think I'm capable of something that sick? Max, you know me. I'm not like that. Please, son.'

'Why deny it?' I said. 'You know what you did to me. To Jessica.'

He snapped his head back at me, then back to Max. To the knife.

'Max, I loved your sister. But Jessica had mental problems. She told stories, and, sometimes, if she got angry, you couldn't believe a word she said. She was always doing that. She could be quite vindictive. You ask your mother.'

'We did,' I said. 'Jo's in a worse state than Max is. Coming apart at the seams. She can't hide it for you any more either.'

Neil barked his laughter like a walrus. 'I can't believe this. Do you have any idea what you're doing? This is libellous.'

'Actually, I think you mean slanderous,' I said. 'Libel is written. But I'll write it down if you want me to. I'll spray it in big black letters up and down the sea wall if you like.'

I don't know where my strength was coming from – I can only describe it as unlocking a door and letting water flood through it. The door had been locked and watertight for so long, but now it was open, and everything was coming out. I could feel the fear leaving me as the truth did. Max was destroyed and I had nothing left to lose now. The worst was over. There was nothing to be afraid of any more.

Max collapsed to his knees on the boardwalk, the knife clattering down beside him.

Neil stepped forward. Max shuffled back one space. He stepped forward again, but again, Max shuffled back. Neil put his hands up and stepped back in surrender. He was so close to the edge of the jetty I could have pushed him into the raging sea with one finger.

'OK. Listen to me. If you want the truth, I'll tell you. But you'll only hear it from me, son. You'll get nothing but lies from that one.' He pointed to me, not looking at me.

'That one?' I said, folding my arms. 'Who are you calling "that one"?'

'Go on,' Max mumbled. I could barely hear him over the waves beneath the jetty, barrelling into the wooden stilts like wrestlers.

'Your sister had problems. We took her to counsellors, therapists, and they all said the same thing: she was angry because of her dyslexia, and how she kept sending her little stories off to publishers, getting nothing but rejections. It affected her badly. She took it out on us. Mainly on me.'

'You're lying,' I said calmly, feeling my fear fizz away, an angry swirl in my stomach taking its place.

'Come on, son. Let's go home and we'll talk about it and I'll tell you everything you want to know. I'll tell you the *truth*.'

The word 'truth' was fired at me like a spit glob. Max mumbled something. 'What was that, son?'

'I said Ella wouldn't lie to me. Not about this.'

Neil didn't skip a beat. 'She would, if she needed the money. I've had this before. Work experience girls at the garden centre. Accusing male members of staff of all sorts, just to get them sacked or to get a bit of compo. This is what girls like her do. You can kiss your sponsorship goodbye, darling, I'm telling you that for nothing.'

'Good,' I said, crossing my arms. 'I didn't fancy another

year with Pervert World emblazoned across my kit anyway, thanks.'

'Everything I've done for you.' He licked his lip again. 'You're done. Your father's done 'n'all. I can afford better lawyers than he can. False accusations can get you in very hot water, my girl...'

'This isn't a false accusation.'

'Your word against mine. I've got clout around here. *You* haven't. You're just a slut.'

'Say it again, Neil.'

'Slut. You wanted it as much as I did. Touching me when you thought no one was looking. Little stolen kisses when you said goodbye. Always wearing the shortest little dresses. Any excuse to wear very little at all around me.' Neil laughed, managing to be patronising even now, with the waves roaring. 'You see things in black and white, love. It's not always the man's fault, despite what the papers say.'

'I was a child!'

'Takes two to tango. If there's blame being apportioned here, you've got to take some of it.' He turned back to Max. 'OK, have it your way. We did have a thing. Briefly. But it was all her, Max. Every bit of it. She wouldn't take no for an answer. You know what she was like; always round our place, always cadging presents.'

Max just sobbed. I laughed. I was on the verge of hysterics. 'I was a child!'

'Yeah, you're a child *when it suits*. You've got nothing on me, little girl. Nothing.'

'I've got everything, actually. I'm going to the police, and I'm going to tell them every single detail about every little thing you did to me, starting with the moment you sat down on the sofa next to me when I was watching cartoons and you shoved your filthy hand down my knickers. Right up to and including the afternoon you pinned me down with your big fat hairy belly and raped me on that island.' I pointed into the thick black night, in the vague direction of where I knew it was. Where it would always be. 'I'll tell everyone what you did to me. And they will believe me.'

He cleared his throat. 'Where's your proof? The diaries of a lunatic and stories about me kissing you at some party and putting my hand down your pants. That's all they are, darling. Stories. Big deal.'

'I never mentioned the party,' I said. 'Did you, Max?' He shook his head.

Neil folded his arms.

'And it's not just the diaries. It's not just "some stories", either. And we've got a witness who swears Jessica walked in front of that bus.'

'And a witness who saw you touch her up,' called a voice. All three of us looked up towards the seafront, to where a figure stood in a white hoody at the end of the jetty.

Zane. Next to him stood Corey. And next to him was Fallon. A bubble caught in my throat. I had never felt so strong.

'What's this, a conspiracy?' Neil fake-laughed, but his nostrils were flaring like his face was fighting itself.

Fallon went to Max's side and bent down to put her arms around him. 'And there's the baby,' she said bluntly.

Neil looked from her to me, back to her. 'What baby?'

'The baby you put inside her. The one she lost.'

He pointed at her. 'Shut your fucking mouth, you liar. Your mother was that old witch woman, at my daughter's inquest. I know your lot. Bunch of gyppos. I'll sue this time, I'm telling you. You'll all look like fools in court.'

She shook her head. 'I'm not lying. I was there when she miscarried it. It was fully formed. It had bones. It had eyes.'

She looked at me. 'I didn't know what to do with it but I couldn't just flush it down the toilet like you told me to. So I buried it. I took a boat out to the island and I buried it.' She turned her attention back to Neil. 'I'll tell the police where it is. They'll be able to tell it was yours.'

'You're bluffing. All of you. This is harassment.'

'You did this to yourself, Neil,' I said. 'You can't complain now it's come back to bite you. You're a paedophile. You're evil. Every one of us knows it now. And if I speak up, they'll speak up with me. It'll be all over this town by the morning. I'm not living with this any longer. You have to live with it.'

He breathed like he was having a heart attack, scanning the boardwalk. Then he strode over to Max, who shuffled back until Neil had a grip on the knife. He came striding back towards me. Zane and Corey started down the board-walk, but I held a hand up to stop them.

'It's all right,' I said. 'I'm not afraid. He's the coward. A coward who hides behind money. He's going to offer me some right now. Aren't you, Neil?

Huffing, he backtracked to stand next to Max, sweating heavily now. He pointed the knife down at him. He was shouting.

'Do you want to lose the house? Do you? Do you want me to lose all my businesses? Your car? Do *you* want everyone to know about this? Because that's what will come of this if you go to the police, son. Do you want your mother to be out on the streets? You're a Rittman. You'll be tarred with the same brush. And for what, eh? This is family, Max. We can't lose that. There's nothing more important, is there?'

'Strange that family was the last thing you mentioned losing,' I called out.

I held fast to Neil's stare. Even if the sea wind burned

my eyeballs, no way was I backing down this time. Zane and Corey were standing beside Max, helping him get to his feet. Strong and mighty, making a wall in front of Fallon.

'I've been so scared of you, for years, but I'm not scared any more. I can see what you are now. The only thing that scares me is Max living for one second longer in your disgusting shadow. You going to prison – it's going to solve all our problems.'

Neil dropped the knife. 'A hundred thousand,' he said, quieter than before.

'What was that?' I said, cupping my ear.

He chewed on both his lips. 'One hundred thousand and you leave Brynstan. My lawyer can draw up the contract. But no repeat fees, no comebacks. We're done.'

I shook my head.

He breathed out – once, twice, three times. 'Two hundred.'

I shook my head.

He scratched his neck, the diamonds on his watch glinting in the moonlight.

'Five. Hundred. Thousand. Final. That'll buy you whatever then, won't it?'

I looked at Max, then back at Neil. 'It won't buy my life back, will it?'

With a snarl, Neil delivered his parting gift to me in a hushed, deep tone, like the one I'd last heard on the island.

'If your father gets cancer again, I'll make sure he dies. And then I'll come for you. That's a promise. You'll see my face in your fucking nightmares.'

I stared back. 'I already do.'

That was the point when I just lost it. I was an athlete coming out of the blocks. I flew, barrelling into him and feeling the boardwalk disappear beneath my feet as we flew through the air and crashed down hard onto the wet sand below. As the tide lapped over us, I straddled his chest, my hands around his neck. I squeezed and squeezed with all my strength but his neck was too strong. So I started punching him instead, both fists. Right hand, left hand. Cross punching. *Bang-bang-bang. Bang-bang-bang. Bang-bang-bang.* And screaming, so much screaming. I was wild. This was the revenge I'd always wanted. This had been the target all along – Neil Rittman. I was going to kill Neil Rittman. I wanted to kill Neil Rittman. I wanted to knock his brain clean out of his skull.

I grabbed his ears and slammed his head back on the sand. If it hadn't been for the wave, I'd have killed him then.

But it ploughed into us, a real strong one, breaking us apart. Then I was in the water, breathless with the shocking coldness of it. I could still feel the sand underneath my feet, but I couldn't keep my feet on the ground; I kept floating away and ducking under the water, gasping as the sandy brine filled my mouth. I came up to catch my breath, and another huge wave came over the top of me. And another one.

I couldn't find the surface again.

Then this black shape was in front of me. Coming at me faster than I could move away. Until…

BAM! My whole body was smashed against a hard post, one of the jetty stilts. Then I heard the dull gurgling of the sea in my ears. And then just – darkness.

Now I'm sitting here with you.

And that's the thing I can't get over.

That trying to kill him took my life.

'It's not fair, is it?'

27

A Shock for All

It's daylight. The clock on the wall of the café says 6.01 a.m. I'm not wet any more. I look out to sea. The tide is way out now, revealing a thick golden bar of sand.

I ask you if you came back just for me. You say yes. Someone always comes back. You say I needed to see a friendly face.

I'm glad it's you, Jess. I'd forgotten how beautiful you are.

The café door chimes, and a woman enters, then another. More staff. The early shift for the lifeboat crew, and the overnighters just coming off a shift on the bypass. Whipped prides itself on being the only place for miles around that opens from dawn until dusk. The radio comes on over the speakers. Some DJ on the South-West's favourite radio station is promising 'non-stop hits all day long', and appealing for listeners to send in their old bras.

I look back through the window and see the boardwalk through the window. Some police are still milling around like luminous ants. It's still taped off.

You tell me it's going to be difficult for me, but that you're here. Everything will be OK in the end. I find that hard to believe. You say that, now I've told you the whole story, I can begin to get over it. I find that hard to believe as well. It's too soon, I say. I'm only seventeen. I did nothing wrong.

You say I already know the answer to that.

I'm sitting beside the café window when I see the man running up the beach and I instantly know it's washed ashore. The sand flicks up behind him as he sprints. And he's screaming.

His face is alive with fear. He's running so hard to get away from it, what he's found. In those brief moments, I am the only person in the café to see him. But, within seconds, the quiet crumbles into chaos.

'Somebody! Help!'

'What's he saying?'

'Did he say a body?'

Someone calls my name, but I don't turn around. I keep walking, out of the café, into the morning air, along the Esplanade, down the steps and onto the wet sand, like the sea is a magnet and I am metal.

People overtake me. Someone shouts, 'Call the police.' Thudding footsteps, snatches of breath. The sand's covered in a billion worm hills and tiny white shells. A group of crows squawks nearby. They're all clustered around an object, pecking at it.

'Let the police handle it.'

'Don't look. Don't look.'

I keep walking towards the mound, until I can see for myself what the man was running from. Until I can see for myself what I have done.

And I do see it. It becomes clearer with every footstep. It's wearing my jogging bottoms. My hoody. It has my hair. It's asleep but soaking wet.

It's me.

I stare down at my bloated, bleached face on the wet sand, surrounded by tiny mirror pools and broken tree branches. One of my arms is slung out. The other is rounded, like I'm singing 'I'm a Little Teapot'. I almost laugh. A tiny crab crawls into my open mouth.

'God, it's so strange.'

I know, you say.

Some other people have gathered round, a couple of builders in big brown work boots and two waitresses from the café. One waitress has her hand over her mouth. One of the builders is swearing, dialling 999. Another builder is taking off his jumper. He lays it gently over my head. One of the waitresses gets out her phone and clicks onto YouTube – one way to get more followers. The third builder rips the phone from her hand and hoys it into the mud.

'Oi!'

'Sue me!'

'Where's Max?' I ask you.

You tell me he's been at the police station all night.

'All night? What happened exactly after I... after the waves?'

You take my hand and, as quick as one movie scene cuts to another, it's night-time again. Last night. Except it's all blurry, smudged at the edges, just a memory. I'm standing on the pavement, between Max's roughly parked Audi and the rusty old Jeep from the farm. I'm watching myself and Neil arguing on the jetty. You stand beside me, on the pavement. Corey's at the top of the jetty. Fallon's next to him. They're holding hands. Neil's brandishing the knife. I watch him threaten me. I see myself launch at him, sending us both overboard onto the sand below. We're tussling. I'm punching. I'm pulverising him. My fists ache, I'm punching so hard. All I can hear is the rush of the tide as it storms the shore and pounds the stilts of the jetty. Then the waves break us apart and I disappear under the water but Neil is washed up. He gets to his feet and starts stumbling towards dry land, spluttering.

I am nowhere. That must be when I died.

Max doesn't know it. He runs to the end of the jetty and dives off, straight into the sea and disappears. His head comes up, he dives down again.

'He'll kill himself. Don't let him, Jess,' I say. 'Please, stop him. Do something!'

But you tell me to watch. The wind howls around us like wolves and there's a thumping noise of someone running down the jetty at full pelt, like a rugby player running for the end zone. I don't recognise them at first – they're in a white hoody. It's not Fallon or Corey, they're both still there. No, it's Zane. He dives in after Max.

'Where the hell are the police?' shouts Corey. 'They should be here by now, Pete called them ages ago!'

Fallon's watching Neil stumbling down the beach, getting away. And she runs after him. Fallon and Corey chase Neil down as he runs with a twisted ankle back up the seafront, sopping wet and coughing up seawater. Corey rugby-tackles him to the ground.

'He's never played rugby in his life,' I say. You smile at me.

Fallon sits on his legs, taking off her belt and handing it to Corey so he can roughly tie Neil's hands behind his back. He's not even fighting back.

'What about Max though? Is he going to be all right?' I ask, going back to the sea wall. I can taste salt in my throat.

You point back to the beach. Zane's pulling him out, dragging him out of the water. He's struggling, he wants to go back in, but Zane's too strong for him. He's out of breath, but shouting at him. I can't hear them at first over the waves.

'She's gone! You'll drown if you go back in there. She's gone, Max.'

*

In a heartbeat, we're back to the daylit beach. My body lying crudely among seaweed and wet branches. More people stand around. More people start getting their phones out. A woman in wellies and a pink anorak rubs a tear from her cheek; yet she won't look away.

They've had search and rescue boats out all night, you tell me, but the sea had swallowed me whole. And now the early morning tide has spat me out again.

There are sirens behind us on the jetty and the builders start moving people back.

'So I died because I tried to kill him?'

You say nothing.

'Why me?'

You won't answer.

'Why won't you tell me? Why am I still angry, even though there's no life left?'

You say, in time, that will go. But I don't believe you.

'I didn't learn my lesson in life, so what's the point learning it now?'

The police set up a white tent around my body and usher all the gawpers back, until they're behind a cordon near the jetty.

'Can I go back?' I ask. 'I mean, if I've learnt my lesson, can I be alive again? I've seen it on films. People learn their lessons and they get sent back. Can we do that?'

You say it doesn't work like that.

'But this is crap. This is a crap way to end a life. To end *my* life. That's it? That's it? No more anything? What about Max? What about my dad, is he going to be OK? And Fallon and Corey? I know I pushed things too far but come on! What about Zane? Zane's not all right, he hurt himself. I need to go back there, Jess. I need to help them.'

You tell me I already have. You tell me everything will be all right.

But still I don't believe you.

'*Trust me.*'

28

Away on Their Own

What the living never find out is that dying is actually OK. It's them who have to do all the suffering, the people who stay behind. I don't feel rage now, or resentment or anything. I don't feel the urge to punch walls or pummel punchbags. And I don't itch. You say we can stay as long as we need to. You tell me the dead don't leave until their living are ready to lose them. I'm glad that's the way it is. I just wish they all knew that. I'm still here with them.

You keep me away from the raw grief, the awful first few weeks. I don't want to see that, anyway; I know how it goes, because I felt it when you died. So we don't hang around our houses and we don't go to the places we know they'll be. Instead, we wander, and we watch other things to keep ourselves occupied. The one good thing about dying is that you can go anywhere, do anything. I'd always thought Heaven was a big white place where everyone sits around in white clothes talking about beautiful things, but it's not; not for me, anyway. My heaven is everywhere. It's walking around, smelling flowers I'd never noticed, going to places I never knew existed. Walking, not running. It's having fun with a friend and laughing all the time. That's my Heaven. It always has been.

I still see the odd thing I'm not meant to in those first few weeks. My dad sobbing as he puts the shopping into the boot in Tesco car park. Fallon and Corey taking the baby down to the seafront and looking at all the flowers people have left. Max going down there and ripping apart the flowers, bunch by bunch. People in the town I never met have left them there. People I went to school with. People who watched me run at Area Trials or County Champs and who've never forgotten it. Pete Hamlin leaves me some roses.

I see Max and Corey and Fallon going to the undertakers with my dad, the day before my funeral. They want to see my casket, lid closed, so it's not such a shock for them tomorrow morning. They're all still sucking on the pastilles my dad gave them in the car. I can hear them clicking against their teeth. I can taste the blackcurrant in the back of my own throat.

My casket is wicker, I don't know why they chose that, but it's quite nice, I suppose. The sides are laced with lemon ribbon and there's little lemon bows all along the lid. Max places his hand on the top, and Fallon puts her hand on his, then Corey too. They stay like that for minutes, until there's a knock at the door and Zane walks in. He looks embarrassed. He's late. His boss at Lidl is an asshole. He puts both his hands on top of theirs, and they all cry together.

I don't go inside the crematorium the next day. I wait outside on a bench, reading an Order of Service someone has dropped and listening to birds in the high trees. They chose a nice picture of me for the front. I'm holding my County Champs trophy and biting my gold medal. I look at the floral tributes laid out in the courtyard. A taxi pulls up about ten minutes into the service and my mum gets out of the back, dressed in a black skirt suit about twenty years too young and two sizes too small for her. She's looking old. Even in death, I am such a bitch.

You come out and give me the edited highlights from the service when it's all over. How Dad and my brothers carried me on their shoulders, joined by Max, Zane and Corey. How Dad broke down in his eulogy when he referred to me as his 'Little Fish'. How Ollie and David and David's husband Jack stood beside him throughout like his soldiers. How they all held hands. How Celestina, my dad's girl-friend, was there too. How she'd cried, even though she'd never met me.

How my four friends recited a poem together, a poem you had written yourself, that Max had found in one of your notebooks. The poem was called 'Five Go Adventuring'. You wrote it about us. How you were always on the outside, while the five of us were 'a solid circle of burning wonder and magic, all on fire with happy youth'.

Max helped Dad and my brothers choose the music and my favourite song played as my wicker casket disappeared behind the red curtains while everyone filed out. Only Max could have suggested that.

They all go to a nearby pub for my wake. Pete Hamlin's there. My dad shakes his hand and pulls him into a hug. He looks strange in a suit. He tells my dad he's moving back to London soon to run a gym with his sister. He says he's never seen anyone my age with as much fire in her belly as me. My dad agrees. They hug again.

I make myself known to them; you can do that, when you're dead. As my brother Ollie stands at the bar, I flick his ear. He looks around, but thinks nothing else of it. I do it again on his other ear while he's chatting to Corey – he looks annoyed when he sees there's no one behind him, and then his face relaxes, like he knows. David comes back from the buffet with two plates for him and Jack. I bite a corner of his cheese and pickle sandwich when he's not looking and watch his reaction – his face trying to work out a reasonable explanation but only coming up with a smile.

Dad's saying goodbye to people at the door. I walk behind him, step on tiptoes and blow slightly on the back of his neck. He stops, his eyes dart from left to right. He closes his eyes, breathes in, breathes out, opens them again and they're watery. He doesn't cry and he doesn't say anything, just carries on saying his goodbyes. But he knows I haven't gone yet. They all do.

29

Five Have a Wonderful Time

I want to go to the trial. It starts at the end of the following summer, almost a year to the day after the night I drowned. My mum comes back from Mykonos for that too. She brings Firat with her this time. He seems nice enough, another pushover like Dad; he tries to shake Dad's hand, but Dad refuses. Mum chooses a quiet moment during recess to ask Dad for a divorce. Dad gets in first and presents her with the papers from his solicitor. Sucker-punched. Neither of my brothers speak to her this time. They stay beside Dad like two marble pillars, strong and silent.

Neil's lost a lot of weight. He has to be helped onto the stand by a couple of guards. Every single detail of what he's done comes out. I'd always been worried that four years and no evidence meant what he did could never be proved – that my selfish silence meant he'd get away with it. But it's been quite the opposite – my death has caused a landslide.

Max gets the best lawyer money can buy, Tamara Strallen-Sheppard, who is based in London but flies all over the world. And brick by brick she dismantles Neil's throne. That's the point of her whole case – Neil has made himself untouchable with his money; a king amongst peasants. "But remove the king's court, remove the sycophants and the money and what is the king but just a man? Just one lone, pathetic man with delusions of grandeur." She makes his defence lawyer look like a small boy on his first day of school.

The police have the diaries – six in all on the book-shelves, two more in the wardrobe and a journal hidden under the bed. Some of it's hard to listen to, but I decide I must. This is where it ends now. Zane gives a witness statement – what he saw when he was a child himself, what I told him that day we went to the island.

Corey gives a witness statement too. He remembers everything about the night I died – Max with the knife, my argument with Neil. The defence tries to discredit him – it was a blustery night, he has hearing difficulties, mobility difficulties. There's no way he could have heard much at all. But Corey is so strong. He knows what he saw, he knows what he heard. His replies are faultless. They don't know how marvellous Corey can be. I almost pity them.

Then Fallon takes the stand and her statement proves to be the most damning yet. She knows the location of my baby's grave – under the smallest stone in the Pirate Graveyard on Ella's Island. She'd placed it in a coil of toilet paper inside a small rectangular biscuit tin she'd found in one of our kitchen cupboards; a French shortbread tin that my parents brought back from their honeymoon in Normandy. Dad had been using it for cookie cutters.

The trial is halted while the police dig up the grave and perform tests. The tests prove positive. It's definitely been there for five years. It's definitely Neil's baby.

And then it's all just a matter of time as more evidence

piles up. Two laptops from Neil's home office, loaded with hidden folders of girls, are presented by the prosecution.

Jo Rittman hasn't spoken since the trial. She had a complete mental breakdown two weeks after he was arrested. Auntie 'Call me Manda' Manda booked her into the Priory. New buyers took over JoNeille just before Christmas. Max hasn't spoken to her since. I don't know if he ever will again. He knows how to live without a mum. He's got that off me.

But the trump card was a living, breathing witness statement from a living breathing witness to Neil's crimes – his niece, Shelby Gilmore. She'd been molested from an early age, earlier than both of us. She was so nervous at the trial that her hands were shaking. She drank a whole jug of water throughout her cross-examination and the defence lawyer was brutal. He brought up her many failed relationships, he knew about her and Max and the six guys she'd slept with in the past year alone. He put all of it down to her being 'naturally over-sexed' and made her go over what Neil had done to her, over and over and over again.

But Shelby is mighty. She's braver than all of us, as brave as a lioness. She does what neither I nor Jess could do in life – she stands up, knees shaking, hands fidgeting, dry-mouthed, and she looks Neil square in the face and she tells him and everyone else in that room the truth about what he had done to her since she was ten. How he had called her a 'deviant' too. How she was the one who trashed his brand-new Porsche at her birthday party. How she'd been at breaking point too, that night – she was just better at hiding it than me.

Shelby got revenge for all of us, all the girls who couldn't speak up. All the deviants whom he held down and forced himself into. All those little girls and babies in his laptop folders or on the CCTV tapes from the toilets at the garden centre, who didn't know what was happening to them or were too young to understand or too scared to stop it.

After the trial, more witnesses emerged. Girls on work experience at the arcades. Girls doing summer jobs in the garden centre café. Girls who didn't like the attention, the touching, the 'after-hours chats'. In all, twenty-two deviants came forward after Shelby's testimony.

They jail Neil for a minimum of seventeen years. The judge calls him 'the only true deviant in this room'. Neil cries out on the stand. Protests his innocence. Shouts at Shelby. Calls her names. Pleads with Max. They both just stare back at him as he is led away.

Two days later, Neil tries to hang himself in his cell, with a torn strip of bed sheet and an upended bunk. A man in the next cell tips off a guard who stops him just in time. Now they've given him stronger sheets and nailed his bed to the floor. They're watching him all the time now.

I ask Jess if we can haunt him, to make him suffer more. She tells me we already are.

*

The fireworks have started by the time we get to East Brynstan, but we're taking it slow. This is the last time so we're making the most of it. We go to Church Lane, passing Pete Hamlin's cottage. There is a new estate agent sign up in the front garden now. Three families have lived there since Pete moved to London. No one ever seems to settle.

I unlock the gate to the churchyard and we make our way up the path towards the Public Footpath sign. There's a burning wood smell on the air, and the tang of cooking meat and tomato soup. A couple of car doors slam in the lane and two family groups emerge at the start of the footpath, chattering to one another, their kids wrapped up in big coats and wellies.

Solar lights illuminate a runway snaking all the way up the side of Brynstan Hill so people know where to walk. Lining the route are candy-floss trucks and popcorn stalls and vans selling roasted chestnuts and burgers. We let people pass us, chattering, excited, kids writing in the air with sparklers, groups of people linking arms. It's cold. I can feel it tonight.

Up on the summit of Brynstan Hill, the flames of the humungous bonfire dance high into the night sky – crowds of people are up there already, beetling around in thick coats and boots, marvelling at the one time of the year Volcano Town's volcano actually spews fire. We carry on walking as the gradient gets steeper and the bonfire grows bigger on the horizon.

'There they are,' I say, unable to hide my excitement as I pick out Fallon in her oversized white puffa jacket and white moon boots on the edge of the summit. In her arms is the little girl I met briefly as a baby and who I've watched grow ever since – this is Ella. She is so wrapped up in woollen clothes that I can only see her little red cheeks and big brown eyes, but she is beautiful. She looks just like Zane only she smiles way more he ever did.

She looks in our direction and points.

'Oh my God, can she see us?' I ask.

You frown. You don't think so. But she's smiling and waving right at us. Saying 'Mumma, Mumma, Ella!'

Fallon's writing her name in the air with a sparkler. Maybe it's that.

When we reach the summit, Zane has lifted Ella into his arms to watch the bonfire.

'Fire fire hot hot hot!' she screeches. 'Corey, nook!'

'I know, big hot fire,' says Corey, who stands beside them, still in his Costa uniform. He must have come straight from work.

Fallon laughs, folding her arms. 'She ate a worm this morning,' she tells Zane. 'She's got this thing about insects. Loves them. Keeps a whole bunch of snails in an ice cream tub out the back, doesn't she, Core?'

Corey nods, pushing his glasses up his nose and rubbing Fallon's arms on the outside to warm her up, like he has ESP when it comes to her being cold. 'Yep. Has tea parties with them and then she kills them and eats them after. It's hilarious.'

'Little weirdo fits right in, doesn't she?' Max roots about in the picnic basket they all stand around and pulls out a large silver thermos. 'Anyone for soup?'

'Yeah, go on then,' says Zane as Ella reaches for him. He takes her and lifts her onto his shoulders where she starts bouncing.

'Did you see the flowers on the graves, Max?' Fallon asks as he pours out her tomato soup. 'Ella picked them out.'

'Yeah I saw on the way up. They're great. What do you think of the new headstones?'

'Beautiful,' says Corey. 'I'm glad they're next to each other.'

'Yeah, so am I.' Max nods, as a rocket zooms up into the air and screams across the sky in a blaze of starlight, finishing in a single resounding *CRACK*.

'That was scary bang,' Ella giggles, still on Zane's shoulders. She reaches out her hand to Corey and he takes it gladly.

I've watched them all over the past two years. I know what they all mean to one another now. Max lives in Cloud now – he bought an old manor house that needed doing up, close to Whitehouse Farm. My dad helped him with the legal side of things – Dad's good like that – and it gave him something to focus on. Corey and Fallon helped with the decorating and for the last six months, Zane's been lodging with him. His mum was a lot more understanding about him being gay than he gave her credit for but he still wanted his own space. He couldn't be himself at home. He could around us. Or rather, them.

'Did Zane tell you he's getting grief from his rugby lot again?' says Max.

'You're not, are you, mate?' says Corey.

'Only a bit of stick from a couple of new guys, yeah,' he laughs. 'Most of them have been all right. It's just the same two who keep giving me static.'

'What do you mean? What are they doing?' asks Fallon, reaching into the picnic basket for a child's drinking cup. She hands it to Ella.

'Trolling mostly. The odd text. Used to be good mates with them at school but they just won't accept it.'

'Danny Leech and Andy Tanner?' says Corey.

He nods, his face illuminated by the fire. 'They're just twats. I can handle them.'

'I said they probably fancy him,' says Max as another round of fireworks starts up, drowning out their voices.

'I doubt it,' says Zane, handing Ella over to Corey. He stands her in front of him and puts his gloved hands over her ears when one, two, three, four, five loud rockets scream out in quick succession. She stares up at them, open-mouthed. Fallon bends down and starts talking to her, telling her that me and Jessica are up in the sky, two stars looking down on her.

'Do you want to do something about it, mate?' says Max.

They all go silent again. 'I meant, go and talk to them. See if they need help understanding.'

Zane dips his roll in his soup. 'When you say "help"...'

'I don't mean heavy stuff,' Max laughs. 'But we can't let it go on, can we?'

'No way,' Zane laughs. 'It's their problem, not mine.' He met someone recently, at the gym. His name is Sam. He hasn't told them all just yet. He's keeping it glowing inside him for just a little bit longer.

Fallon smiles and squeezes his forearm. 'We've got your back though.'

Zane nods, before bending down to Ella and whispering something in her ear. Then they start chasing each other through the grass around the Iron Age remains.

'How's the application going, Max? Any more news?' asks Corey.

'Yeah, actually,' he says, standing up. 'I've got an interview.'

'Oh that's amazing!' cries Fallon, pulling him in for a hug.

'Yeah. Zane's been training me for my bleep test for the past month. I'm still a long way off becoming a full policeman, but, well, ball's rolling. Least I know what I want now.'

Corey smiles and pats him on the back. 'Well done, mate. That's brilliant.'

'Yeah. If all goes well, I could be pounding the beat a couple of years from now.'

'Do you know what area you want to go into yet?' asks Fallon.

'Rape prevention,' he says, without a moment's hesitation. 'You know, eventually.' Neither of them says anything, even though their heads must be full of words. Fallon looks as proud as she did when Ella took her first steps. Corey just nods.

'So what are we doing after this then?' asks Zane, coming back over to them with Ella on his back like a little monkey. 'Do you want to come back to the house for a bit of Disney and a curry or summing?'

'Yeah, that place in the high street was good last time,' said Corey. 'The Chandni. We've still got the leaflet somewhere, haven't we?'

'Somewhere,' says Fallon. 'Yeah, that would be nice. Can't be too late tonight though cos I've got a ton of homework to do for college.'

Max nods. 'We could pick it up and bring it round about eight. Same as last time?'

'Ooh yeah, get more naan bread this time though,' says Corey, as Zane puts Ella down and she appears at his side, asking for her drink, which he gives her.

'I'm gonna eat *all* the poppadums,' says Ella. 'And *you* can't have any.' She points at Max and giggles into her little purple gloves.

'No, *I'm* having all the poppadums,' says Max. 'You fart when you have curry.' She cups her mouth like he's said something very naughty and Max grabs her and tickles her off the ground.

'Naughty Uncle Max,' she laughs.

'No, naughty Ella Bella Spinderella.' And she laughs even harder. She asks for 'Snuggly Duddlies' and he lifts her up and they squeeze each other tightly as another lot of rockets scream skywards.

She's the perfect mix of all of us – she's got Zane's eyes, Fallon's courage, Max's intelligence, Corey's sense of wonder – and my name.

Max still misses me. I still see those moments in the

mirror where his mind is wondering what the point is and his face crumbles. The few times of day where he's without one of them and he crawls into himself like a crab, but little by ever so little, it's becoming less of a habit. Zane is there with the tough love and the early morning jogs. He's kept him off skunk too and even helped him fill out his Deed Poll forms to change his surname – he's Max Walmsley now; his mum's maiden name. Corey and Fallon are there with the counselling sessions and takeaway pizzas and trips to the zoo or town or some farm with the baby. Every day they all do something together, even if it's just to go round and watch TV or have dinner. There's no secrets now. They tell each other everything. It's like their code.

Five more rockets scream up, one after the other, screeching, howling and streaming over their heads, louder and brighter than any that have gone before. I look at the faces of my friends, illuminated orange and full of wonder. I look at Ella. I know she can see me now. I wave at her and she waves back. She can see the magic. I hope that lasts.

I feel a tap on my shoulder and turn to look at you. You tell me it's time for us to go.

I don't want to leave them, of course I don't, but there isn't a place for me here any more. If I don't leave them, they won't be able to get on with their lives.

Dad won't put that new framed quote up in his office – the one from Great Expectations - 'You are in every line I have ever read' – the photo of me with my medals beneath it. And he won't ask Celestina to marry him.

Corey and Fallon won't ever truly be happy.

Baby Ella won't thrive.

Zane won't move in with his boyfriend.

Max won't join the police, and save more girls like me

from men like Neil. So I have to go. I think they're ready for me to go.

They've never stopped being the Fearless Five. Those years in between, they just got lost for a while. They don't ever need to be lost again. I've made sure of that.

And that's enough for me now. Just enough.

★ ★ ★ ★ ★

Acknowledgments.

Jenny Savill at Andrew Nurnberg Agency for keeping the faith and for all the metaphorical chamomile when I've had too much Red Bull.

Anna Baggaley, Clio Cornish, Lisa Milton, Taryn Sachs, Jen Porter and everyone at HQ for taking my little Monster, my lonely Deviants and my fragrant Sweetpea under your wing.

Imogen Russell-Williams, for your vital advice just when I needed it most. Your Samurai editing technique is breathtakingly bloodthirsty and I love it.

My early readers – especially Penny Skuse, Matthew Snead and Barry Timms.

Laura Myers for your steadfast friendship, constant enthusiasm for my books and for never being afraid to tell me when I'm being a twat.

Jamie Skuse, because he always looks for his name in the back of the book.

Julia Green and the entire creative team at Bath Spa University, home of the finest MA in Writing for Young People in the UK. I wouldn't be published without it.

All the UKYA book bloggers who have supported me from the word go and who continue to spread the word of the Ceej, especially Laura @ Sister Spooky, Michelle @ Tales of Yesterday, Sally aka The Dark Dictator, Ray Reads a Lot and Jess Hearts Books.

All my author mateys who encourage me, calm me and generally Retweet the crap out of me, especially Christi Daugherty, Keren David, Fiona Dunbar, Hilary Freeman, Helen Grant, Emma Haughton, Zoe Marriott, Keris Stainton and Lee Weatherly.

And the soundtrack for this one was as follows: Arctic Monkeys, Birdy, Busted, Calvin Harris, Death Cab for Cutie, Devlin ft. Ed Sheeran, Echobelly, Ellie Goulding, Fall Out Boy, Feeder, First Aid Kit, 5 Seconds of Summer, Foxes, Gorillaz, Imagine Dragons, Kesha, Hoobastank, Linkin Park, MCR, Prodigy, Radiohead, Skrillex, Sleigh Bells, Slipknot, 30 Seconds to Mars and Youth in Revolt.